UNITED

WE

FALL

BROOKE RILEY

ISBN- 978-1-7348329-2-1

To my mom, who always believes in my dreams
even when I don't.

PROLOGUE

Carissa
SATURDAY, OCTOBER 14TH, 2023

INHALE.

Exhale.

My racing heart grasps for any form of calm. Any feeling of peace.

Years of practicing all forms of self-defense and meditation should be helping me now, but my mind repeats the sound of the gunshot. The sound of the scream. I can't erase the events of my past, but I can control my future.

Two weeks have gone by. I have yet to find any peace or feel any calm. My mind is like a desert, where I search for the thirst-quenching water in the oasis but can't find any. Despite my many breathing techniques, my heart continues to pound rapidly in my chest. I even try controlling my breath to calm my mind. Nothing.

A muted yellow glow from the streetlights leaks

through the broken blinds on the window. I couldn't afford a nice motel with the money I had left. So, a dingy motel with no modern comforts it was.

I don't mind. I don't deserve anything nice or comfortable.

I lie on my back on the scratchy motel sheets and stare up at the ceiling. Peeling beige paint combines with its popcorn texture; little crumbs of it have fallen here and there around the room. It's all I can afford with what little money I have left. In a matter of days, I'll have nothing. I'm running out of options. Evan will be tracking my steps, closing in on me. I know too much for him to let me get away so easily. Even if he did let me go, the president would never let this slide.

A gunshot sounds outside my window. I dive to the floor beside my bed, my pulse pounding in my ears as I hear the screaming. It echoes in my ears, just as it has for the last two weeks. It takes me a moment to realize it's not another delusion from my nightmares. There was an actual scream outside the window, an actual gunshot. Another person from some other resistance that had begun to form, taken down by the soldiers, I would assume. No one disobeys when they know what the outcome is —no one except the rebels, that is. And my father never had rebels here before. Smaller resistances existed around us, but we never aligned ourselves with them. Often, they were more violent, more volatile when it came to taking action.

I exhale all the air from my lungs. My neck begins to cramp, but I don't dare rest my head on the floor. This place is infested with roaches and mice; I'm sure of it. Gathering my strength, I slowly rise from the floor. I don't know what I'll see when I look out the window, but I look anyway. Peeking past the cracked plastic blinds, I see nothing too violent.

Outside, two soldiers restrain a man; a gun lies on the pavement a few feet away. The man has blood dripping down the side of his face, though not from a gunshot wound. No, the soldiers have beaten him with their fists. One soldier is kneeling on the ground, blood gushing from his shoulder. He must be the one who met with the bullet. His wound doesn't seem fatal; he gets slowly to his feet, though looks shaky at best. Another soldier helps him to a patrol truck where he begins to apply first aid.

I back away from the window, my stomach turning within itself. The last thing I need is for the soldiers to see me watching them. They don't

3

appreciate witnesses.

I return to sitting on the bed, my heart still pounding against my chest, threatening to break out. The cheap alarm clock on the nightstand says it's only 4 a.m. I sigh, running a hand through my newly dyed brown hair. I'm ready to get moving, but the curfew doesn't end for another hour and a half.

So, I sit cross-legged, trying to meditate and begin my daily practice of training. It's been a few days since I've been able to train. After meditation, I begin practicing my self-defense maneuvers. By the time I'm finished, it's 5:45 and I'm dripping with sweat. But the anxiety has subsided... for now. I walk into the small bathroom, step into the shower, and let the hot water rush over me. I let it burn my skin. I run the cheap motel shampoo through my hair. Something is better than nothing, I guess. I soap up and shave my legs, trying to feel like a human again. When I finish, I grab the towel hanging just outside the curtain. I shake it out to make sure no bugs are hiding in it before wrapping it around my body.

I drag my hand against the smooth, cool surface of the foggy mirror, creating enough space to see my face. My now very wet hair brushes the tops of my shoulders and clings to my neck. It's been growing since I haven't had time to keep it trimmed. I always kept my hair short for missions. To be less of a weapon to be used against me in a fight.

I dress in my last change of clothes and grab my things. My car needs gas, and that will eat up quite a bit of my money after I pay the remainder for the motel room. The only two options I have left are both dangerous. I could return to Evan, maybe even spare my life if I play by his rules. Or I could go home. Dad will lock me up, but it's safer than the alternative. He'll protect me from Evan, even if I'm locked away.

I load up my car and walk to the small building in the parking lot that serves as the manager's office. An unenthused teenage boy sits behind the desk, his face in his phone. I wait, but he never looks up. I clear my throat and he finally takes notice of me.

"If you've come to pay, you'll have to wait for the manager to return. I can't accept any method of payment."

I cross my arms. "Will he be returning soon? I have to get out of here." The boy shrugs, his attention already back on his phone. I groan. "Look, kid, I only have cash anyway. I'll put my payment on the desk and go. I can't stay here and wait around."

The boy says nothing. He's not paying attention at all. If I leave now, I can keep my money. It's not as though I've enjoyed my stay here. I turn to the door, but the manager appears.

"Come to make your payment?"

I smile innocently. His arched brow and glare indicate he knows what I was about to do. "I'm skipping town, so I figured I'd pay for yesterday and be on my way."

I can tell he doesn't believe me, but I don't need him to. It's not like I'll ever see him again, anyway. His opinion of me won't matter in the end. I hand him the cash, and he walks around the front desk to print out a receipt.

"We hope you enjoyed your stay at Economy Inn. We would be happy to have you again soon."

I laugh dryly. "My room was full of roaches and mice droppings. I think I'll pass."

His lip curls in distaste at my comment, but I don't bother waiting for a response. I walk out the door, letting it slam shut behind me. I get into my car and drive far away from the motel. I'm so far north of Cyrus, I'll need to find a gas station if I plan to make it all the way home before sundown. I drive for half an hour before finding one and pulling in. It's mostly empty, save for one other car. I park and go inside to pay cash. The guy behind the counter looks bored. Another person walks around the store, grabbing snacks.

I walk up to the counter, handing the clerk twenty dollars. "I'm at pump two. I need to fill up my car."

The guy nods, not saying anything as he counts the money. My stomach growls, clenching from lack of food. I haven't eaten since yesterday around lunchtime.

I consider the amount of money I have left. I need to eat something. I sigh. "I'd also like to get a glazed donut and a coffee."

The guy sighs as if this is a burden to him. He punches the keys on his computer before looking at me again. "That will be an additional $5.62."

I look down at the six dollars I have left. I give him the six and he gives me the small change and the wrapped donut. I walk to the coffee machine in the back corner and take a small cup. I fill it up, taking it black.

I sip at it as I walk outside to my car. It's not the worst coffee I've ever tasted, so I take that small victory. I fuel up and eat the donut. It's more sugar than my body is used to. I never indulge much in sweets, trying to maintain my health, but my options are even more limited now.

The pump stops right at the twenty-dollar mark. I sigh. My car isn't quite full, but it will have to be enough to get home. I finish up, take my receipt, and pull away from the gas station. I'm ready to go home. I drive for another two and a half hours before finally pulling into the strange, yet familiar driveway.

To my surprise, the gate rolls open for me, even though I was sure the code would have changed.

Everything is the same, except the leaves on the trees have begun to change and fall, giving way to bare branches and a trail of red and brown on the driveway.

I reach the house and step out of my car. I know they'll be awake by now. But they'll most likely be downstairs in headquarters. I exhale a shaky breath, a chill racing up my spine. Maybe this is a bad idea. But I have no other option. I walk the few steps up the porch, lifting my fidgety hand to knock.

A moment passes. Then another. My heart begins to beat rapidly. I question whether I've made the right decision, but before I can turn away, the door swings open, and Spencer stares back at me. His eyes widen at the sight of me.

"Carissa?"

The sight of my cousin breaks whatever is left of my resolve. I collapse against him, hugging him. I no longer try to stop the tears that I've held back for these past two weeks. I'm home. And for now, that is enough.

CHAPTER ONE

Peter

SATURDAY, OCTOBER 14TH, 2023

"IT IS NEVER AN EASY THING, HOLDING A funeral inside this church. But it is even harder when a young life is taken from us. Today, we remember a young woman we all knew well, Raegan MacArthur. A bright soul, always radiating light to anyone she met. Though she was a quiet person, I've known Raegan to become a feisty spirit when confronted with something she genuinely believed in."

Pastor Moore's words hit something in me. Something I haven't quite buried yet. Two weeks. It's only been two weeks, and yet it feels like an eternity. The wooden pews of Bent Ridge Bible Church offer no comfort. Pastor Moore—Sawyer's father—knows everyone in town. Everyone knows everyone here.

Everyone knew Raegan. So, the news of her death sent a shockwave through our humble town.

In the pew in front of me, Mrs. MacArthur sobs into her husband's shoulder as he rests his head on hers, likely fighting tears of his own. Pastor Moore's words bring light into the dark, but not enough to drive out the grief or the pain.

Across the aisle, in the back pew, Andre Williams sits with Maya and Spencer. Spencer's head is bowed, his eyes closed. Maya's hand absently rubs her nephew's shoulder.

Up ahead of them, in the frontmost pew, sit Sawyer and Nicole. Nicole sobs into his shoulder, and he has both his arms wrapped around her. But these are the only people I recognize in the crowded church. The whole town showed up, even those who don't believe in any religion.

Everyone knows everyone here. And when one of us falls, we all mourn the loss.

I glance up to the front of the room. The casket is closed. Some think the accident left Raegan's body bruised and beaten. They don't know the accident is a fake story devised by Andre Williams to cover up what happened. They don't know that the only thing in the casket is a picture of Raegan chosen by

11

her parents, along with her favorite stuffed teddy bear from her childhood. The one I gave her when she turned nine. They don't know that her body was never recovered from the abandoned warehouse. They don't know about a bullet piercing her, about the blood on the floor. And they certainly don't know that Andre Williams' son is the culprit.

I try to focus on Pastor Moore's words.

"Life is a gift. We're blessed with the time we have here, each of us making a difference in some way or another. And at the end of life is an eternity in peace for those who believe. I know Raegan's faith will carry her through. She's more alive than those of us here today."

Everything in me burns with a deep desire to give Evan the same fate he chose for Raegan. All I can think about is the unsuccessful effort to find her body. There was so much searching between the first battle and now. That monster did something to hide the evidence, and I don't want to know what he did with her. I just want her back.

I feel a hand take mine. I look over at my sister, Emilee, who came for the funeral. She knows the truth. She was never interested in working for the resistance. It wasn't like she didn't care, but the idea was daunting to her. Emilee is more like our father in that way. She prefers the life of a student, studying business like our dad. She likes the hustle of the city, the office she works at in California, over the quiet small town of our childhood in Texas.

The resistance isn't for everyone. Maybe it's for no one. At this point, I question if it's even for me. No actions have been taken in the sea of empty promises by Mr. Williams. I'm losing my faith in a resistance made of broken ideas.

Emilee squeezes my hand, tears shining in her eyes. I squeeze back, a code we created as children when one of us was in distress and needed comfort. I glance over to see how my mom is. She doesn't cry like some of the other women in the room. But I've heard her sobbing late at night. I know she hurts, too. But she's too reserved to cry in front of others, even at a funeral.

I look at the casket again and think of how I failed. I could have done more to save her. I close my eyes, but every time I do, I hear Raegan screaming she loves me. I hate myself for not telling her I love her, too. I worried at the time it wasn't true but losing her has made me realize how much I loved her. *Love* her. And I'm a fool for doubting I ever did.

Her sky-blue eyes made my heart skip a beat. Her determination to find the traitor was something I admired. She was stunning, and now she's gone. I failed her.

Pastor Moore's service on life and eternity ends, though I hardly heard any of it. A few men from the congregation rise, ready to lift her casket and carry it on to the gravesite. The casket is rigged to feel as though someone is in there, to keep up the ruse. But the truth is it's emptier than me.

We begin our march to the hearse. My sister keeps her arm around me as they load it up. Then begins the drive to the gravesite just on the edge of town. My mom drives and Emilee sits up front with her.

"Peter," Emilee says, glancing back at me.

"Yeah?"

"Just breathe. It's going to be okay."

I look out the window, unable to bear the weight of any pity, especially from my sister.

We arrive at the gravesite. The pallbearers carry the casket to the spot the MacArthurs reserved.

Emilee holds me with one arm, trying to comfort me. She's four years older than me, so she thinks she's so much more grown-up. But at this moment, I feel as though I've had to grow more than I care to admit.

Raegan's casket is lowered into the ground. There's a bouquet of roses, poppies, and lilies standing on a table nearby. Everyone pauses near the vase, each taking one flower delicately. Mostly roses or lilies are dropped down to the top of the casket. I grab a poppy, Raegan's favorite, and let it fall from my hand. The flower floats down the six-foot distance, landing with a soft thump on the lid of her casket. I stare down a moment and whisper, "I love you, too."

I walk away from the others, down the dirt trail leading to the graveyard, facing away from the rest of the congregation. I refuse to let anyone see me cry.

I hear the gravel crunch behind me. I wipe my eyes and turn. Emilee gives me a small, sad smile. She puts her hand on my shoulder. "You can't blame yourself, Peter. You did everything you could."

I shake my head. "If I had done everything, we wouldn't be burying an empty casket and laying her soul to rest beneath the ground. She would be standing with me in town, and we'd be distracting ourselves, at least for a few hours, from everything happening around us. If I had done everything I could have, she'd be alive, Emilee."

I don't realize I'm sobbing now until my voice cracks on the last word.

Emilee pulls me into a hug, and I cry into her shoulder. She doesn't say anything at first, and for this moment I'm her little brother, hiding from the nightmares that haunt me as she hugs me and tells me it's going to be okay.

But nothing is okay.

After a few moments, Emilee sighs and holds me at arm's length. "I know you're hurting, and I know your first instinct is to jump back into the action and find a way to bring down the people who took Raegan from us. But you can't just go into this with clouded judgment. Raegan would want you to take a breath, to know you've done your best and that you are good enough. So, don't do something stupid. I don't want to bury you next, okay?"

I know she's right, but I won't dare admit it out loud. I know she worries. She's my older sister, and they tend to do that far too much. I finally give her a small "Okay" before she goes to join our mom and the others again.

As the crowd moves away, people move toward the hole to fill in the rest of the dirt over the casket. I go back one more time, looking down at the spot that represents Raegan's final resting place.

"I love you, darlin'. Your death will not be in vain."

MONDAY
OCTOBER 16TH, 2023

MY MOM PULLS INTO the parking lot of my school. I look at the students rushing from cars of their own, wishing now more than ever that I could be alone. I love my mom, but I need space to think. Her constant barrage of questions doesn't help me, especially when she's quizzing me on what to say if people ask about Raegan.

I hate it.

Slipping out of her car, I grab my backpack from the floorboard. Slamming the car door harder than I intend to, I pull the hood of my jacket over my head. My mom rolls the window down and calls out to me. Stopping, I take a few steps back to hear her.

"Peter, I know things are going to be harder going back in there, especially knowing word got around already, but—"

I hold up my hand. "You mean the cover-up got

around? Mom, I know you're trying to help, but I can't handle talking about this anymore."

My mom nods, looking a bit disappointed. I hate disappointing anyone, but I can't take another talk about what to say if people ask, or what to do if there are questions. I know the lies I have to give. I know I have to protect the resistance, the very resistance I'm beginning to doubt. I walk away from her car and approach those big glass doors leading into the school. People stare at me like I'm some anomaly. Like I don't belong.

The joke's on them. I don't.

No one truly belongs here anymore. Invisible lines are being drawn; people are beginning to choose sides. Even if they can't see it yet. Everyone here fears the word rebellion. Whispered rumors and faint conversations fill the halls, all centering on that one word they fear the most. A few people are lingering in the main hallway, staring at me as I walk past them. I ignore their sympathetic glances. I don't need the pity. I need action.

Opening my locker, I slowly start organizing the few things I'm allowed to keep here. Pens, pencils, notebooks, my textbooks... I have time to kill and nothing else to do with it.

Footsteps echo off the walls, coming closer. I assume it's a soldier patrolling the halls, as they always do. Lately, soldier activity in the area has increased, something I take to be a bad sign. They patrol the streets day and night, always watching. In school, there seems to be more of them, lurking around corners, waiting to hear one wrong word, see one wrong move. I don't know why, but the feeling in my gut—the feeling that something wicked is coming—never fades.

As the footsteps get closer, I risk a glance up. Instead of a burly soldier, I'm greeted by Nicole.

"Where the *hell* have you been?"

She stands in front of me, her arms crossed against her chest. She's in an oversized gray pullover, most likely Sawyer's, black yoga pants, and sneakers. Her red hair is in a messy bun, and the dark circles under her eyes give away the lack of sleep as much as the absence of her usual makeup.

"Good morning to you, too, Sunshine."

A pang of hurt hits my chest as I remember saying the same thing to Raegan whenever she complained about being awake too early.

Nicole's glare burns holes into the side of my head. "Don't give me that crap. You've been hiding out since the funeral. I assume you've been avoiding me."

I exhale slowly, gripping my locker door until my knuckles turn white. "I haven't been avoiding you. I just haven't been to school."

Her eyes soften, and I can see the tears she's holding back. She rubs her eyes to prevent them from falling.

"Fine. I just…" Her words trail off. She looks ready to break apart. Gathering herself, she says, "I know there's more to Raegan's death than a car accident. She never rode along with anyone else besides me or Sawyer. And she usually drove herself. And even if the story is true, you would have been with her wherever she was. Please… I can't take these lies anymore. What *really* happened?"

It's clear from her distress and desperation that this has been bothering her for a while. But I don't know what to tell her. I'm scared to make the same mistake again and put her in harm's way.

"She was with some people from church. The driver lost control. That's—"

Nicole puts her finger to my lips, stopping my scripted answer. "You know, that's the same story

20

everyone is telling me, but I just can't find anyone in the church who's been in an accident recently. Besides, I can see it in your eyes, Peter. You don't believe that bullcrap, either. So, tell me what you know."

I push her hand away, gently. "I already did."

"Peter, please. I know there is so much more to this. The evidence is there. The casket was closed. Don't lie to me like everyone else. Please...I trust you."

I glance around. A couple of sleepy teenagers are standing just out of earshot, oblivious to this conversation. Other than that, the hallway is clear.

I sigh. "We can't talk about this here. I'll give you the answers you're looking for soon, Nicole. But not right now."

Nodding slowly, she says, "You're hurting just as much as I am, if not more. I'm sorry. I shouldn't have come after you like that."

I try to offer comfort, but it's weak. And Nicole doesn't buy it. I don't have any message of hope or anything motivating to say. Everything sucks.

Nicole lingers a little longer, so I say, "I promise I'll give you answers. But not now."

Skepticism is etched on her face, but she doesn't

say anything more. Giving me a weak smile, she turns and walks away. I don't know where she disappears to, but soon the hallway is just as silent and cold as before. The other two students have disappeared. I sigh, slamming my locker shut, the sound echoing down the hall before fading to nothing.

I find myself walking to my first class, math. There are a few other people here, talking quietly. Others are studying the whiteboard. I find a seat in the back of the room, my hood still pulled up over my head.

Whispered conversations fill the air, finding their way to the back corner that I've claimed for myself.

"He was friends with that girl they said died a couple of weeks ago. That's why he looks all depressed."

"I heard about that. She was in a car accident, right?"

"Yeah, she had gotten sick right before and was gone for a bit. I heard she was just getting better before that happened. It's really sad."

Hearing this is torture. I hate how they talk about her as if they care. They didn't know her. They never tried to.

I want to shout the truth right here, right now.

It wasn't an accident! She was killed. You're all being brainwashed.

But I know how that would end for me. Soldiers marching in, ready to take me down before I say too much more. I'd be dead before sunset. Captured and taken to the torture bases, then killed for believing something different.

I rest my head on my desk, closing my eyes. Counting my every breath, and every beat of my heart, to calm my mind. It doesn't do much, but it stops me from doing something I'd regret.

AFTER THE DAY IS half over, I find it easier to fall into a state of numb nirvana. I do all my work, and I keep my head low. All that awaits me after lunch is English and history. One of those being better than the others. English is an easier pill to swallow when history class is no longer the same.

Hiding in the back again, I pull out all my stuff. My English teacher, Ms. Whites, begins writing a line of poetry on the dry-erase board. The loudspeakers mounted to the ceilings crackle to life, startling the girl sitting a few seats ahead of me.

"Good afternoon, Cyrus High. This is Principal Hughes speaking. I want to draw your attention to a tragic loss that our school has suffered. As many of you may know, one of our students, Raegan MacArthur, was killed in a car accident two weeks ago. There have been some rumors floating around about why she hasn't been in school, and my staff and I have decided that it's time we put those to rest. We would ask you to please respect her family's wishes for privacy at this time. And remember, a loss like this is something we all grieve. If you feel like you need to talk to someone, we have counselors ready to speak with you before and after classes. Thank you."

I roll my eyes. No one took the time to get to know Raegan. No one cared about her. But she didn't mind. She was always kind to everyone, even though it was never repaid. She didn't care that no one showed the same respect to her. She still did it because that was who she was.

I feel eyes fall on me with the hush in the room. I keep my eyes focused on my notebook, tapping my pencil rhythmically on the table, trying to keep my cool. Everyone knows I was always with Raegan. I was by her side whenever we weren't in class. I feel my eyes water again, but I blink back the tears. I won't let anyone see my emotions, especially not here.

I start copying the poem, even though Ms. White hasn't begun the lesson yet. Anything to distract my mind from this cruel reality.

School drags on at a snail's pace. A few of my classmates approach me, their pitying condolences grating on my nerves. They never cared for me before. Why start now? Still, I play nice; I thank them, and accept the hugs when they want to give them. Everything feels fake.

School is finally over, and I rush outside, feeling as if the walls are closing in on me. I expect to see my mom's car somewhere, but I can't find her. I check my phone. There's a text from her on the screen.

Running late, honey. I'm sorry. I'll be there as soon as possible.

I groan. I want to go home, away from this hell. A truck pulls up to the curb and the window rolls down.

Spencer. "Do you need a ride?"

I shake my head. "My mom's running late. She said she'll be here as soon as possible."

Spencer sighs. "We both know that means she's going to be super late. I didn't drive all this way over here for you to refuse a ride."

I open the passenger door and slide in. While I buckle up, Spencer pulls away from the curb, turning onto the main road out of here, and I text my mom that Spencer came to pick me up. Not that she's rushing to get me. I lean back in the seat and close my eyes, though all I hear is the gunshot and the scream like a broken record in my head.

As Spencer pulls onto the highway, I open my eyes and say, "Don't you usually give Hannah a ride?"

Spencer's hands grip the wheel a little tighter. "Let's just say we're on a break right now."

"Oh. I'm sorry," I say.

Spencer doesn't reply. I don't try to make any conversation for a while, not sure how to change the subject. He doesn't seem to be in a hurry to say anything, either.

So, most of the ride is in silence, which I don't mind.

Finally, Spencer breaks the quiet.

"How are you holding up? You haven't been around, and I didn't get to talk with you at the funeral."

I shrug. "I'm fine."

"Bull crap. Try again, this time with the truth."

I don't say anything. He's not wrong. Spencer continues talking as he pulls in front of my house. "I'm really sorry. I know you loved her."

I still can't find the words. Not for someone else, anyway. I can't say them without saying them to her. So, I settle for nodding. "We grew up together," I say instead. "Friends since we were little in the church nursery. We were inseparable. Then my dad took a promotion my mom begged him not to take. We moved to California and she still managed to stay closer to me than any of the friends I made there. Living life without her is hell. And it's only been two weeks."

Spencer nods. "So, what are you planning? I'm worried about you. I overheard you and your sister at the funeral. Hunting Evan down and making him pay won't solve anything. Not at this point."

"Why not?" I can feel my anger rising steadily.

He hesitates, then says, "I can't tell you yet, but

27

we have a lead into things happening with the government. If you act too soon, it could mess things up."

I shake my head, opening the door, and grabbing my bag. "I have to do my own thing when it comes to this."

Spencer sighs. "Yeah, I knew you would say that. Don't get yourself killed, all right?"

I step out of the truck, close the door and walk up to my house. When I'm inside, I sink against the door and my resolve crumbles completely.

CHAPTER TWO

Evan

MONDAY, OCTOBER 16TH, 2023

I SEAL THE LAST BOX OF MY ITEMS AS I look around my office. Everything I'll need in DC has been packed up. My door flies open, nearly slamming into the wall before the hinges catch it. Samantha stands in the doorway, looking like an absolute mess.

Her strawberry blonde hair is down in waves past her shoulders. She's in jeans and a t-shirt rather than her usual business casual attire. No high heels adorn her feet; she's wearing black Converse sneakers. I don't know if I should be alarmed, but I *do* know I'm staring much longer than I should.

She enters the office, all fire and rage. "I'm being relocated."

"Oh really? I didn't know," I say, gesturing around my office. "Relocation? What a shock."

Her glare could burn holes into my head if she

wanted it to. I think she wants it to.

I turn and stack a few boxes on top of each other. "We're all being relocated. Except for Jackson, who told me to get all my stuff the hell out of his office."

Samantha groans. "I know you're aware. I'm saying if we're pulled in different directions, how are we supposed to take President Morgan down? Did you think of that yet, oh Wise One? Or were you too busy staring at me?"

My mouth opens to defend myself, but I quickly shut it. There is no defense I can come up with that will ever be enough for this woman.

I sigh, resting my arm on the stack of boxes in front of me. "We will figure something out. We're both going back to DC first, so I'll talk with him. I'll tell him I want a personal assistant and that you've been such a good help to me. Maybe he'll let me keep you."

"You say that as if I'm a pet. You don't own me, Evan Williams."

I rub my face with my hand, bothered that my name sounds good coming from her lips. "You know what I meant. Don't take it wrong or twist my words. I thought we were beyond that by now."

She nods. "I suppose we are. I guess we can see how that goes."

She falls silent for a moment, and I label the final box with a sharpie.

Finally, she says, "How does it feel leaving your family like this?"

There's something soft about the question. Something innocent. Every emotion I've had is flooding through my body. I'm leaving everyone I love behind *because* I love them. What a twisted, wicked world this is.

I shrug. "I've had to put my feelings away for a long time now. What I want isn't going to be what I get. I must obey orders and do as I'm told. My family wants nothing to do with me now, anyway, so it's not like it matters. They hate me."

That last sentence nearly chokes me.

They hate me.

They hate me.

They.

Hate.

Me.

"What about Carissa?" she says. "You don't know where she went."

I tense at that. I regret what happened that

night. At least if I'd let Jackson go with her, I'd have known she made it somewhere safe. But my threats kept him here, like a dog obeying his master.

"She can take care of herself."

At that, Samantha lets a small smile slip. "Oh, you misunderstand me. I know she can take care of herself. But *you're* her older brother. You need to know if she's safe. Where would she have gone? She's hated at home, too. She can't go home; she can't run to Jackson's house. She's alone. She doesn't have money—at least not enough."

I shake my head. "I don't need you repeating my thoughts out loud, okay? Why did you come in here? Is it because you're worried about Carissa, or because you're worried about being relocated where you can't keep your eyes on me to report back to your own master?"

Samantha steps closer to my desk. "Neither. I'm worried about you. Killing someone for the first time is… it's not easy. Most people would lose their minds. They'd flirt with the edge of insanity. But you seem to be acting as if everything is normal, and I guess I worry you aren't letting yourself feel the emotions you need to feel."

I think back to the moment, the dark place in

my head I refuse to let my mind wander to. I find my emotions have run cold; there's nothing there for me to feel about the situation. What does she expect me to feel? To think? I can't ask. She's practically an assassin. She's taken the lives of many, all at the snap of her fingers.

She won't understand what I've done.

"I don't need your concern. I'm fine."

She comes closer, passing the desk and standing in front of me. She rests her hand on my chest, right above my heart. It pounds fast, hard. "This says otherwise."

My pounding heart has nothing to do with what I've done. Her hand moves up, finding itself on my shoulder. "It's okay to feel something. If you're numb to it, that's when there's a problem."

"You're numb to everything. Why should I be different?"

"Because you still have a heart left. Mine was broken too long ago; it died with my parents and… someone else. But you… you still have something in there. You still have the luxury to think for yourself, to feel emotions you can't control. You haven't been made into a robot for the bigger machine."

33

I bring my hand to her cheek, but she withdraws, taking a few steps back. "W-what are you doing?" she says.

I look down at my feet, unsure what to say. Whatever just happened feels like a punch to the gut. She exhales carefully, slowly.

Her eyes fill with tears as she says, "I'm sorry."

I shrug. "What for?"

"I can't feel the same way you can. I'm not... I'm numb to everything. Just like you said."

I step around my desk, closer to her. "I didn't mean it like that. I meant to say that you've become used to going on missions and killing people if the president bids you to do so. I didn't mean you aren't human."

Samantha turns and walks to the door, but I rush after her, holding it shut with my hand. She turns, our proximity not lost on her. Refusing to meet my eyes, she says, "Let me go. Please."

"Not until you tell me what you can and can't feel."

She sighs. "I can't love someone. I don't have that emotion."

"Love is something everyone feels."

She shakes her head. "No, you don't

34

understand. Love is a weapon to be used against someone only when they least expect it. Love is dangerous. Evil. Look at what you've become because of it."

I step back, but she doesn't make a move to leave yet. She can't feel the way I feel. I don't even know why I'm feeling attracted to her. We have no connection beyond our mutual agreement to take the president down. But as she stands here, biting her lip in nervousness, I wonder if there is something deeper between us. We've been working together for a while now.

"What if it isn't?"

She looks up. Hoarsely, she says, "What?"

"What if love isn't dangerous? What if no one uses it against you? Then what? Would you allow yourself to feel something for someone?"

"No," she says softly, almost inaudibly. "Because my ability to love died when my parents did. I've been exposed to the cold for too long."

With that, she leaves, closing the office door behind her. I exhale slowly, trying to figure out how we got here. I shake my head, running a hand through my hair. This is not how I imagined my confession would go.

I brush everything off for the time being. I can't think about it, any of it, when I have so much more to focus on right now. I call Jackson to help me move some of the boxes to my car. We're flying to D.C. in Air Force One, but the drive to the nearest airport will still take a good half of the day. It gives me time to think, to plan. Samantha will be coming with me. We are supposed to come up with a game plan, but now things might be awkward.

After loading up the final box, Jackson offers for me to stay at his place for the night. We don't leave until tomorrow morning, and this warehouse will be too easy for the resistance to find me, to retaliate. Even though it's been two weeks, and everything has been quiet, I don't trust is enough to stay here.

I park at Jackson's apartment. His black car is parked a few spots away. An old lady sits on the porch outside the building. She looks at me and says, "Finally, someone who knows how to pull into a parking lot."

"Um, thanks?" I say.

She points to Jackson's car. "The boy that

owns that car speeds right into the parking lot. He could hit a kid or some innocent bystander."

"Oh."

The door to Jackson's apartment opens and he steps outside. "Hey, there you are. Come on in. I just had pizza delivered."

I follow him inside and say, "Your neighbor has such fond things to say of you."

He scowls. "Yeah, I'm sure she does. She's crazy. Talks to herself a lot. I'm not talking about the normal amount. I mean full-blown conversations as if she's actually talking to someone."

"All right, then."

Jackson leads me to the small living room. The couch has extra pillows and blankets. "This is yours, for now. And anything in the fridge or pantry is yours, too."

"Thanks. I'm pretty tired and not very hungry, so I think I'm going to get some sleep."

Jackson nods. "Sure thing. I'll be in my room. Pizza's on the counter if you get hungry."

Jackson takes his slices of pizza and walks down the hall to his room. I kick off my shoes and pull off my shirt. Pulling the blanket up over my shoulders, I close my eyes. For a moment, there is peace.

Until my nightmares replay everything I don't want to see.

CHAPTER THREE
Peter
THURSDAY, OCTOBER 19TH, 2023

I LEAN AGAINST THE STONE PILLAR AT THE entrance to the school, waiting for my mother, who is running late. *Again.* Every day this week she's been late, and I don't want to bother Spencer for another ride. I glance across the parking lot and see Spencer's ex, Hannah. She's talking to a football player I've seen around the halls. He's not the jerk-jock stereotype. He's quiet, much like Hannah is.

Hannah's eyes meet mine, then she quickly turns away and gets into his car. I'm glad Spencer isn't here to see this. I'm sure seeing Hannah move on so quickly would not be fun for him.

But then. Spencer pulls up to the curb in his truck, the window already down. "Looks like you need a ride."

The car with Hannah and her new boyfriend is

already gone, and I can't tell from his expression if he saw them or not. I hope for his sake that he didn't notice. "Why are you here?"

He looks at me like it's obvious, but says, "I already said it looks like you need a ride. So, are you going to get in, or did I waste a forty-five-minute drive to get here?"

I sigh, pushing off the pillar and shouldering my backpack. I open the truck, throwing my stuff in the back seat before sliding in. "I guess you know my mom is running late?"

He doesn't say anything. He doesn't have to. It's become routine. My mom runs late, Spencer takes notice and comes to the rescue. I buckle up as he pulls away and I watch the school get smaller and smaller in the rear-view mirror.

We're silent for a while, but I dread what might come. Every time I ride with Spencer, there's something he wants to say about how I'm handling things. Deep down I know he's right. But I'm tired of sitting and waiting for Evan to be caught. I'm tired of Mr. Williams not being willing to do anything to retaliate. We must show them we aren't going to back down.

Instead, Spencer says, "How long has Hannah

been hanging around that guy?"

My eyes widen as I look at him. His jaw clenches and his knuckles turn white from his grip on the steering wheel. For a moment, I think I see something akin to sadness in his eyes, sadness mixed with anger and perhaps jealousy.

"Honestly, I only saw them today. I haven't seen her around school much, and I don't know much about him. I don't even know his name. I know he plays football, but he's not much of a jock. He's pretty quiet."

Spencer nods, not saying anything for a while again.

I say, "Do you... want to talk about it? I thought you told me it was just a break."

Spencer laughs, but there's no humor in the sound. "Hannah texted me two days ago saying she doesn't want to get back together and that the break made her realize she needs to work on herself. I guess by 'work on herself' she meant she found someone new."

We're at a stoplight. Spencer lets his hands fall from the wheel for a moment as he stares blankly out onto the open road ahead of us. I stay silent, knowing that's what he needs for this moment.

He shakes his head. "There are bigger, more important things going on in this world right now. Like how your mom is so busy lately. She's put in more hours than most of the resistance. Combined."

"I guess she figures that's more important than coming to get her son," I mumble.

Spencer says nothing to my comment. I grab my notebook out of my bag and begin on the homework that I need to catch up on from missing two weeks. I hope it will keep Spencer from talking about Raegan. I don't like talking about everything that's happened. And remembering the good times is just as hard; every memory is tainted with the outcome.

I get some homework done, making a dent in all the overdue assignments. Spencer pulls into my neighborhood, so I pack my things up. I know it's rude not to have talked to him, and I feel the guilt gnawing in my gut. So, I say, "I'm sorry about Hannah."

He gives me a sideways glance. "Oh, he does speak."

I sigh. "You're right. I didn't mean to ignore you the whole ride. You didn't deserve that. Especially considering all you've done for me lately."

He nods, turning down my street. "You're right, I didn't. But I get it. You've got a lot going on in that head of yours, too. It's fine."

As he pulls in front of my house, I see my mom's car is still in the driveway. I look at him. "You said she was busy working."

He smirks and punches my arm. "Happy birthday."

"What?"

"It's your birthday, right? That's what your mom told me when she came up with this plan."

I run a hand through my hair before pulling the hood back over my head. "Well... yes. But what does that have to do with anything?"

He smirks. "Why don't you go find out for yourself?"

I get out of the truck and walk across the lawn to the porch of my house. Spencer is behind me, and I'm curious to see what it is my mom has planned.

"I don't think I like this," I say.

Spencer leans against the brick of our house. "Yeah, well, you need to let yourself be happy, even if it's just for one night."

"Happy? How could I ever think about being

happy when Raegan is dead?" I choke on the last word. Clearing my throat, I say, "I'll be happy when Evan has paid for what he's done."

Spencer shakes his head, tucking his hands in his pockets. I start to dig for my keys in my backpack. He steps up onto the porch, placing his hand on my shoulder. "I know why you don't want to be happy right now, but she'd want you to try."

I grip my keys harder than I need to, my mind spinning. I don't have it in me to be happy. And I certainly don't want people telling me what Raegan would want. But instead, I don't say anything. I jam the key into the door and turn the lock.

Spencer follows me inside the house, the open floor plan of my home giving me a view of the living room and kitchen. I don't see my mom, but I smell food cooking. Spencer says, "You aren't the only one that misses her, you know. I miss Raegan, too. And yeah, maybe I wasn't close to her, but I know she wouldn't want you spiraling out of control. And I know why you're spiraling. I spiraled when I lost my parents. I just want to help you make better choices than I did."

His words hit me hard. I let my backpack fall onto the couch. "You're right. You're right, I've been acting like I'm the only one affected by this. And I'm not. But I'm not ready to be happy yet. I'm not ready to let myself forget for a moment what's happened to her. I will do my best to enjoy the evening, but happiness is a stretch."

Spencer nods. "That's fair."

My mom comes in from the garage; she was probably getting something from the freezer we keep out there. "Peter! You're back. Surprise! I thought I would be done cooking by the time you got back, but unfortunately, I didn't have everything and had to run to the store. But I'm making your favorite Italian dishes. I've got chicken alfredo already made, and some fettuccine pasta. Oh, and for dessert, I'm working on the chocolate cake!"

I walk around the counter and hug my mom, really hug her. We haven't exchanged many words at all this week. I've been too busy drowning in my grief to see that she has her own. And now she's worked hard at making a meal for my birthday.

Mom hugs me back and says softly, "I'm sorry I haven't been around enough for you, Peter. This isn't going to make up for that, but I hope you're surprised."

I smile, wiping at my eyes to keep a few tears at bay. "I am. Thank you."

Spencer claps his hands. "Well, this has been touching, but there are too many emotions in one room, so let's talk about how I tricked you into thinking your mom was too busy to come and pick you up."

My mom frowns, probably knowing that's a little too accurate to be called a trick. Spencer keeps smiling, trying to change the subject again. "Mrs. Daniels, whatever you're cooking smells amazing."

My mom smiles again, stirring some pasta. "Thank you, Spencer. You can call me Michelle. It's been so long since I've been married to Mr. Daniels that I don't use his name anymore. But I think we're on a first-name basis at this point."

Spencer inhales sharply, realizing his mistake. "On that note, I'm going to borrow Peter for a moment, if that's okay."

My mom hugs me one more time and says, "Of course. I'll call you boys when dinner is ready."

I lead Spencer out onto the back patio. The sun has started its slow descent. It's October, the autumn season not quite in full swing for Texas, but there's a chill to the air.

"What did you want to talk about?" I say once the back door is closed.

Spencer crosses his arms. "Your mom is inviting a few of your other friends. And apparently, they've been asking questions. The red-haired girl doesn't seem to take the cover story seriously."

I lean back against the pillar holding the cover to the patio. "And where did you hear that?"

"She asked your mom after you promised her some answers a couple of days ago. You know you can't give her anything, right?"

"And how do you know that?"

Spencer shrugs. "Your mom tells my uncle a lot of things. She tends to ramble off when she's exhausted. I happened to be with my uncle when she started talking about all of that. My uncle trusts that you know what you're doing, but I know you better than that."

I don't say anything, looking out into the backyard instead. Spencer sighs. "I don't want to get into an argument with you because it is your birthday, but you have to be rational about this."

"I am being rational. If Nicole doesn't know anything, she'll go hunting for the answers herself.

I have to tell them something."

Spencer pinches the bridge of his nose as if this is stressing him out. "Again, I don't want to argue with you because it's your birthday. But think about the danger you could be putting them in if you tell them anything."

I nod, but I don't make any promises. We head back inside, just in time for the doorbell to ring. My mom, still finishing the cooking, asks me to get it. I walk over and am greeted by Nicole and Sawyer, both carrying gift bags.

"Y'all didn't have to get me anything," I say.

Nicole hugs me quickly. "Of course we do! It's your birthday, silly."

I give a small smile, the only type of smile I can afford these days. Nicole and Sawyer set the gifts on the cherry wood coffee table.

Nicole looks better than she did the other day. She's back to her fancier clothes and makeup. The two of them walk to the kitchen table. Sawyer starts a conversation with my mom. I turn to see Spencer looking a little *too* long at Nicole. I elbow him in the ribs. "She's got a boyfriend and you have no chance."

Spencer rubs his side. "Ha. Ha. I was in

thought, thank you very much."

"Yeah, sure," I say before making my way into the kitchen. Spencer follows me, making a point now of *not* looking at Nicole.

The table is covered with all my favorite Italian dishes. A chocolate cake sits in the center. Spencer and I sit down as my mom begins dishing out the pasta. She is smiling, something I haven't seen her do in a while. It makes me almost want to smile, too. Almost.

Instead, I say, "You didn't have to do all of this, Mom."

"I wanted to, Peter. I want you to have something special on your birthday. Today is a big day. You're an adult, but you've been an adult for longer than any of us realize. I wanted to give you something that would make you happy, even if it's just for this evening."

I nod and offer a sad smile. I don't know what to say. And anything I might say will only come out wrong. Nicole must pick up on my lack of words because she says, "Michelle, this is quite the amazing spread of food you've made. I didn't know you could cook like this."

My mom beams at the compliment. "Well, I

haven't been cooking much recently. We haven't been here for too many meals lately since we're always on the move. But I do love to cook."

I want to say that it's not that *we* haven't been home. I'm hardly ever out of the house these days, except for school. But I don't say any of that. My mom went to a lot of effort to give me a good meal with some good friends. I won't ruin it because of my own emotions.

At first, no one speaks. The room is deathly silent. I hear the *tik, tik, tik* of the wall clock that hangs above the pantry. Forks and spoons scrape against the plates; the salad tongs rattle against the bowl, and my mom smiles as though that will bring enough light to the darkness that covers us all.

Finally, Nicole says, "So, how has work been for you, Michelle? I know you've been super busy lately."

My mom gives her automatic answers about accounting, which I can see Nicole studying for inconsistencies. But she never questions, only adding a bit to the conversation, filling gaps so it isn't so awkward. Spencer glances up at me and mouths *Are you okay*? I shake my head. In my mind, I hear Raegan's last words to me over and over.

They are my heaven and my hell all at once. Regret grips my heart. I can't take this pleasant conversation any longer. I feel as though I'm suffocating. I stand up.

"I need to take a moment," I say abruptly before rushing out of the kitchen. I breeze through the hallway and enter my room. I shut the door as quietly as I can and walk to the window. I feel the tears sting my eyes again, the familiar ache of unbridled pain. When I'm not angry, the grief is intense.

I hear my door brush open. I glance back, fully expecting it to be my mom checking up on me. But I find it's not my mom at all. It's Nicole.

I wipe my eyes. "I just need a minute."

She steps inside, her heels clicking on the honey-colored floor. The door falls shut behind her and she leans against it. "Peter, you're one of my best friends. I know you were always closer to Raegan. And honestly, I didn't mind. But that doesn't change the fact that I want to be here for you. I'm sorry for how aggressive I was to you earlier this week. It wasn't fair of me to expect anything from you right now. I didn't mean to make things harder on you."

I shake my head, turning fully to face her. "No, Nicole... it's okay. I forget we *all* lost someone to this. I'm not the only one grieving, and everyone deserves the truth."

Nicole nods and silence falls upon us for a moment. Then she says, "You're right. Sawyer and I lost a best friend. The MacArthurs lost their daughter. The town lost a neighbor. But you... you lost someone more than that. And you can deny it all you want. I saw the look in your eyes just as I saw the look in hers. Maybe it wasn't that you were in love, but that the connection was so much deeper. You understood her and she understood you. You lost your soulmate. We all hurt, yes. But that doesn't take your pain away, either."

I sigh. "This would be so much easier if you knew the truth."

Nicole looks at her feet. "Yeah, it would. But it's your birthday. I'm not going to bother you with it tonight."

I desperately want to tell her everything right now, but I know I won't be able to handle giving her the story. Not after Spencer begged me not to. Not with the knowledge that I'd be putting her life at risk. So instead, I say, "Her last words to me were that she loved me."

Nicole's eyes go wide. "What?"

I sigh. "She told me she loved me. And I didn't say it back."

With no context, it makes no sense. Yet I've had to hold onto this for so long.

"I wish I'd said it back," I whisper, my voice cracking on the last word.

Nicole doesn't say anything. She closes the distance between us and wraps her arms around me. "She did love you. And you loved her. And now it's time for you to let go for the night and live a moment of happiness before everything falls apart again."

She's right. The world is falling apart outside. I need to give in and just live this moment, though it hurts so much.

Nicole pulls away and heads for the door. I follow behind her, slowly. The hallway is dark, but soon we're in the light of the kitchen. I take my seat by Spencer again, and my mom and Nicole fall back into the conversation as if nothing happened. I appreciate this. I can't handle the sad looks my mom gives me whenever our eyes meet. I don't meet her eyes this time, finding my seat at the table again.

Dinner carries on. I'm even able to join in on talking about things happening at school, about the fluctuation of soldier activity.

Finally, my mom rises to gather the dishes and says, "It's a nice evening. Why don't the four of you go outside for a little bit? I'll start cleaning up in here."

Nicole offers to help her first, but my mom insists that we all go do something outside. I can tell that means she needs time to think things over without interruption, so I tell everyone to follow me.

Outside, everyone stands on the patio, but I go to the middle of the yard. The crisp autumn air is a welcome break from the usually hot weather. The sun is dipping down fast beyond the horizon. I turn back to Nicole and Sawyer, who look at me as though wondering what could be going through my head. I sigh. "I promised you an explanation."

Rubbing the back of my neck, I return to the patio. Spencer watches me. He gives a slight shake of his head, the small gesture begging me not to say anything. But I'm done lying to people who deserve answers.

"Raegan didn't die in a car accident."

Spencer shuts his eyes and pinches the bridge of his nose. "You can't do this," he says in a tight, yet stern voice. "You compromise things when you do this, Daniels."

I lean my back against the cool brick of the house. "I can't lie to them. I've done plenty of lying and I'm tired of nothing ever-changing. They deserve the truth as much as everyone else."

Nicole looks a little baffled like she's not sure if she wants to hear the words I might say now that they're so close. I close my eyes for a second, and the last words from Raegan repeat in my head. Those four words. I need to block them out to focus on this, yet I don't have the heart.

Finally, I meet Nicole's blue-green eyes. "Raegan was killed because of her involvement in the resistance against the government, one I introduced her to. Her parents were already involved, and so is my mom. It killed me to hide that part of me from her, so I chose not to. Eventually, she was recruited. And to get back at me for rising in the ranks, someone who I thought I could trust took her."

I struggle as I tell the rest of this story. I don't

hide anything about my involvement in the rescue and how I defied orders. Spencer looks thoroughly annoyed, but eventually helps me by lending information whenever I need to pause. The truth falls out of me until I am both numb and out of breath. My heart pounds at the memories of betrayal and death.

A few stray tears have fallen from my eyes. Nicole's face is red and puffy from crying. A couple of times as I spoke, she turned and cried into Sawyer's shirt, as he stroked her hair and comforted her. She and Sawyer stare at me now, stricken. Even Spencer, who lived through it all, looks sickened at hearing the whole story again.

A silence falls upon us all. I can't look any of them in the eye. Not when hot tears sting my own. Not when I replay Raegan's last words and her scream over and over in my head. I turn away, leaning my side against the house, watching out in the backyard at nothing. Enough to keep me from falling apart in front of them.

Finally, Nicole steps over to me. I look down at her as she touches my shoulder. "Raegan loved you. She wouldn't want you… to stay like this. She loved your vibrancy. Your heart. So why do you insist on hiding those away now?"

I step away from her, from everyone. The sun has now dipped completely past the horizon, though the rays of light struggle to poke through the dust that stays in the air. "I can't have peace knowing her murderer is still out there somewhere. He has to pay for what he's done."

The words fall so easily from my mouth. But Nicole's words have prodded something inside of me to wonder if I want justice for Raegan, or if I'm looking to have my revenge on Evan.

I RINSE THE PLATE in my hands before putting it in the dishwasher. Everyone left ten minutes ago, and I'm helping my mom clean up what was left in the kitchen. We don't say much. Everything feels broken apart as if no words can fix the silence that falls between us.

Finally, my mom says, "I'm worried about you."

"I know. You're my mom. You always worry about me."

"No," she says. "I mean... you're eighteen. That means a lot of different things. There's the draft if Andre can't rig your name out of the system in time. There's the fact that you can go on missions... I'm..." She pauses. "I'm not ready for you to be an adult."

I look up from the plate in my hand; my mom looks weary. I set the plate down and say, "Mom, I'm not going anywhere. I'm sure Mr. Williams will get my name out of the system soon enough. And if you haven't noticed, I haven't been working lately. I doubt he'd send me on a mission yet. I won't accept any if it makes you feel better."

She dabs her eyes with a paper towel. "So much has changed, and I—"

My phone rings from the table. My mom goes over and glances at it. "It's your father."

I dry my hands and grab my phone. "Hello?"

"Happy birthday, son."

Even with the two-hour time difference, I can't help but feel like it's late in the day to bother making a call. I suppose it's better than nothing. I lean against the counter. My mom goes down the hall to give me privacy. I wish I could tell her to stay, so I could talk to her some more.

Instead, I focus on the phone call. "Thanks, Dad."

"I sent you a gift in the mail, but I'm thinking it's running a little late. Sorry about that."

I don't want a gift to replace the absence he's created for years. My dad is punctual for many things, but holidays and birthdays are not one of them. "No problem. It'll get here when it gets here. How have you been?"

"Busy. Work has been killing all my free time. But, um, I wanted to apologize for not making the funeral. I know it's a big deal with what happened, and I was packed and ready. But things came up, and—"

"You don't have to make an excuse, Dad. You couldn't come, and I'm not mad about it. Emilee was there. She told me you tried to get away. It's okay." I exhale slowly, hoping the tightness in my throat isn't obvious.

"Thank you," Dad says. In his voice, I hear relief. I know he probably thought I was mad at him, but honestly, I'm not. I've come to realize, after all these years, that his work takes first place ahead of everything else. And I think there's a part of me that's accepted that's how it will be. Even during tragedy, you can find my father at work. It's a quality both of my parents unfortunately share, and I can only hope the trait skipped me because I never want to be that way for my future family.

My dad talks about work and his new intern. He talks about Emilee and her boyfriend and anything he can think of to fill the silence. I offer up a few "oh's" and "ah's" as he speaks. Thankfully, after a couple of minutes, he has to go, ending the call for another business-related thing. I couldn't handle it if we talked for much longer anyway. I'm thankful for the silence as I finish the dishes. When I walk down the hall, I see my mom has fallen asleep on her neatly made bed. I retreat to the living room, grabbing one of the blankets, and cover her with it. I know she's not sleeping much at all these days. I glance at her one more time before quietly shutting her door.

I need to clear my head. I need to run. But the sun has long since set, meaning curfew has been in effect for a good while.

A perfect way to get the adrenaline up.

I lace up my sneakers and zip up my hoodie. I start by walking from my house to the entrance of our neighborhood up the road. Then I begin running down Main Street, on the sidewalk, of course. The blood thunders through my veins, pumping me full of that addictive rush.

I push myself farther, faster, and harder than I ever have. My mind, for once, is clear and peaceful. It won't last long, but for now, I take it in. The crisp autumn air, the rush of blood coursing through my body, my feet pounding against the pavement… it's enough to make me feel less alone.

I find myself running to the park track, doing one lap around before veering off the track. I don't run through here, but carefully make my way to the clearing. I'm panting as I dodge branches and brush, but I keep going. A lone tree sits in the center, the leaves gold, red, orange, and brown. Some have fallen, but a majority still hang on to the branches. It's a wonderful sight to behold, even in the dim light of the moon.

"Look, Raegan, the leaves are how you like them," I say, mostly to myself, though the words seem to catch in the air. Maybe she hears me. Maybe she doesn't.

The wind rustles the branches, and I shake off the thought that it's her way of saying hello. It's a stupid idea, but oddly comforting, nonetheless.

My breathing is heavy, my heart still pounds against my chest, and I feel the ache of lack of use in my muscles. I take a seat under the tree, closing my eyes and breathing in the crisp air.

I hear a rustling noise from the bushes, causing me to shoot up to my feet. If a soldier passes through here, I'm screwed.

The bushes move and make way to reveal... a dog.

I laugh, despite myself, because I was close to climbing the tree to evade whatever danger might be here. He's furry, his coat a mix of whites, grays, and browns. I take a step forward, wondering if he has a collar. The dog comes to my feet and sits, looking up at me with big, sky-blue eyes.

Raegan's eyes.

I sigh, crouching down to check for tags. Nothing. I move past the dog, and he follows.

I shrug, figuring he'll find a distraction and leave, especially when I start running again. He chases me for a little while, never aggressive. I slow to a walk once I reach my neighborhood. He's kept up with me. The temperature is dropping.

When I reach my home, my mom is out on the porch. I don't know what could have woken her, but she stands there with the same blanket I put on her wrapped around her shoulders. Now I am really screwed.

"Peter, you had me worried. Get in the house before someone sees us." She sees the dog and says, "You have a shadow."

I nod. "Yeah, he found me in the park and wouldn't stop following me."

My mom usually is against animals in the house, but she says, "Bring him in."

I tilt my head to look at him, then back at her. "Really?"

She nods, turning to open the front door. "Yeah, he looks like he belongs to you. We'll put up flyers in the morning to find the owner, but I have a feeling he's a stray."

I smile. When I wait by the door, the fluff ball walks right inside as if he's done this a thousand times. My mom finds some paper bowls and fills one with water. The other she fills with leftover chicken we didn't finish the night before.

I go to shower while the dog eats. When I return, my mom is on the couch, typing away at her laptop. The dog sits at her feet. She looks up at me and says, "He's an Australian Shepherd. At least, mostly. I was curious."

I look down at him. He doesn't raise his head but blinks to acknowledge my presence. "Okay, and what does that mean?"

Mom shrugs. "I don't know. Whatever you want it to mean, I guess. I took a picture of him and did a little research. I also made some flyers to print out for tomorrow. He looks like he hasn't eaten in a while."

I nod. He is a bit skinny, and his fur is matted with mud in places, but he doesn't seem to care. I yawn, turning down the hall to go shower. I don't take too long, my body is exhausted from more than just the run.

I return to the living room ten minutes later to find my mom still on her computer, probably doing more work. The dog has curled up on the rug in front of the coffee table. His head perks up when he hears me. "I'm pretty tired, so I'll probably go to sleep soon."

My mom smiles. "Okay, honey. Good night."

I walk down the hall to my room and hear the little click of paws behind me. The dog marches past me, making circles and lying down on the floor by my bed. I shake my head, a small smile escaping past my defenses. I climb into bed, peeling off my t-shirt and throwing it onto my lounge chair by my window. I roll to my side, closing my eyes. Then the screams begin.

CHAPTER FOUR

Peter

FRIDAY, OCTOBER 20TH, 2023

MY ALARM CHIRPS, BUT I'M ALREADY awake. I sit up, seeing a mass of fur on the floor. I forgot about him. I chuckle to myself and he lifts his head. "Well, buddy, time to get you some food."

I slide out of bed, grab my shirt from my chair, and head down the hall. I pour some water into the Styrofoam bowl my mom used the night before. Then I get some more leftover chicken. I'll stop by the store on Main Street later and get him real bowls and kibble. And a leash. He can join me on my run tonight.

The dog comes around the corner and begins eating. I tilt my head. "I don't want to call you Dog every time I see you. You need a name."

He lifts his head, eyeing me for a second before turning back to the chicken. "All right, then. I'm going to go get dressed... Fido?"

The glare I receive makes me believe dogs do understand what humans say. I laugh and turn, walking up the hall. I grab some clothes and change. My mom is in the living room, ready for work when I return. She taps her watch.

"We have to get going."

I follow my mom to the car, leaving the dog-naming for later.

School is another day of hell. Everyone still follows me with looks of pity. I hate it. I don't see Sawyer or Nicole too much, except in class. Whenever I do see one or both of them, I hide. I have to avoid them now that they know the truth about everything. Maybe it's just the heaviness of the situation or the way it feels to know that they see the very raw parts of what hurts me. It's too hard to face them.

It's probably better I don't see them here, anyway. Nicole always has questions and being overheard in the halls is the last thing we need.

As the school day draws to a close, I think I've made it almost to safety. I'm standing at my locker, grabbing the things I need for my final class when I hear the all-too-familiar click of heels on the hard floor. I glance up. Nicole is at my side.

"You've been avoiding me, Peter."

She doesn't say it like a question. No, she knows exactly what I've been doing. "Yes, I have. Your point?"

She laughs dryly. "Don't give me that attitude." Then, in a lower voice, she says, "I need to talk to you."

I shut my locker a bit harder than I intend. "Not here, Nicole. You know better. We can talk after school."

She groans but turns and walks back up the hall. I head in the opposite direction to my class. It's my elective for the semester. Government. I hardly pay attention, and when the bell rings, I'm the first one out.

I throw my things in my locker and rush outside to the front pillar. I'm hoping my mom will be here before Nicole finds me, but I know the odds of that are slim.

Sure enough, Nicole is there in an instant. "You tried to leave before talking to me?"

I sigh. "Nicole—"

"No, no, it's fine. But I need to talk to you. I want in."

I don't even look at her. "No."

"Why not?" she asks, her heels clicking on the concrete steps as she descends two, then turns to face me.

"Because I didn't tell you what happened so that you'd want to join in. I told you so you could know the truth. We're not having this discussion."

Nicole crosses her arms. "It's not up to you what people do, Peter. I want to make a difference. Please. Tell me what I need to do."

Before I can deny her request again, Sawyer comes out. "Oh, there you are, Nicole." He turns and sees me. "Hey, Peter."

I know Sawyer will take my side on this. "I was just explaining to Nicole why she can't join the resistance."

His head whips toward her so fast, I'm surprised his neck doesn't crack. "Nicole... I thought we talked about this last night."

Nicole closes her eyes a moment. "I know, baby, but I can't sit here and do nothing. My best friend was killed. I know you're not oblivious to everything going on around us. I need to do this."

Sawyer looks a bit hurt. "But I thought we agreed you wouldn't do anything crazy until you've thought this through."

I open my mouth to say something, but just then Spencer pulls up to the curb. His expression is unreadable. He motions for me, so I approach the truck. "Your mom said you'll need a ride. I had nothing better to do, so I figured why not be your taxi now?"

"You're always a ray of sunshine," I say, opening the door and sliding in before Nicole can stop me. Not that she's paying me any attention. She's too busy arguing with Sawyer now.

Spencer glances out at the couple. "What's that about?"

"Oh, just Nicole wanting to join the resistance. Sawyer is against it. I told her no. The usual everyday normal high school life discussions."

"I told you not to tell them, Daniels. But hey, what do I know? It's not like I'm wise or anything."

I give him a look that says shut up, then glance back at Sawyer and Nicole. They're still arguing. Sawyer looks mad now, something I've never seen before. Nicole has her arms crossed and won't look him in the eye. She's trying not to cry, then, if she refuses to look at him. I don't think we need to stick around for this lovers' spat. Spencer seems to agree; he pulls away from the curb, leaving them behind.

I'll pay for it later, but for now, I can't handle the idea of anyone else that matters to me joining the resistance.

Spencer is silent—something I'm used to at this point. I've grown accustomed to his company on the way home from school, too. My mom is still unreliable as ever in that department.

He gives me a sideways glance. "So, are you going to keep sitting there quietly, or are you gonna talk?"

"I don't know. Not much to talk about. I ignore all my classes and do enough schoolwork to get me through without suspicion."

"I meant about Nicole," Spencer says.

I smirk. "You mean about how you were staring at her at dinner last night?"

Spencer's face goes bright red, and his hands grip the wheel harder. "I did *not* stare at her."

"No? You looked like you were checking her out. I'm sorry to tell you, but they've been dating for two years. They're arguing now, but they'll work it out."

"Have you seen Hannah with that guy again?" he asks, completely ignoring my statement.

I think back through my day. "No. I haven't

71

seen them again. Not together, anyway. Hannah and I share a class, and I have two classes with the guy. But I assume they leave before me since his car is never in the parking lot when I get outside."

Spencer turns right at a stoplight, taking us out of Cyrus and onto the country roads. I watch the trees move, just like Raegan used to do. My heart aches.

"It's not like it matters," he says. "She isn't coming back to me."

I look over at him. "I'm sorry."

He shrugs. "It's fine. We weren't a good match anyway. Back to more important matters. What are you going to do about Nicole?"

"What do you mean? I'm not getting involved."

He smirks. "You'll have to. You are Nicole's key to get in, or the door keeping her out."

I shook my head. "I got one person involved. I won't do it again."

Spencer sighs but doesn't say anything else. There's something else on his mind; that much I can see. I can't tell if it has to do with Hannah, or if it has to do with something else. He's not the easiest person to read.

After some time has passed, I say, "What's wrong?"

He doesn't say anything. I don't bother poking, knowing he won't open up if he doesn't want to. I turn in my seat and grab my backpack. I begin my homework, deciding it will help pass some time.

When we finally pull up to my house, I pack my things back into my book bag. Spencer says, "I need to tell you something. Something I've been keeping from you."

"So, he does speak," I smirk at the use of his words against him.

He glares. "Listen to me."

I unbuckle, sliding out of the truck but not closing the door. "Hey, I tried to listen earlier. You're the one who didn't say anything."

He rubs his eyes with his hand. "I know. I was trying to figure out how to say this because I don't want you exploding on me. Besides, I'm not supposed to tell you this information, but I feel wrong not telling you."

"What's up?" I ask, a little twinge of uneasiness in my gut now.

"Well, the day of the funeral, the morning actually, my family had a visitor."

I lean my arm on the roof of his truck, resting my backpack on the floorboard. His eyes darken on me; his mouth is a thin, straight line. "And my uncle didn't want to deal with it at the time. He still doesn't, but I feel like you deserve to know what's happening."

He looks away and I sigh. "Spencer, what's going on?"

"Carissa came back, and she's being held in HQ.

CHAPTER FIVE

Jackson

FRIDAY, OCTOBER 20TH, 2023

I WATCH FROM THE DOORWAY OF THE warehouse as Evan and Samantha pack up the rental car with boxes and bags of belongings they need to take with them to DC. I stay out of the way, having already been yelled at by both of them for trying to help. I step out and lean against the wall, watching them go back and forth, arguing with each other and repeating the cycle over and over. I sigh.

Samantha yells at Evan as he retreats inside, slamming the door behind him. I look over at her, but her warning stare tells me not to say anything. Valuing my life, I go inside.

I find Evan in his office. Soon to be my office, but I digress. Evan says, "I need to ask a favor of you since you'll be staying here with your team."

I shrug. "You own my soul, anyway. Why ask

a favor when you can command me to do whatever you want?"

He glares but says nothing. He told me the other day he knows where Carissa is and if I don't do everything he says, he will send agents after her and have her detained. I don't believe him for a second. She's great at slipping off the grid. But I don't take chances when it comes to her, so I follow orders like a good little servant. Interesting how our roles have reversed.

He breezes past me into the hall, motioning for me to follow him. I have nothing better to do. I don't see Samantha during our walk around to the other side of the warehouse. She must've run off after their last argument. I wonder if they'll kill each other before reaching the airport.

I wonder if I would care.

I follow Evan down the hallway towards the locked room we've never entered since Raegan's death. Evan says, "The favor I need is something you need to do every day. It's not something you can just neglect."

He goes to unlock the door and I say, "Fine. I'll feed your cat and make sure she has plenty of water."

Evan shakes his head, clearly unenthused

about the sarcastic comment. "I don't have a cat. This is serious. You have to swear on your life you won't breathe a word about what I'm about to show you."

The twinge in my gut is unwelcome. I don't know what's behind this door anymore. I don't know what the crime scene looks like. I know by the time the resistance finally broke through the door, trying to find her body, there was nothing. But I've never been in this room since that day, knowing there was more to it than that.

I swallow the lump in my throat. "Swear on my life? What are we, knights?"

He turns on me as he pushes the door open. "Enough joking around. Do you swear?"

"I already told you, you own my soul. I have nothing left. What more do you want?"

This seems like enough for him because he motions for me to step inside first. I brace myself for anything. A body. Blood on the ground. Bullets.

But there's nothing besides boxes and the fallen, severed ropes in the room. The chair is gone. The ropes lie on the floor, along with broken zip ties. The room smells mildly of bleach. I look at him. "What's in here that you need to show me?"

"When we first came here, I had a bunker built beneath this room. That's where we're going."

He leads me over to a stack of boxes. Behind them, he moves a tile aside. A ladder descends into the murky blackness. "How safe is this bunker?"

"Safe enough. I'll go first so I can hold your hand in the darkness down there."

I glare at him. "Funny. Get your ass down there. I'm not going first."

He begins going down and I wait until I can barely see the top of his head in the darkness before starting my descent. The ladder shakes slightly but doesn't seem unstable. I finally see light at the bottom. It's bright, like an LED. Evan stands in the corridor. It's a bit narrow—we wouldn't fit side by side. But it's still wide enough to not feel like the walls are closing in on me. He points down the corridor to another steel door. I'm beginning to hate those doors. Too many secrets lie behind them.

Secrets wrapped in lies.

"You're keeping your cat down here? It's not in bad condition, right? I'm not going to have my nightmares haunted by a poorly cared-for cat?"

Evan rolls his eyes. "Go on and open it."

My stomach lurches and I feel like I might lose

the lunch I didn't eat. I reach for the doorknob and turn, but I don't push the door open yet. "You aren't going to kill me down here, are you?

"I wasn't planning to, but if you keep asking questions I might be tempted. Hurry up already, will you?"

I exhale slowly and push the door open. The air smells strongly of mildew, but that's not the thing that distracts me the most. What distracts me the most is the figure lying on the cot, looking up at the ceiling. The figure turns her head. Sky-blue eyes meet mine, and a face I can barely recognize looks over at me.

I stumble back to lean against the doorjamb in shock. My heart begins racing along with my mind as it tries to wrap around this possibility. The scream, the blood, the ropes...

Reagan's alive?

CHAPTER SIX

Carissa

FRIDAY, OCTOBER 20TH, 2023

I DON'T KNOW HOW LONG I'VE BEEN locked up in here. I know it's been a couple of weeks. Spencer tells me what day it is whenever he comes in, but soon I let it leave my memory. I belong here for my crimes. Most importantly, it's safe. Evan won't come looking for me here.

If he is even still looking.

Along with my traitorous ex. I guess I shouldn't have expected Jackson to come with me. I believed in his love, in his heart. Everything I shared with him and everything he shared with me wasn't something I took lightly. He promised me forever. I was naïve to believe he meant it. To believe he loved me. His loyalty will always lie with my brother first.

I sit, hugging my knees to my chest on the small cot. It's cold in here, or maybe it's me. I don't know.

I let the tears fall, the ones I've held back for days. They come easily now. I saw the disappointment on my dad's face as his men hauled me down here, locking me up. I've asked for him, but he refuses to see me. I tried to speak to him that morning, tried to explain my side, but he'd hear none of it. Only watched as his men brought me to the cell.

Only Spencer cared enough to stay around and listen. He understood and even accepted me back. Maybe not entirely, but he didn't turn me away or call me stupid for even going along with Evan and Jackson. I had been blind to the fact that I thought I loved Jackson.

No, you did love him.

I hated that I loved him. *Still* love him despite everything. I can't turn off my heart so quickly, even when he hurts me in ways only a lover can.

My emotions wash over me, and I'm so distracted by the tears that I don't hear the door open. But then I hear the footsteps echo off the empty cells. When I look up, I see Spencer standing outside my cell with a tray of food, his light brown hair slightly disheveled. He stares inside for a moment, waiting for me to acknowledge his presence. I nod slightly at him and he slips the tray to me through the slot in the bars at the bottom. I don't move over to it.

"She went a while before eating food," I tell him. "I deserve the same thing."

"What do you mean?" Spencer says.

"Raegan. She refused to eat most times we brought food to her because she thought we'd poison her."

Spencer is silent for a moment, tucking his hands in his pockets. After a moment, he takes one out and runs it through his hair, making it messier than it already is. Finally, he sighs. "And do you think I'm poisoning your food?"

I shake my head, but I'm sitting in the shadows of my cell, so I don't think he can see me. I finally say, "No."

He motions to the tray. "Then eat. What happened in the past remains in the past, unchanged. Whether you eat or not, it doesn't bring justice to the situation."

I hate that he's wise sometimes. He's lived a rough life, and it's aged his mind and soul beyond his physical nineteen years. Spencer sighs again. "Well, if you don't want to eat, that's fine, but I brought you someone who wants to listen to your side of the story."

I perk up slightly. Could Father be here right now? I stand from my cot, leaving the safety of the shadows. Walking into the light, I push the tray of food carefully aside with my foot. I hear the door to the holding room brush open and then a new person arrives, turning the corner and approaching my cell. Not my father. No, this is the last person I'd want to face right now.

Peter Daniels stops behind Spencer, his eyes intent and burning with a mixture of emotions. Spencer says, "He has questions, but he's also willing to listen to your side of the story."

My eyes haven't left Peter. He's worse for wear. The lively, electric boy I last saw is gone. Instead, he's darkness, doubt, and despair. His eyes hold a fire of burning anger. Dark circles show his lack of sleep. He looks exhausted but stands tall, asserting his dominance over the situation. Or at least trying to.

I cross my arms to keep myself warm and prevent my shivers from reaching my spine. My pride refuses to let me show my weakness to him. "What do you want to talk about?"

Peter comes forward and stops only a few feet

away from the cell bars dividing us. "I think we both know what I want to talk about."

I glance at Spencer, who leans his shoulder against the wall outside another cell, watching our interaction. Peter says, "You should eat your food before it gets cold. Tell me everything you have to say and then I'll ask my questions."

I decide to do as he says. I sit on the concrete floor, the tray of food in my lap. But I don't touch the food. Instead, I talk.

"It started only a few months ago when Evan and Jackson recruited me. Evan introduced me to their new world of power and glory. I never was one for seeking those things, but I believed Jackson genuinely loved me. And I love him, so I followed blindly. I did the things they told me but mostly stayed out of the way. Evan went on a 'mission' for four months, but I found out that he was back in DC doing work there for the president and not our father. I stayed here training some people and working for my father. Then Evan came back, and things only escalated from there. Soon, everything was moving so fast, and because Jackson was there, I went along with it."

I shake my head. Hearing the words fall from

my mouth only makes me feel more stupid than I already did. Following Evan's orders because of a boy who said he loved me, who lied to my face... I was a fool.

I sigh, finally sipping the water Spencer brought me. "That night, after Raegan was killed, only four of us remained. I decided I couldn't be with them anymore. Jackson almost came with me, at least that's how it seemed, but in the end, he stayed with Evan and I left. I've been on the run ever since. I ran out of money a few days ago and knew I'd be in danger. Evan will never stop looking for me. I know too much. So, I came home. I knew I'd wind up here, but this is safe and it's far more luxurious than what I deserve for the crimes I've committed."

Peter nods, and I see something working inside his mind. I feel a weight lift from me, if only slightly. He finally says, "I want to know how she was taken to that warehouse. How did Evan get her there?"

I set the food tray aside, barely touched. I don't eat much these days. I grip the iron bars in front of me and stand to meet Peter's eyes. "A team was sent to take her. One of Evan's operatives, Marty, threw a rock at Raegan's head. She had a mild concussion, but she was never permitted to lie down. We kept her wrists and ankles zip-tied to a chair…" The words sound evil coming from my mouth. I'm horrified by my actions. Yet, I continue. "I took care of her, helping her to the bathroom and watching over her. I fed her and made sure the concussion didn't cause further complications."

Peter doesn't say anything about my answer, only asks, "And how was she treated? I heard you say she refused to eat."

"She thought the food had poison in it. We never would have done that. But she didn't believe us. She ate some days and others she didn't."

Peter nods, rubbing his face with his hands. He doesn't look up or speak for a long time, his face still in his hands. Spencer takes a step forward, but Peter shakes his head. His eyes are rimmed red with exhaustion.

I run a hand through my silver hair. "Raegan was so intelligent. And I'm sorry for your loss. I —"

Peter stops me. "Thank you for your time. I will see if I can convince your father to speak to you, but I won't promise anything. He's very upset by your presence here right now. It'll take time. I need to get going. Have a good night." With that, he leaves.

Spencer sighs, taking the tray from me. "Never

give him pity."

I tilt my head. "Why?"

Spencer heads for the door, then turns back to me and says, "Because then he has to acknowledge that his best friend—the girl he loved—is dead. And it's too much for him to take."

Spencer leaves, and the door slams shut. All too soon, I feel cold again. I take the blanket from the cot and wrap myself in it, sitting in the shadows once more. I start to cry again. I feel as if I'm in a lonely form of hell. And I can't say I didn't have it coming. I deserve this mess. I deserve to be lonely.

I'm a monster, only capable of evil.

There's no hope for me.

CHAPTER SEVEN

Jackson

MY STOMACH STILL FEELS UNSETTLED AS I sit across from Evan in his office. The way Evan has been treating Raegan this whole time as if she's more a pet than she is a human. The way he's keeping her locked up is much worse than one would keep a pet.

"Why is she still alive? I thought you killed her."

"I have my reasons," he says, though he doesn't look me in the eye. "You're the only one I can trust with this. Please don't tell anyone."

I lean back in my seat. "You could lose your position as heir to the country for this. Why are you doing this to her, anyway? What you're doing is far worse than death. This is torture."

Evan hands me the paper schedule. "Because she can still be used later. Right now, I have other things to work on. Bigger things. You have to keep her presence a secret."

I'm still shocked. "How is she even here?"

"I thought I made that clear," he says, annoyed.

I run a hand through my hair. "There was blood. And the scream?"

I remember the smell of bleach; someone must have cleaned the room recently. The very sound of her scream has haunted my nightmares since the day Evan killed her—made it seem like he killed her. Perhaps it was my conscience, or whatever was left of it. Carissa leaving…the blackmail… all for what? She's alive and Evan lied to everyone. I'm surprised he'd pull a stunt like this. And angry. If he had told Carissa, she wouldn't have left and I'd know if she's safe.

Evan stands, pacing the small length of his— my—office. "I did shoot her. I shot her left shoulder. I hadn't intended to shoot her at all; I was just aiming close to her, to scare her enough that she'd scream. But my hand was shaky, and the bullet hit her shoulder. She screamed, but shortly after that, she fainted. I unbound her, and she fell to the floor. I caught her before she hit the ground, then laid her there to stop the bleeding. That's why there was blood on the floor."

I stare at him, mouth agape. He goes on. "I bandaged her up as fast as I could and then carried her down to the bunker. We hid there while the agents finally broke into the room."

I don't know what to say, only that death might have been a mercy to her, a sweet release after the misery he's put that girl through. But of course, I say nothing.

Evan sighs. "I've changed her bandages a few times, but everything looks like it's healing. I feed her only once a day to keep her weak. Sometimes, she refuses to eat, thinking I'm going to poison her."

"Huh. I wonder why?"

His glare makes me snap my mouth shut. But I know that, deep down, there is a side to Evan that refuses to kill anyone. Maybe underneath the rough exterior he's built up around him, he has a soft side. And I genuinely want to believe that. The fact that Raegan is alive nearly proves it. But then again... he threatened to harm his own sister if I followed her. He used my love for Carissa to make me stay away from her, and now I don't know where she is, or if she's even okay. My heart aches not knowing if she's at least safe.

Evan waves a hand in front of my face. "Are you still in there, or did your mind leave us again?"

"Funny," I say. I don't tell him where my thoughts wandered. He doesn't get to know the inner workings of my mind. "Anything else I need to do while you're gone? Any other humans you're keeping as pets, perhaps?"

This earns me another glare. Again, I shut up fast. He stands up from his chair, holding a stack of papers. "I can add you to the list of human pets quickly if you don't stay in line. Do I make myself clear?"

"I can't blame anyone for wanting to keep me as a pet. I mean, look at me." I gesture dramatically to myself. Evan stares me down until I look away under the scrutiny of his gaze. I groan. "Fine. Yes, I understand. Take care of your human pet, don't tell anyone, don't fall out of line. I know how to do my job."

Evan walks past me. "That's debatable, but I'm glad we've reached an understanding. Now, I need to finish helping Sam with the car before she gets too suspicious."

I stay seated, my mind battling between the options I now have. I'm in charge of this place, and my team won't arrive for another few days. This gives me time to contact the resistance, to let them know Raegan is alive and that they need to save her. I only saw her for a moment, but it was plain to see she wasn't in good health. Her skin seemed to cling to the bone as if that were all it had to hold onto. Even the light in her eyes was fading. Life was slipping from her quickly.

What am I thinking? *Save her?* I want to scream at myself for such a thought, but now I realize my loyalty to Evan died the moment he let his sister disappear into the night. When he made the woman I love walk out of my life and shattered my heart.

I know exactly what I'm thinking. I want revenge on Evan, but more than that, I want to do the right thing for once in my life.

Finally, I leave his cursed office and walk down the hall toward the front door. I don't open it yet; instead, I stand to one side, watching Evan and Sam. Evan slams down the hatch to the trunk of his car. He walks to where Sam stands, and they have a conversation. I wonder if Evan realizes how their proximity speaks of something more than business partners. I wonder if he knows he's setting himself up for heartbreak. How she'll never be attracted to him the way he is to her.

Lydia, the receptionist at the warehouse, told me some things about Samantha a while ago. How she lost her ability to love anyone, the emotion wrung out of her after years of hurt, anguish, and brutal training as a top assassin in the government. I've seen the glint in Evan's eye when Sam walks into a room. The tension between them is always thick, two strong forces bound to collide. To Evan, there's something else, something like attraction. But she doesn't feel it. At least, not in the way he does. She's been brainwashed for years, something that's hard to reverse.

After a few moments, I decide to break it up. The least I can do is try to repay the torment Evan has put me through by annoying him in any way possible. It is hardly enough, of course, but for now, it suffices. I step outside, though they don't notice me yet. I clear my throat, and Evan jumps back from Samantha. She doesn't budge, not realizing what scene he was creating. I cross my arms. "You're just going to leave without saying goodbye?"

Evan rubs the back of his neck. "I didn't think you cared so much, Maverick."

I hope Evan translates the glare in my eyes. I

hope he sees that my intention was *not* merely a goodbye. I tuck my hands into my pockets. "I don't care, but this will be our last time working together. You're moving on to bigger things, and so am I. This ends our long chapter together. I guess I'm a sentimental person like that."

Evan crosses his arms and shrugs. "I guess it does. It's been nice working with you."

"Wish I could say the same."

He rolls his eyes and opens the passenger door for Samantha. She glances back at me, giving me a small wave before sliding into the car. Evan closes the door and I say quietly, "You know she can't give you what you want, right?"

"What are you talking about?"

"Do yourself a favor and don't fall for her. While I think you deserve the heartache you've caused me, I'd be a horrible person to not warn you."

Evan doesn't look pleased by my words. He steps away from the car and gets closer to me, lowering his voice. "Look where we stand. You're already a horrible person. We both chose this life despite that. I don't need you telling me what I need to do in my personal decisions."

He backs up, walking around the car. As he rests his hand on the handle of the door, he looks up at me one more time. "Goodbye, Jackson."

When I don't say anything in return, he slides into the car, puts it in reverse, and drives off down the road. I stay out here, watching them disappear into the distance, the autumn breeze comforting me for a moment. Then I realize I have the place to myself for a little while. I don't have time to wait if I plan on getting Raegan out of here. I need her help to come up with a plan.

I find myself wandering back down to the bunker. Raegan is still on the bed. She doesn't move much when I enter. She's weak.

"Hey," I say. She moans slightly. I step closer, but I don't want to startle her. "I'm going to get you out of here."

"If this is a sick prank on me that Evan's put you up to, I don't want to hear it." Her voice is faint—I have to strain to hear her—but her anger is loud and clear.

I sigh. "This isn't a joke. Evan's left for DC. The president is making him his heir to the country. I'm here now, and I want you to be free."

She's silent for a moment, and part of me

wonders if she's fallen asleep. But then her quiet voice speaks again. "I'm going to die here anyway. I've been without food and water for a couple of days."

"I'll go get you some food and water. We need to get your strength up so you can leave the cot."

Raegan sighs, and it sounds painful. "Whatever helps you sleep at night."

I smirk. "It's nice to know you haven't lost your sarcastic side being down here alone."

"Oh, I'm not alone. The mildew on the wall and the rats love my company."

"Oh, pardon me. I didn't mean to disrespect your friends like that. Obviously, the mildew and rats mean something to you."

She coughs, then says, "You're not funny."

"I know."

I go back upstairs and begin looking for good food. I find some chicken and veggies from the night before and decide that works. I heat it in the microwave while I fill a glass with water. I load it all on a tray and take it back down to the bunker. I help Raegan to a sitting position, but she won't eat.

"Could be poisoned," she says sharply, then clamps her lips together.

I shrug. "Yeah, maybe it is. But wouldn't that end your misery a lot faster? I mean, if you don't believe me about getting you out of here, then why bother trying to survive?"

She glares at me. Her eyes have sunken into her head. She's frail, thinned out from lack of nutrients. Her skin has become a new type of pale due to lack of sunlight. Or any light. Her hair and skin are dirty, and I wonder how long it will be before she's strong enough to shower. To sit on her own. To do anything.

I break off a tiny piece of chicken and put it to her lips, and to my surprise, she takes the food, chewing slowly, almost as if she's forgotten how. She coughs at times and even hacks some food back up. It's a slow process that takes nearly two hours. Her stomach can't handle much. When a decent portion of the food is gone, I put the plate aside, satisfied. Her eyes fall shut, so I help her back to a comfortable sleeping position.

As I leave, I turn to her one more time; her breathing has evened out and I know she's asleep. "You may not believe me," I say softly, "but I'm going to find a way to get you out of here. I promise."

With that, I leave, locking the door behind me. Not that she'd be able to get out on her own. I take the dishes back up and wash them, leaving them on the drying mat. I go to my new office and plot how I'm going to approach Spencer. He'd be the easiest to corner since he's always picking up Peter or his girlfriend at the school down the road. I've spied on the school, keeping tabs on everyone. He'll listen to me. I know he will.

Ironic how the very office Evan used to plan how he was going to take Raegan is the same office where I plan to free her from his clutches. I decide to approach Spencer tomorrow. I know he'll be at the school early to wait for Peter. I know I can talk to him then, let him know Raegan's alive. She's fading fast and doesn't have much time. My team will arrive in a few days. We have to do something before they get here, as it will be too hard to keep them away while Raegan is rescued from this hell. And I don't want to explain anything to a bunch of new people.

With my plan in place, I decide it's time to get some rest. I feel wrong leaving Raegan here, so I decide to use one of the spare rooms we used for sleeping. I won't go home tonight. But hopefully, in two days, Raegan will be reunited with her family and I can abandon this place. And maybe after that, I can find Carissa and at least learn whether she's safe. So much to do. So little time.

CHAPTER EIGHT

Peter

SATURDAY, OCTOBER 21ST, 2023

CARISSA'S WORDS HAUNT ME LONG AFTER our talk, though I don't mean for them to follow my every waking moment. I wish I had listened to her longer. I wish I had asked her more questions. But instead, I fled the moment she started to show pity or sympathy. I'm mad at myself for reacting like that, but I couldn't stand to be there any longer. No amount of sorrow or pity will bring Raegan back. People don't understand what's going on. They just throw out empty words, assuming they can feel my feelings, and understand my loss.

I sigh, leaning my head against the couch. I'm sitting on my living room floor with the dog. My mom bathed him this morning, for the second time this week, so now his fur is fluffy and soft. I stroke his head. "What should we call you?"

He lifts his head, sky-blue eyes staring into my soul. I frown. "Well, I'm not just going to call you dog. How about... Max?"

He lowers his head, uninterested. I roll my eyes. "Picky. Fine. What about... Spot?"

He still refuses to look at me. I run a hand through my hair. I don't know why I'm so fixated on giving this dog a name, but he looks like he has a deeper soul than most of the humans I know. I'm out of ideas, so I turn to a friendly internet search for dog names. More of the same names come up. Spot, Max, Fido, Fin... it's all the same.

Finally, one takes my interest. I glance over at the mass of fur and say, "Gunnar?"

To this, he lifts his head, looking at me again. I smile. "Gunnar it is." His new name suits him well. No one stepped forward to claim him during the week, so he's mine now. He's very well behaved, and never really barks. Always obeys commands.

I rub his head and am contemplating my next move when the doorbell rings. Gunnar rises with me to walk over there, curious and cautious. I open the door to find Nicole and Sawyer. Nicole looks infuriated. Behind her, Sawyer doesn't seem all that happy, either.

"What are you doing here?" I ask, not unkindly.

Nicole glares up at me. "Well, hello to you, too."

She pushes past me and stalks into the living room. Gunnar starts to growl, but I nudge him. He immediately stops. Sawyer waits for me to step aside before coming into the house. I close the door and face them.

"I'm not really up for company right now."

Nicole crosses her arms. "Too bad. You're getting it."

Sawyer gapes at her, then turns to me apologetically. "I'm so sorry about this. If you need us to, we can come back some other time."

Nicole's eyes bore into mine. "No. We have to do this now."

"Do what now?" I ask though I can already tell I don't want to know.

Nicole sighs. "You've been avoiding us. Why?"

I rub my face with my hand. "Because I know you want answers on how to get into the resistance and I don't want to fight with you. I'm not giving you those answers, and you know that."

Nicole glances at Sawyer before her gaze

returns to me, seeming to scrutinize my every move. "You're right. I do want answers. Because my boyfriend has been unwilling to answer any of my questions, even though I know he's aware of things I'm not. Why is my fight for freedom such a bad thing?"

Sawyer flinches. I feel bad for him. I can see the pain in his eyes, the fear of losing someone he loves. He doesn't want her to become another Raegan, lost in a pointless war. But avoiding Nicole's questions has not been the answer.

I look to my feet, to Gunnar, then outside the back door at the yard. Anywhere but at them; anything to not feel the guilt coursing through my veins. Nicole deserves better from me. They both do.

Sighing, I make my way to the plush chair and take a seat. Gunnar follows me and flops down at my feet in silent solidarity. I can't meet Nicole's eyes. She reaches forward and pets his fur, and he edges a bit closer to her.

"I didn't know you got a dog," she says.

"I found him during a late-night run.," I say, not willing to talk about the tree. Raegan and I always kept it a secret between us.

Nicole glances up. "Late night? You mean... after curfew?"

She seems astonished by this. Maybe she's not so far gone that she can't be talked out of trying to get into the resistance. Maybe the idea of having to break rules like curfew will scare her away.

Nicole and Sawyer take a seat on the couch, and I take my sweet time finding an answer to why I can't get Nicole into the resistance. The truth is I could get her in there. But I'm too scared to lose more people. And I don't know if I want to betray Sawyer, either. Nicole looks at me expectantly, waiting for the answer to the question she's asked many, many times.

I run a hand through my hair, messing it up further than it was. "You know what? You're right. I could get you into the resistance. I could set something up for you. You'd be able to train for missions and fight and do all the things you seem to think will be great. But you don't understand how life-altering this is."

Nicole leans back in her seat. "I'm not naïve, Peter. I know it won't be all rainbows and sunshine and fun times. I've tried to get Sawyer to tell me all he knows, but he's holding back. You have been one of my dearest friends for ten years. Give me the answers I'm looking for."

I glance at Sawyer. In one look, he begs me not to do this. I don't blame him. I stand and begin pacing in front of them. "Fine. You really want to know everything there is to know? I'll tell you. The resistance is run by a wealthy man, Andre Williams. It's all underground—literally. And Andre doesn't truly fight for anyone. It was his son who killed Raegan. If Andre had done more, Raegan wouldn't be dead right now."

I know that's not entirely true, but I'm too bitter to admit it. I keep talking, trying to connect every detail of what I'm saying to Raegan's death, because, truthfully, it all had a part to play in what happened to her. When I finish, I stop walking and look at her. I'm hoping I've scared her away. But no such luck. The fire in her eyes hasn't diminished. If anything, it's grown. She's now more determined than ever to fight. And I know there will be nothing I or anyone else can do to stop her.

Nicole is quiet for a few moments, then looks up at me and says, "I'm a terrible person. I stopped believing her when things were falling apart. But look at where we stand now. She's gone and I can't apologize. I just want to do something to make it right. I want to fight so her death isn't in vain."

I touch Nicole's hand. "She didn't hold it against you. Your anger at her only made her sad. She wanted so badly to tell you everything, to not have secrets. But in this line of work, that's not possible."

Nicole nods, but the guilt is still evident on her face.

Sawyer says, "So where exactly is Evan Williams now?"

I shrug. "He escaped that day. So did most of his team, but we have one of them in custody. And then a few of his henchmen were put in jail for other crimes they did, violent crimes, robbery, other petty theft… they weren't good people."

Nicole frowns. "Why did you quit, then?"

I pace again. "I didn't quit. I'm on leave right now. I was deemed 'mentally incapable' of focusing on my work. Long story short, they didn't trust me to remain calm if we came across Evan's whereabouts, so they put me on leave."

Nicole stands, too. "You just let them push you aside like that? After everything you've fought for by their sides?"

Sawyer touches Nicole's hand. "Nicole, stop."

"No. The Peter I knew never gave up, even after life hit hard. He always fought for freedom, happiness, and peace. He always knew what he wanted. The Peter I knew would never sit back down because something bad happened. He'd find a way to keep pressing on and fighting for what he believes in. The Peter I know—"

"The Peter you know died when she did!" I yell.

Nicole falls silent as abruptly as if I've struck her. She looks at me, eyes brimming with tears. I exhale slowly, turning away from them. "The Peter you know is gone," I say softly.

I feel a hand touch my shoulder. Sawyer stands beside me now. "You aren't giving up, Peter. You went through a very traumatic event. No one should expect you to be okay right now. I haven't known you long, but I know how loyal you are. I know you'll keep fighting for her. But it's okay to need time. Whether you go back or not, Raegan's death won't be in vain."

"Her death won't be in vain because I will find Evan Williams and make him pay for the damage he's done, for the pain he's caused. He's not getting

107

away with killing the girl I loved."

That last part slips through my defenses faster than I can stop it. It's the first time I've been able to say I loved her out loud for someone else to hear me. And it feels bittersweet. I fall back into the chair I was sitting in a moment before. Gunnar comes over and pushes the top of his head against my hand, and I pet his silky fur.

"Her final words to me were that she loved me. And I was too much of a coward to say it back. I regret it every day." I feel my eyes sting and fill with tears. I close them, trying to prevent them from falling past my walls. I fail.

Nicole comes over to hug me. "She knew you loved her, even if you didn't say it."

I shake my head, pushing her gently away. "That's not enough. I should have said it then. She was brave enough, so why wasn't I?"

Nicole sighs. "There are reasons behind it, so don't regret what happened. Just learn from it and make sure you tell people when you love them. You never know when something could happen."

I rub my face with my shirt, drying the tears, trying to wipe away the pain. Nicole sits by me, resting her head on my shoulder. The action makes me think of Raegan, and the pain deepens further, squeezing my heart. "I can't believe she's gone. And I'm ready to make Evan pay for the things he's done. You don't understand how tortured she was there. She barely ate because she thought they'd poison her. She barely moved because they tied her to a chair."

Nicole nods. "I know, and it hurts. But what do you mean by making Evan pay?"

Sawyer takes a seat on the couch again, leaning forward with his elbows on his knees and clasping his hands together. "Yeah, you can't go seek revenge on the guy who killed her. You're only going to get yourself killed in the process. Revenge won't give you the satisfaction you think it will, and it most certainly does nothing to bring her back. Avenging her is a dangerous game that I don't think you want to play."

I stand up from the chair. "No, I know exactly what I'm saying. What he's done is inexcusable. I have to do something to bring him down. Who knows what comes after this? All I know is this isn't an isolated case. They'll keep taking people one by one, killing them off until Andre surrenders. Andre isn't strong enough to fight back against his son, and I can't put him in a position like that. But I refuse to sit here and do nothing. Not only for me but also Raegan's parents."

Nicole sighs. "You haven't even gone to see them lately. I've been over there a lot and they've told me they haven't seen you since the funeral. How do you truly know what they want? And how do you know Raegan would want you to do this? I don't think she would."

I feel my anger rising. "You didn't know Raegan like I did, so don't act like you know everything. You avoided her for the last moments of her life."

The moment the words are out of my mouth, I want to grab them back. Nicole's mouth opens with a retort, but I hold up my hand. "I'm sorry. That was wrong of me to throw at you. I—"

Sawyer stands. "I know you're hurting, but seriously, man. Think of Raegan. What would she do if this were reversed?"

Nicole stands, too. "She would fight for you, yes, but she'd do it the way you refuse to do. She wouldn't play dirty like you want to. She would keep fighting for the resistance so their accomplishments could benefit everyone. She'd expect the same from you. Maybe you should think about that for a little while." Her eyes are blazing with anger and hurt.

I look at them. I can't stop the feeling of betrayal. No one understands exactly how bad all of this is. No one sees that it's my fault. "I don't need you telling me what you think she would do."

Nicole steps back as if she's been slapped. Her eyes burn with a new pain I've never seen in her. Sawyer doesn't meet my eyes. He's frustrated but not nearly as much as Nicole. She takes a step toward me. Gunnar gives a low growl, but I quiet him with a look.

Sawyer holds Nicole back, his hands on her biceps. "Baby, calm down. He's hurting, too."

She's sobbing now. My words from before hit their target. And I hate myself. "Nicole, I—"

"NO!" she screams, pulling away from Sawyer and coming right for me. I start to back away, but she's in front of me in an instant.

Her hands grab my t-shirt; her eyes burn into mine. "I may not have been there in the end, but who was there for her when you were gone? Who got to know her through the biggest years of her life? It sure as hell wasn't you, Peter. And it's not your fault entirely, but you don't know her like you think you do. You're stuck in your selfish lust for revenge on someone who could kill you in an instant. Help me fight, or don't. I won't let you die. I can't lose someone else."

She's sobbing against me now. I let my arms go around her. My resolve begins to crumble as I realize that I neglected my friendship with her in those years, too.

Sawyer sighs. "I'm going to lose this argument with you now."

Nicole turns to him, stepping away from me. "What argument?"

"If I beg you to not do this, it won't matter. If I give you the truth, it won't change your mind, only reaffirm what you feel. You wanted my truth?" He pauses for a moment, regarding her evenly before plunging ahead. "My mom died because of the resistance. She worked for Andre Williams. It put a target on her back. She died because two opposing agents caused her car to crash. They were chasing her, and she lost control. When it came down to it, Andre turned it into a reason to fight harder. My father refused to take part in anything that took his wife and my mother away from us. Especially when the leader won't look around to see what's going on around him, and what needs to be done. If I can't keep you from joining in this pointless fight, so be it. But I refuse to have anything to do with it."

Nicole steps towards him. "What do you mean?"

"This isn't an ultimatum, Nicole. I'm not going to stop you. But I can't stay with you. I can't be the person you need me to be for this. I'm sorry."

Sawyer is out the door before Nicole can stop him. She runs after him, but he's too fast. I stand in the doorway as she runs across the yard. As he drives off.

Without her.

Nicole falls to her knees in my front yard, hugging herself as she sobs. My heart drops. There's a strong urge inside me to say something, anything.

"Nicole, he just needs to cool his head," I say lamely.

I step outside, closing the front door behind me so Gunnar won't run out. I kneel next to her as she sobs, leaning against me. Her voice thick with tears, she says, "How… how could he leave me like this, Peter?"

"I don't know. The resistance took his mom from him. He's holding on to a lot." But I would've never expected this. For Sawyer to walk out on Nicole as she sobbed about losing people.

Nicole rises, her blue-green eyes still filled to the brim with tears. But there's a resilience inside of her now. Something fiery. Something brave.

In a quiet, yet strong voice, she says, "I have to fight, Peter. I can't keep living like any of this—" she gestures wildly around us— "is okay. Because nothing of this is okay."

I sigh, leading Nicole inside and closing the door. I anxiously run a hand through my hair. "To fight this war will break everything in you. Losing Raegan has destroyed everything in me. I'm barely hanging on. Life without Raegan is not a life I ever wanted to live, and yet day in and day out, I live it because maybe I'll figure out how to avenge her. Maybe I'll find my purpose in this crazy, messed-up world."

Nicole looks up at me, eyes full of tears and pain. "I could leave right now and do things your way. Live a life of lies. One day bring children into this world and lie to them, too. I've... I've just lost my anchor. Sawyer has been the only person

114

keeping me steady. Please..."

The tears fall from her eyes, but she doesn't let the sobs escape this time. She walks over to sit down on the couch, and I take a seat beside her.

"Please," she says again. "Just... just see if they'd be willing to let someone else enter. I can't be what my parents want. I can't be what Sawyer wants. But I think that for once in my life, I know what I want. And I have to chase it."

I rub my hands over my face, hardly believing the words as they come from my mouth. "Okay. I'll talk to Spencer and Andre. I'll... I'll see what I can do. I make no guarantees that anything will happen. But I'll try. I can't decide what you should do with your life. If this is what you want, then I will help you where I can."

She smiles softly, leaning her head against my shoulder. "Thank you, Peter. I know we've never been as close, and I know I'm not Raegan, but you mean a lot to me. And I'm glad in all of this, I have you."

I can't bring myself to smile, but I say, "I'm glad I have you, too."

I offer to walk her home, but because she doesn't live too far, she decides to walk alone to clear her head. When she's gone, I close the door and return to the living room, my fist clenched at my side. Gunnar walks up to me and presses his head against my hand, making my hand relax against his fur. When the real yelling began, he ran into the kitchen. Loud noises, I have discovered, are not his favorite. I sit on the floor, petting him.

"What am I doing?" I say.

Maybe to him.

Maybe to myself.

I press my face into his fur, ready for this day to end. Ready for my misery to end. Every day, I wake up to the same nightmare as before. Only it's my life, and I have to live it when my eyes are open instead of when they're closed.

CHAPTER NINE

Raegan
DATE:UNKNOWN

YOU MAY NOT BELIEVE ME, BUT I'M GOING to find a way to get you out of here. I promise.

Jackson's words echo in my head on repeat. They're all I have to hold on to at this point. Seeing as he thought I was asleep, his words must be true if he bothered to speak them at all. I shouldn't let myself hope for some impossible fantasy, a distant wish that had once been the only thing on my mind. But... the idea of returning home, being with my family again, is very appealing.

And seeing Peter again.

My heart aches at the thought of my last words to Peter. *Peter, I love you.* I spoke too fast, believing death was upon me. In a way, it was. I've felt dead these past... days? Weeks? Months? I'm not sure how long I've been here. It could be an eternity, as all my time runs into one painful cycle of sleeping and wakefulness that's never consistent. I know I'm ready to escape, but my mind is more able than my body, and even that strength has begun to fade quickly.

I must have dozed off for a while because I feel myself awaken by the sound of the door swinging open. I glance over to find Jackson setting a bowl of something that smelled of sugar and cinnamon on the small table next to my cot.

Again? "You're only supposed to feed me once a day."

"That was Evan's rule. This place is all mine now, and we play by my rules, which include three square meals a day. Or more if you ask nicely. As I said, we need to get your strength up. I went to the store and bought all kinds of things for you to eat. Oatmeal, mashed potatoes… things that will be lighter on your stomach than full, heavy meals. I also got a big pack of bottled water so you can grab as many as you need."

I struggle to turn my head to look at him as he walks back to the door, lifting the big package of water bottles and setting them on the other side of the bedside table. "Why are you doing all of this?

Aren't you worried about the consequences of helping me?"

My throat is dry; the words come out barely above a whisper. He opens the plastic wrap and hands me a water bottle.

His face is full of anguish. "My loyalty to Evan ended the moment he threatened Carissa's life if I went with her when she abandoned ship. I wanted to leave with her after she ditched him, and now I don't know if she's safe, or if she's even still alive... I'm ready to do the right thing for once in my life. I'm ready to be done with all of this."

When he sees me struggle, he helps me sit up on the cot and lean against the wall behind it. He places the tray in my lap, and I reach for the first bite of the oatmeal on my own. "What's been happening up there? How long have I been down here?"

"This will be the third week you've been kept here. A lot has happened. Hopefully, you'll regain enough strength to get out before my team arrives in five days. I'm going to go hunt Spencer down and get him to listen to me. I know he'll believe me."

"Spencer hated you," I say after swallowing a bite of the warm cinnamon oatmeal. "Why would

119

he believe you?"

Jackson smirks. "I can be very persuasive. Besides, I'd rather not cross Peter again." He holds up his left hand, and it's only then I notice a strip of white gauze wrapped around his palm.

"Wait, what happened to your hand?"

Jackson grimaces as he glances down. "Your boyfriend put a knife in it trying to get to you. As far as you're concerned, Peter will do anything."

My heart leaps at the mention of Peter's name. "He... stabbed you?"

Jackson nods. "As I said, he'll do anything to protect you. I was already going in and out of consciousness, but the moment you called out to him that you loved him... The look on that boy's face was pure and utter determination. He would've probably broken the door down, but that FBI agent had him thrown out. He's much more capable than Evan ever gave him credit for. I didn't know he had it in him. The boy has guts."

I shake my head, though the action makes me slightly dizzy. I breathe, in and out, for a long time before I can speak again. "I don't know if he feels the way I do, but he's my best friend. He's always fought for me."

Jackson tucks his hands in his pockets. "Whatever you need to say to yourself so you sleep at night. Anyway, keep eating. I'll be back to get the dishes in a few minutes. I know Evan will probably be expecting a call from me any minute now since he told me to check in with him frequently. Got to keep up appearances if we don't want him to suspect anything. Will you be okay?"

I nod, even though a wave of nausea rushes through me from the food. "I'll be fine."

As he turns to walk out of the room, I say, "And Jackson?"

He looks back at me. "Yeah?"

"Thank you."

He smiles. "No problem, kid. Take your time. I'll be back soon."

With that, the door shuts. I don't hear it lock, but it doesn't matter. I can't get up from the cot anyway. Besides that, I'm not going to ruin his plans to get me out of here. I want freedom. Slowly but surely, I eat all the oatmeal in my bowl. My stomach still clenches in pain at the feel of food, but it's not as bad as earlier.

A new thought begins to take shape in my mind. All the time I've been down here... I missed

Peter's birthday. I can't stop the ache in my heart at that realization. He's eighteen now. He can go on missions. Even if Jackson does get me out of here, there's no guarantee Peter won't be drafted. He could already be gone.

Don't let him be gone...

I try to focus on something else. I can't get lost in the what-ifs right now. I think about going home and showering, just letting the hot water burn off everything that's clung to my skin down here. I wonder if a doctor will have to check the bullet wound in my shoulder. It's improved slightly, but it's rather disgusting to see. I asked Evan to show me when I first was brought down here. Right after he—very painfully—removed the bullet. I wanted to cry from both the agonizing pain and the sight of my bleeding shoulder.

I set my tray aside on the floor by my cot. I try to wriggle forward on my butt to sit on the edge of the cot; it's slow going, but finally, I'm there. It feels nice, sitting almost normally. I let my legs hang off the side of the cot. They feel dead. So much disuse has left them numb. Eventually, I want to walk around this room. I want—*need*—to feel normal again.

Jackson returns to the room, sees me sitting, and says, "I guess eating like normal is helping."

I nod. "Yeah, a little. I can't move much more from here, but I feel like I'm slowly going back to who I used to be."

Jackson smiles. "Evan thinks everything is going according to his plans, so we're in the clear for now. He's too busy fighting with the girl who went with him, anyway. I don't know if you ever met her, but it's not important."

Jackson bends down to pick up my dishes.

I say, "What day is it?"

"Saturday, October twenty-first. Why?"

I feel the tears prick in my eyes. "So, Peter's birthday did pass. I was hoping…"

Jackson frowns. "I'm sorry. But don't worry; as soon as you can walk mostly on your own, we can get you out of here. I promise—you're not going to suffer much longer."

Fear grips me from within. "But what about Evan's other plans? He said he was going to kill off resistance members one at a time. Why is he going to DC now?"

"Your death proved to President Morgan that Evan was loyal. It had all been a test. Evan knows I won't do anything to sabotage his future, so he trusted me to watch you. Not like he had much of a choice. I'm the only one left here."

I exhale shakily. "What else should I know?"

Jackson shrugs. "Not much else, at least that I know of. A lot will be different when you reemerge into the world, though. A lot of people believe you're dead. I can't imagine this will be easy for Andre to explain away to those who weren't part of his movement."

I hate to agree with him on that, but I do. My presence now is a ghost haunting from the dead. I won't be able to join the rest of the world again, not without bringing too much attention to being very much alive.

He continues. "I mean, from my understanding, they held a funeral for you. Buried a picture of you in a casket since they had no clue where Evan placed your body. They made most of your friends believe that you were in that casket and you'd died in a car accident."

I study him now, suspicious. "How do you know all of this?"

"I got bored and spied on the funeral. Bent Ridge is the same as when you left it, though, so that should please you. Although I can't see you being able to go home when you get out of here, at least not for very long. Eventually, Evan will know what I've done, because as soon as you're safely out of here, I'm going into hiding."

"You aren't going to keep playing a part?"

He shakes his head. "No. As soon as you're safe, I'm going to search for Carissa. I need to find her before Evan does. She's a traitor, and she knows too much. He won't leave her alone for too much longer, even with his promises."

He backs up to the doorway, dishes in hand. "You should get some rest. Tomorrow, I'll go track down Spencer and tell him the plan. In the next couple of days, you'll be out of here and you'll need to be ready."

I nod, bringing my deadweight legs back onto the cot. I scoot down and lie on my back. Jackson closes the door and once again, I'm left alone with my thoughts. They held a funeral for me. Everyone I know and love thinks I'm six feet underground. They don't know I'm far deeper, yet still alive. I feel scared, for the first time in a while. What will it be like to reemerge? If anyone finds out, the resistance won't be a secret anymore. There would be no easy explanation for me showing up alive.

And Carissa abandoning Evan after thinking he'd killed me... I wonder where she went. Maybe she went home. It would be safe there, at least, away from Evan.

I think of my family, of Peter, of Nicole and Sawyer. They've grieved me. They're still grieving me. And I'm still alive. It's a weird feeling, to be assumed dead. To know the people who loved you are grieving over an empty grave. A shiver rushes through me as I realize how dead to the world I am.

But soon, I start fading into sleep. My last thoughts are of home.

CHAPTER TEN

Evan

SATURDAY, OCTOBER 21ST, 2023

I LEAN AGAINST MY CAR AS THE GAS pumps slowly into the tank. Samantha disappeared inside the small building about ten minutes ago, claiming she needed to use the restroom and get some snacks. We'd only been driving for four hours, so I didn't believe her entirely, not when the ride here was misery. It was painfully silent. And we have yet another four hours to go before reaching the airport the president has chosen for his plane to land at. Hopefully, the private jet can put more space between Samantha and me.

My phone rings and I pull it from my back pocket. I see Jackson's name on the screen. I don't feel like talking, but I did ask him to keep me updated until his team got there. Finally, I slide the icon to answer. "Hello?"

"Hey, it's me."

"Yes, that is how smartphones work. I see your name and number on the screen. Exceedingly high tech."

I practically hear him rolling his eyes. "Whatever. You asked me to call and update you frequently, so here I am."

We must be careful. If I were to believe I'm exempt from having my phone tapped, I'd be a fool. "Yes, I did. How are things going with... my cat?" I cringe immediately, wishing I didn't use his previous words about Raegan.

Jackson pauses a second, then seems to catch on. "She's doing fine. She loves to eat, but I'm making sure to follow the strict diet plan you have for her. I'm hanging around the office since I have nothing better to do. I cleaned up the space a bit; I want to make it clear to the newbies that it's my office now. I've even personalized it a little."

"Great," I say, rolling my eyes. I finish pumping gas and lock up the cap on my car. I slip back into the driver's seat, shutting my door. Sam has yet to return from inside. I suppress a groan. "We're at a gas station now," I tell Jackson. "The airport is about four more hours' worth of driving.

We're supposed to arrive around 8 PM so there'd still be some daylight. But it's getting dark much sooner."

Jackson mumbles something about the weather, and I can see he's struggling for conversation. Finally, I say, "Have you heard from Carissa?"

This is a delicate subject, of course. I can almost feel him tense on the other end of the line. It's probably not a good idea to ask him about her, but I must know if she's reached out. I suspect he might not tell me if I don't ask.

Finally, he says tersely, "No. Maybe I should ask you the same question."

"She won't reach out to me. To you, however... she might," I reply.

I imagine Jackson running a hand over his face like he does whenever he's stressed out about something. He says, "I have to go. I need to get some food and then lock up for the night. I'll talk to you... at some point, I guess."

He hangs up before I can reply. I know that, in his eyes, I'm unforgivable. It doesn't matter. I did what I had to.

Samantha slides into the car at that moment, a

plastic bag full of chips and candy in hand.

"What took you so long?" I ask carefully. "I was getting a bit worried."

She sets the bag on the floorboard by her feet and hands me a bottled water. She doesn't say anything to me. Our last conversation, which took place many hours ago, was an argument over directions to the airport. This is how the trip progressed. Arguing, silence, talking, repeat.

We're still in silence mode right now. I decide to try and break it again. "Can I get a bag of chips?"

She reaches down to the floorboard wordlessly and hands me a bag, not making eye contact with me. I guess it'll take more than that to get her to talk to me. That's fine. I prefer driving in silence anyway. I pull away from the gas station and back onto the main road.

It's about fifteen minutes when she finally says something. "How long until we reach the airport?"

I glance at the GPS screen of my car. "Maybe four more hours? Three and a half if I speed? I don't really know at this point."

She nods slightly. "Have I ever told you the

story of my first kill?"

I guess we're in talking mode again. I shake my head and glance sideways at her. Her head rests against the window as she watches the road pass by us. I say, "No, you haven't."

"I was sixteen. I was asked to keep an eye on this boy. He wasn't much older than me. Brown hair and black eyes. He was a bit of a nerd in his school, though he was eighteen and behind. He'd missed too many days of school due to his mother's illness. When she died, he dropped off the face of the earth for a while, then decided he wanted to finish high school. So, he was on track to graduate at nineteen instead of eighteen."

I don't know what that has to do with anything, but she's talking to me again, so I don't dare question or speak up. I listen as she continues. "Anyway, I thought he was cute. Of course, I was sixteen and barely had a normal life, so any boy around my age, whether he was a nerd or not, was hot to me. I got to know him more, learned his name was Xander, and found he was working two jobs to pay rent and eat. He worked one job as soon as he got off school and then worked the second one until about three a.m. He'd sleep until about seven a.m. and go to school, only to repeat it over and over. Never had free time, yet he managed to somehow make time for me. I was placed in the same school, so during school hours, he was mine."

She exhales slowly, and I can hear the tears that threaten to spill by the tone of her voice. "I got too close to him. Soon, we were falling in love. We were young, but we were planning our future together. My commander at the time warned me against this, saying I needed to keep my emotions out of it. It was already too late. I didn't tell this boy about my life, of course, only my cover story about abusive parents and wanting to escape town. He did, too. And we agreed that when I turned eighteen, we'd elope and run away together. I thought I had found my way out, if only for a few more years. But President Morgan caught wind of our plans and he knew I wasn't faking."

I glance over at Samantha. The tears are falling steadily down her cheeks now, but her voice is still oddly firm. "He ordered Xander to be brought in. Then he told my commander to kill him. I was in the room next door, listening to his screams as they interrogated and tortured him. They thought I had told him things about my life, and they wanted to know what he knew." Her voice cracks, and she pauses a moment, collecting herself. "I consider it my first kill because his death is my fault."

We're both silent for a long time. My heart hurts for her. The pain she's endured from such a young age... She deserves better. Maybe we both do. She finally speaks again.

"I vowed never to fall in love again. Only Xander holds my heart. After he died, I couldn't sleep for months. Not without hearing his screams echo in my nightmares. I was so sick to my stomach at that time, too. No one understood what had happened to me. Eventually, President Morgan pulled me from that school. Emotions are a weakness that he does not tolerate."

She stops talking now and turns back to the window.

I don't know if there are words to help with something like this. I'm not sure I know what to say to her. Helplessly, I watch the road ahead of me, unable to speak. The rest of the drive passes in silence. I keep wondering if she wants me to say

133

something. But what do you say to something like that?

As the sky darkens, Sam dozes off, her head resting on the window. I keep thinking of her story, of how many times she's been broken before. Jackson's warning flares in my head. He's right. She'll never see me the way I see her. But I will fight for her. And I will fight to avenge everything that has happened to her, and to me. Everything I do will be to protect her as well as my family. Every threat ever aimed my way will come back to haunt President Morgan when I am through with him. I will fight for justice and revenge, no matter who gets in my way.

THE REST OF THE DRIVE moves silently as Sam doesn't back up from her sleep until we arrive at the secluded airport. Air Force One awaited us, without the president, of course. He never traveled anywhere, even for business. It was too dangerous. There were too many assassination attempts already that it was decided he wouldn't leave his safe house until every last resistance member was dead.

The private flight gives Sam and me plenty of space from each other, just as I hoped. Only now, it feels lonely. I shake off the thought and begin working out a plan. We need a way to get around DC without being noticed. I also need to figure out where the safe house is, and how much security detail exists around it. The president rarely comes to the White House anymore. Going into the safe house is probably a death wish unless he invites us himself. So if we are going to do this at the White House, we'll have to be quick. No one knows where he's staying for the night, so it will be impossible to get that information unless it comes from him.

I must've fallen asleep at some point because the next thing I remember is feeling someone poking my arm repeatedly. Sam stands there, waiting for me to wake up. "We've landed."

I sit up, gathering my things quickly. The agent who flew with us stops me. "The rest of your personal items will be collected by attendants and brought to your respective rooms. You don't need to worry about getting it yourself."

I need to meet with the president right away. I explain this to the first person I see inside the terminal, a secret service agent. He says nothing, just nods slightly, then says something into his earpiece.

I'm taken by limousine to the White House, where an escort of four agents guides me to the president's office. I feel as though I'm important. All things considered, I am. Other agents and soldiers line the halls, straightening as we pass. Two secret service agents stand outside the president's office, a man and a woman. The female agent whispers to her partner, who nods and knocks three times on the president's office door.

The door clicks unlocked and opens. The secret service agents, and the other ones that led me here, step aside to let me walk inside. Two more secret service agents are inside the office, standing at attention on either side of the door. The president is sitting in his office chair. His brown hair looks windblown, but as if on purpose. His face is nearly clean-shaven, with only a little stubble left behind. He's young, maybe forty-five.

His youth was part of his campaign. The ads emphasized over and over that he's young and therefore knows what the country needs, unlike the old politicians who have been at it for a while. The power went to his head at some point, though, and now, he rules like a king; he's taken over the country. He took power ten years ago and hasn't left office since.

President Morgan looks up at me and smiles. "Welcome, Agent Specter. It's nice to finally see you again. Please, have a seat."

I sit in the chair opposite him and wait for him to finish his paperwork. Finally, he sets the pen down and clasps his hands in front of him on his desk. His blue eyes are icy cold. They're nearly the same shade as Raegan's, which sends a shiver down my spine. Her eyes—her everything—will haunt me forever.

I give him a small smile. "It's nice to finally be… home."

The word tastes bitter on my tongue, but I don't dare show it. President Morgan nods. "Yes, it is good to have you back. I'm glad you finally came to your senses during our time together. Your skills are greatly valued. I'm immensely proud to have you as my heir, which we do need to talk about, but seeing as you've just returned,

I'm sure you're ready to get some sleep. We will meet very soon and discuss how to announce to the country who you are, as well as your new tasks as heir to this kingdom."

Kingdom. The word sounds foreign. But he is the metaphorical King of the United States, and that's scary. No more term limits. No more voting. Just him, running the country. And me, standing right by his side. Even though it shouldn't be, the idea of running a country, or part of it, is so tempting, so alluring.

He rises, as do I. I don't tell him everything I planned to say. His quick, dismissive behavior means he doesn't want to talk and I can't push past his defenses if I try to talk to him now. Instead, I shake his hand, thank him, and leave. The agents that led me here lead me away. A car is parked outside the gates, waiting for me. I get in and the driver takes me away, already knowing where my hotel is. I suppose I'll get a house near here, or maybe even live in the White House soon. Or maybe I'll be hidden in the hotel forever. I don't know how all of this will work.

But I know that, soon, I'll have my answers. Like it or not.

I PARK MY CAR A FEW BLOCKS AWAY FROM the school. I don't want anyone to see it. Spencer and Peter will easily recognize it if I park too close. I start walking, and as I get closer to the school, I pull the hood of my black hoodie over my head. The air has chilled slightly as autumn approaches.

I stand at the side of the school, giving me a perfect view of where Spencer's parked his truck. He's sitting inside it, waiting for Peter to get out of school. I tuck my hands into the pockets of my hoodie. I'm wearing sunglasses, despite the fact it's cloudy. I double-check to make sure I'm out of view of any soldiers or cameras.

I start waving erratically, motioning for Spencer to see me.

He glances over at me through the windshield,

not recognizing me yet. He's too far away. I motion with my hand again, beckoning him over here, keeping my head down slightly. He looks hesitant as he glances at the school doors. Finally, he gets out of the truck and starts to approach slowly. When he's about five feet away, realization comes across his face.

"You've got some nerve showing up around here," he says. He takes two quick steps closer and swings at my face, but I catch his fist in my hand, twisting his arm behind his back. He struggles against me, but I'm stronger than he is. I shove him against the brick, then glance around. No one sees us… yet.

With my free hand, I restrain his other arm that he keeps swinging back at me. I sigh. "Look, do you think I'd come here to see you without a good reason? I have something important to tell you. Something you're going to want to hear."

"I seriously doubt I'd want to hear anything you have to say." He tries to use his body weight to push back against me, but I hold him firmly, twisting his arm tighter. He yelps slightly. I glance around again. No one is around. The only sound, besides Spencer's heavy breathing, is the wind in the bushes.

Then the bell rings, signaling school is over. I need to make this fast. "Listen to me. I need your help. Raegan is alive."

He stops fighting for a moment, his body going stiff. Then he kicks his right foot into my shin— hard. I double over, losing my grip on him. Suddenly, it's me pinned to the wall, Spencer's hand holding me there by my throat. He's more skilled than I gave him credit for. Anger laces his voice as he says, "Is this some sort of sick joke? Because I swear, once Peter gets out of there, this will not end well for you."

I shake my head. "No. I'm serious. You have to believe me."

Spencer starts to apply slight pressure against my throat. I take in a breath, holding it, rationing the oxygen. This isn't my first street fight, and I doubt it will be my last. I wait for his anger to subside, for his curiosity to take over. Finally, he lessens the pressure against my throat and says, "Explain to me how she's alive."

I glance around uneasily. The pressure on my throat lessens more, just slightly. "I can't explain here. Besides, Peter will be looking for you soon.

She's still at the warehouse, except Evan has left. It's just me now. My team will be arriving any day now. I want to help get her out of there before it's too late. She's weak—very weak. Evan has made sure of it. Please, gather a team and get out there as soon as possible."

Spencer backs up a few feet, his arms crossed. I rub my throat with my left hand. Spencer smirks. "I see you still have your little gift from Peter."

I roll my eyes. "Yes, a stab wound doesn't heal within two weeks, nitwit. Anyway, do you believe me?"

Spencer shakes his head. "I don't want to believe you. In fact, I want to kick your ass back to wherever you came from. However, I can't take that risk if you are telling the truth."

I sigh. "You have no reason to believe me. But she's going to die there if we don't get her out soon. She needs medical attention, too. He did shoot her."

Spencer glares at me, sizing me up. I keep eye contact the whole time. Finally, he says, "I hope you know if you're lying, you won't have just me to deal with, but Peter, too. And he's very unforgiving when it comes to what's happened to Raegan."

I nod. "I know. That's why I came to you first."

Spencer eyes me a moment more before finally conceding. "Okay. I'll talk to Peter and the others. How soon does your team arrive?"

I feel relief wash over me, but the hard part has yet to begin. "Maybe four days. You'll have to work fast. I'm doing everything I can to keep her nourished, but she's incredibly weak."

Spencer sighs. "All right. I'll see what we can do."

He walks back to his truck and I rush around to the sidewalk by the road, praying no one recognizes me. Especially not Peter. I keep my head down and my hands tucked into the pockets of my black hoodie. I know Spencer believes me, despite not wanting to. And for now, that is all I need.

I get to my car, climb in, and drive back to the warehouse. I park behind it so that no one will suspect anyone is here. The last thing I need is attention. I enter through the side door, the one that conceals the trap door to the bunker. I want to check on Raegan and make sure she is okay, but I hear a noise outside the steel door.

I reach for the knife in my pocket and head down towards the main hallway. That's when I see two advanced agents and a group of three younger, newer ones. Two girls and a boy.

I sheathe my knife. "Who are you?"

The male agent says, "Agent Maverick, I'm Agent Phoenix. We're here to bring you your new team."

I glance at the group of... kids. "Them?"

Agent Phoenix nods. I scoff. "They're not even old enough to be here."

The female agent steps forward. "They have been trained for this moment. You are to show them what it means to be an agent in field training. We were told you were informed of their drop-off being moved up."

Of course, they'd be scheduled to come sooner. I can't help but suspect Evan has something to do with this. I clear my throat. "Oh, yes. That's correct. I was informed they would be coming here today. I was also informed my team would be highly trained, the best of the best. I was not told that they would need training from me to accomplish anything. I didn't sign up to babysit."

Agent Phoenix levels a steely gaze at me. "Are you saying you cannot fulfill your orders from President Morgan?"

That shuts me up fast. "No, sir. I'm saying more

information would have been nice. However, I will see to it that they are trained well and can complete missions in the field."

Agent Phoenix nods and then turns to the new agents. He gives them a curt nod and then turns smartly and heads out the door, followed by the female agent, who has not mentioned her name.

I look at the new students—agents—and decide this means a major change in my plans.

But first, I need to find a way to check on Raegan. I clap my hands together, calling their attention to me now. "Welcome to your new home. Show yourselves around and familiarize yourselves with the layout. One warning: the steel door around the corner is off-limits. If I catch any of you even lingering near the door at any time, there will be severe consequences. Do I make myself clear?"

It's been a while since I've used my threatening voice. It feels kind of good. The newbies all nod quickly. I smile. "Excellent. If you'll excuse me, I have some things I must take care of."

I hurry down the hall, trying not to look rushed and making sure no one is following me. I unlock the steel door and slip inside the storeroom. I lock the door behind me and make my way down to the bunker. I left the door to Raegan's prison open so newer air could circulate through. It wouldn't help much, but I figured maybe it would be enough. As I get closer, I can hear the coughing.

I rush to her side. "Whoa—are you okay?"

She nods but is too weak to speak. I touch her forehead. She's burning up. "You have a fever."

I take the blanket off her. Her body is very frail and her clothes are wrinkled. I look away, focusing on grabbing her a water bottle instead. "I talked to Spencer today," I tell her. "He's going to talk to Peter. You'll be home soon enough. Of course, I need to find them again. My team is already here, which means I won't be getting down here as often. Of course, you'll get your food for every meal. I mean, if you want it," I add quickly.

She shrugs, coughs again, and finally finds the energy to speak. "I don't know. I feel so sick. What's happening?"

"I think the sudden intake of nutrients is messing with your body. We'll take things a bit slower. You'll be out of here soon, though. They're fighting for you."

Her eyes slowly close, and I back away. She needs rest. I crack the door behind me to block the light from the main area of the bunker and start the climb back up to the storeroom. After securing the tile in place, I leave the room and go to check on my new team. I find that they have all settled into different offices. My office is untouched.

Perfect.

I hide in there, for now, unsure of what to do next. If I'm honest with myself, I know exactly what I need to do, but I don't want to address them or deal with any of this.

I know I need to set the rules, create the boundaries, and figure out a way to get them out of here when Peter and his team come to rescue Raegan. Yet I can't send them anywhere without express permission. I leave my office and stand in the center of the lobby. I call out to see if anyone can hear me. Turns out they all can. I ask them to gather around and, once they're all in a half-circle around me, I smile confidently. It's been a while since I've faked that, too.

"Hello again, everyone. I thought we should set some ground rules while you stay with me."

One of the girls groans. "Stay away from the steel door in the left wing. We know."

I study her for a moment. Dark hair, dark

clothes, and a look of rebellion on her face. She looks young… not much over fifteen. I smirk. "Okay, good. But there's more to it than that. You need to understand I'm in charge. You can't question what I tell you. Trust me, that will not go well for you."

The girl rolls her eyes. "Yeah, okay. Whatever you say. When do we get to take care of business? I'm ready to get my hands dirty."

Her enthusiasm is amazing. "What's your name?"

With the same confidence, she says, "Linley."

"Well, Linley, what brought you here to this fine establishment? We all have a background story, right?"

Linley shrugs. "I suppose, but who says I'm in the habit of telling anyone where I came from?"

I study her a moment longer. She reminds me so much of myself that it hurts. I see the pain that lies behind that air of confidence. Finally, I turn my attention to one of the boys. He looks older, maybe twenty. His dark hair and brown skin have the other girl staring at him longingly. I point to him. "And you. What's your name?"

"Trevor Gonzalez." He has a slight accent to his

voice.

I nod at him. "Do you have a story to tell, Trevor?"

I don't know why I'm suddenly interested in these people's stories. I guess I wonder how they were so easily tricked by the president, how they wound up in this place at all. Now that my eyes are open, I see the faults, the cracks in everything I've ever believed.

Trevor smirks. "Well, my skills surpassed those of everyone else on my level. Eventually, my commander decided I must be put on a team."

I want to scream. So many blind people, and what can I do to save them? I turn to the other girl, who has finally pulled her googly eyes away from Trevor. I nod at her. "And you?"

She runs a hand down her long black braid. Her skin is so fair, but her lips are painted bright red. "Genesis Clark. I've been in training for government agencies for two years. This is part of my field training."

She can't be more than nineteen years old and already they've brainwashed her, too.

This is it? This is my team? An emo girl barely willing to listen, a man so full of himself he can't

149

possibly focus on much, and a girl in training. This is what they see my worth as.

I pinch the bridge of my nose. "Look, we're out of time to do much of anything today. Why don't you all return to wherever you're staying and then come back tomorrow? We can start then."

Genesis rolls her eyes, but she follows Trevor out the door. Linley doesn't budge.

"If you don't mind," she says, "I'll stay in one of the offices for tonight. My home is pretty far away, and I'm too tired to call a cab."

"Home? Wouldn't you be staying in a hotel?" She doesn't say anything. I cross my arms. "All right. I can probably get you home. Where do you live?"

"I'm pretty sure you can't," she says, heading back to the office she claimed earlier.

"Linley," I say, stopping her.

She turns. "Yes?"

"Where do you live?"

She looks to her feet and mumbles something, but I can't hear her. "Speak up."

Finally, her brown eyes meet mine. "I live in California. I ran away from home because my mom is marrying some guy she's been seeing for a few months. I didn't know until a couple of days ago. She didn't bother to tell me she was dating anyone. Next thing I know, I'm rolling with this group of runaway teens and they tell me about someplace that'll let me stay for the night. I met a girl there. She was cool. And one thing led to another. I'm here now."

I nearly sag with relief. She's not too far gone. She can be saved. "I'm sure your mom is worried about you."

"I doubt it. I tried to tell her I wasn't comfortable with her marrying this new guy so soon. But she didn't want to listen to me."

I know the feeling all too well. It stings deep. I remember my father marrying Noah's mother without asking me how I felt about it. But Linley is young, and mistakes happen when you're young and irrational. She can still save herself from the tragedy that waits for her here. "Can't you stay with your father, then?"

She's silent for a while, looking down at her feet again. Finally, she shakes her head and looks back up at me, her eyes filled with sadness. "He died two years ago."

I decide I've questioned her enough. "Okay,

Linley. You can stay in one of the offices. I'll be here, too, but in my office."

She nods and rushes away from me. I sigh. I need to find a way to get her out of here, too. But first, Raegan. Before it's too late for either of them.

CHAPTER TWELVE

Peter

MONDAY, OCTOBER 23RD, 2023

SPENCER PULLS IN FRONT OF MY HOUSE. I begin to thank him for yet another ride home, but he interrupts me. "Something happened when I was waiting for you to leave school. I didn't want to tell you while we were still there because I knew you'd react too quickly, and it might jeopardize everything."

I look at him, seeing a hesitation in his eyes. I don't like where this is going. "Okay. What's up?"

He opens his mouth as I see my mom come outside, waving for me to hurry inside. I sigh. "I'm sorry, Spence. Can I call you later and you can tell me? My mom needs me."

Spencer shakes his head. "This isn't something I can tell you over the phone."

I slide out of the truck. "It'll have to wait until

tomorrow. I'm sorry."

"Peter, you're going to want me to tell you now. Your mom can wait."

I glance over at my mom. "No, she needs me. Tell me tomorrow, okay?"

I shut the door before he can argue with me further. A slight pang of regret fills me, but I can't do anything about it right now. I'll make it up to him somehow. I walk across the yard to my mom, who is holding an envelope. "Mom, why are you home early?"

She sighs. "I need to talk to you. It's important."

We go inside and she says, "I got something in the mail today. Well, you got something in the mail today, but I need to explain myself before you open it."

She hands it over to me, and I see it's from my dad. I rip it open without waiting for her explanation, wondering what he would mail to me instead of calling me. My mom's words come out in a rush: "I wanted to tell you the truth right away, but your father told me he would tell you. And I guess he never did because when that came in the mail, and you hadn't said anything…"

I barely hear a word she says. It's a picture of my father and some lady who looks slightly younger than him. They're holding each other in a tight hug, all smiles. I open the card. *You're invited to the union of Greg Daniels and Carlie Matthews.* They look like they're in love. I look up at my mom. "What the hell is this?"

My mom looks shocked. "Watch your language, Peter."

"I'm sorry, but why am I getting invited to a wedding I didn't know was happening?"

"He wanted to tell you and I thought he would. It *is* his news, after all."

"Yeah, but he didn't even tell me he'd found someone. I didn't even know he was dating anyone. Why didn't Emilee tell me anything?" I hate how my voice sounds right now, like I'm just a kid again, whining about a divorce and a move across the country.

My mom's eyes water. "We worried about how you would react since losing Raegan."

Something inside me breaks. "He should have told me he was dating someone. He should have told me he proposed. Yet he expects me to come back after high school, live with him again, go to the college he wants me to go to, and be okay with this?"

I hear the click of Gunnar's claws on the floor. He edges up beside me, bumping my clenched fist with his nose. I don't budge. "Did you know any of this was happening, Mom?"

She nods, not meeting my eyes. I turn, leaving her in the living room, and storm into my room. Gunnar slips in with me before I close the door. I pace back and forth on my floor and realize I need to get out of here for now. I grab my phone from my pocket, remembering Spencer needed to tell me something. He answers on the first ring.

"Yes?"

"Can you turn around and come get me? I need to leave."

"What happened?"

"It's a long story. But you were right: my mom could have waited. I'm sorry. Can you come back?"

Spencer sighs tiredly. "Yeah, I'm not that far away. I'll be there in ten minutes."

I glance down at Gunnar, who's curled up in the corner, almost asleep again. Must be nice, I think. I slip out of my room and find that my mom has disappeared. Her car is gone, so she must have gone somewhere to think. I don't bother leaving a note for her. I make sure Gunnar has food and water, then step out as Spencer pulls up to the curb.

I climb in his truck and he says, "What's going on?"

"My father decided he's going to get married without telling me he was even dating anyone. My mom knew all along. So did my sister. No one bothered to tell me about it."

Despite his earlier frustration with me, he seems shocked, too. "Why would they do that?"

I shrug. "They thought because of Raegan's death, I wouldn't want to hear it. It doesn't matter. I'm not going to the wedding."

We're both silent for a while as Spencer drives on, leaving Bent Ridge behind. Finally, I say, "You had something you wanted to tell me?"

"Yeah, and you're probably going to be mad at me for not forcing you to listen earlier."

"Why?"

"Raegan's alive."

My heart stops. I stop. "What?"

Spencer sighs, running a hand through his hair. "When I was waiting for you at the school, someone called me to the side of the building. It turned out

157

to be Jackson. I tried to take him down, but he overpowered me and explained that things have changed. And Raegan isn't dead. But she's not in a good state, either. We have to get her out of there soon."

"Why didn't you make me listen, or tell me when this happened?"

"You've got to be kidding me. What, did you want me to hop out and beg on my hands and knees at your feet for you to stay and listen to me?" He shoots me a sideways look. "I also worry about getting your hopes up if Jackson is lying. But honestly, I don't think he is. He told me we need to get her as soon as possible. He has a team arriving there soon, but not for another couple of days. We have to act fast."

Spencer stops at a red light, letting his hands fall from the wheel. My heart is racing, and I'm ready to go now. "Let's go get her."

"Hold on, now. I already told my uncle I need to meet with him. I'm going to tell him, and you're coming with me."

"What will he do about it?" I ask suspiciously.

The light turns green and Spencer speeds up, heading down the country roads that lead to

Williams' Ranch.

"What will he do about it?" I repeat my question.

"He'll know what action we need to take to investigate this further. He needs to know what's happening. Besides that, he trusts me, and I'm all he has left."

I don't try to argue with him. I know his home life has been shaky, even before living with his aunt and uncle. But now with Evan's betrayal and Carissa's return, Mr. Williams has looked to him for help more than usual.

It's another twenty minutes of silence and listening to my heart racing in my ears. The idea that Raegan is alive seems daunting and unreal. How? How could she still be alive? I heard the gunshot. I heard the scream.

So many questions race through my head. I want to know what's happened. It's been a month now since the incident.

Raegan could be alive.

Spencer pulls into the driveway of Williams' Ranch and drives down the long path toward the garage. When the door closes behind our truck, the floor lowers, taking us down below to headquarters.

Spencer parks and gets out of the truck. "Come on," he tells me. "We're going to talk to my uncle, but you need to control yourself about this."

I sigh and get out, then follow Spencer to the door. He puts in a code, a new code since I've been here, and we enter. We walk past some people leaving training and my heart lurches a little. Training used to be my job. But after I left, Mr. Williams assumed I had no intention of returning and put someone else in charge of training recruits. I see a few familiar faces, like Marcus and Kyle. They nod towards me, looking a bit surprised, but don't say anything.

Spencer knocks on the oak door to his uncle's office. The door is ajar, and Mr. Williams looks up from his desk. He permits us to enter and smiles.

"Hello, Spencer. And Peter, it's nice to see you again. If you want to go back to training our recruits, I can get you in there." As usual, his focus is only on the resistance.

Spencer shakes his head. "Uncle Andre, we have something big to tell you."

I tuck my hands in my pockets, listening to Spencer recount everything that happened. Mr.

Williams keeps an unreadable expression on his face the whole time. When Spencer finishes, we're all silent for far too long.

Finally, Spencer says, "I think we need to investigate this further. I feel like he was telling the truth."

Mr. Williams rises from his chair. "I don't. This is obviously a trap to lure someone out, most likely Peter."

"But he didn't even approach me," I say. "He went to Spencer."

Mr. Williams nods. "Yes, because he knew Spencer would tell you. And he knows you'll run to the rescue. Brett and his team investigated every room after the incident. Raegan wasn't there. Neither was Evan. There was plenty of evidence that she had been shot. But even if she was still alive at the time, there's no way she's alive now. I'm sorry. I know it's hard to hear, but I'm not going to send a team to be hurt or killed to look for a dead girl."

Spencer speaks up angrily. "Uncle Andre, how could you say that? I thought we didn't leave anyone behind. What if he's telling the truth?"

"And what if he's not?" Mr. Williams retorts.

"I'm sorry. But my decision is final. Now please, get to work. And Peter…" He trails off. With a shake of his head, he dismisses us.

I storm out of the room, not caring if Spencer is behind me or not. I stop in the lobby, realizing I have no way to get home right now. Spencer appears beside me. "I can take you home first. I don't mind doing my work later."

I shake my head. "It's okay. As much as I don't want to be here, I don't want to go home right now. I'll wait in the workroom while you do your assignment."

Spencer leads the way. "It should only be an hour, anyway."

He places his hand on a sensor outside the door. The door slides open, letting us through.

"That's new," I say.

"My uncle increased the security measures here to prevent Evan from having a way back inside headquarters if he were to try. According to Jackson, Evan left for DC, but we have to be careful."

I nod, following Spencer to his usual back-corner table. We pass Stella and Noah. Stella still has her lavender hair. They're in deep conversation when Noah glances up at me.

"Whoa, Peter? You're still alive?"

"Barely." The anger from my conversation with Mr. Williams still drips from my voice.

Stella stands up. "Are you okay? Is something wrong?"

I don't trust my voice anymore. I glance at Spencer, and he comes to my rescue.

"Jackson approached me today," he tells them. "He claims Raegan is alive, but my uncle won't look into it."

"But I'm going to. I'll go by myself if I have to," I say.

No one looks surprised. Instead, Spencer turns to me and says, "How can we help?"

I look at him with surprise. "You aren't going to try and stop me?"

"Why? That would be pointless. I know you well enough now to know you will fight for the ones you love. Especially her."

I look down at the table. I don't know how we can do this.

Then, Noah says, "I'm in. But we need to come up with a plan of action. We can't run in blindly."

I look up at them, feeling a bit lighter.

Stella nods. "Yeah, and we can't meet here to talk about it if Andre isn't going to support us. We need to meet somewhere else."

Noah says, "We can meet at my apartment. It's on the bad side of Cyrus, but it's safe enough to meet at. No one will suspect much."

I smile, a genuine smile for once, and say, "Thanks, but you have to know the risks. If Jackson is lying, we could get hurt. Or worse."

Stella smiles in return. "We know the risks, Peter, but if Raegan is truly alive, we have to take it."

Finally, I feel a weight lift from my shoulders. I have a team that is willing to help me. And we're going to save Raegan.

TUESDAY
OCTOBER 24TH, 2023

I SEE NICOLE GETTING out of her mom's silver car, standing on the front walkway of the school. I glance around to see Sawyer heading toward the school from his truck. It's cold and windy out, but I need to catch them both before they go inside. I decided last night after talking with Spencer that we should include them. He was reluctant, but I had already made up my mind.

I start running to the front of the school. They're avoiding eye contact with each other. I quickly run up the front steps, two at a time. I reach the doors before they do, turning around and stopping them from going inside. I glance around to make sure there are no soldiers nearby. Most of them will already be inside, patrolling the halls.

Both Nicole and Sawyer look up at me at the same time. "We...need to... talk," I say, out of breath.

Nicole says, "Peter, are you okay?"

"I will be. Look, we're going to be discussing something big, something that changes... well, everything. This evening, we're meeting somewhere."

"Who's meeting?" Sawyer asks, clearly confused.

"Some people from the resistance. I want you there because we're working on a plan. You're not going to believe this, but Raegan's alive."

Nicole pales and looks as though she might faint. Sawyer reaches a hand out to steady her. She pulls away, taking a few steps to lean against a pillar. Sawyer, obviously hurt by this, turns to me.

"What do you mean she's alive?"

I sigh. "I can't explain much now, but I'd like you guys to come with me tonight. I know it might be a bit... uncomfortable for you two. But I could use your help."

Nicole and Sawyer share a look, and then Nicole says, "Of course we will. We can all ride together, and you can guide us to wherever you're meeting."

I smile. "Thanks."

SCHOOL DOESN'T HOLD MY focus at all. In my notebooks, I write out ideas for ways to infiltrate the warehouse. When the final bell rings to signal the end, I'm the first out of my class. I rush past my locker, already having everything I need for the night. I wait outside for Sawyer and Nicole, who catch up quickly.

I give Sawyer the address Noah gave me, and we drive ten minutes to the darker side of Cyrus. Some buildings are tagged with crude words and sayings. The streets are dirty. Some of the apartment buildings have broken windows. We pull up outside Noah's building. He's waiting outside with Stella and Spencer. When we approach, he turns and leads us inside and then up the rickety stairs to his apartment.

Noah opens the door; his apartment is a surprisingly bright contrast to the outside. The walls are painted cream white, and he has house plants everywhere. "I like gardening," he explains when he catches Spencer looking at the plants on the bookshelf.

We head over to the kitchen table and begin discussing the situation, catching Sawyer and Nicole up on things they don't know about. A few minutes later, the doorbell rings, more like buzzes, and Noah stands. The apartment is small, so we can see over to the front door as he opens it.

"What the hell arc you doing here?" Noah says angrily.

I look up to see the last person I ever wanted to see right now.

Jackson.

CHAPTER THIRTEEN

Jackson

I PULL INTO THE PARKING LOT OF NOAH'S rundown apartment complex. It's like mine: all the doors face outside, and metal stairs lead up to each building. But unlike mine, weeds are growing between the concrete, a lot of broken windows, and some empty units tagged with spray paint.

My car will stand out too much here. I need to be quick. I walk up the shaky stairs to Noah's apartment and knock on the door. My heart is beating rapidly against my ribs.

The door swings open and I'm face to face with my stepbrother. He crosses his arms. "What the hell are you doing here?"

I glance behind him. I see Spencer standing not too far back, studying me. Peter, Stella, and two people I've never seen before sitting at the small table.

My eyes fall on Noah again. "Look, I know I'm not welcome here in any normal circumstance, but there's been a new development that will change how you rescue Raegan."

Noah pins me with a glare that could kill me if looks had that power. He opens his mouth, likely to tell me to leave his home now, but Spencer steps up behind him. "Let him in. He has the information we need."

Noah eyes me carefully, angrily, as he steps aside. I enter cautiously. Peter stands, coming around to stand in front of me. "You have one minute to say what you have to say. Then you need to leave before I do something I will *not* regret."

I hold my hands up in surrender. Peter glances at my left hand, and I see a flash of something in his eyes as his gaze lingers on the scar… Remorse? I put my hands back in my pockets. "Don't worry. I won't take too much of your time." I take a breath. "My team arrived yesterday."

Spencer eyes me closely. "You said we had four days."

I nod. "I know. I thought you did. When I got back to the warehouse after talking to you, two agents were there with my new team. It's hardly an advanced team, but they've been in training for a long enough time. The drop-off date was moved up, but no one told me about that."

Noah crosses his arms, still very put out by my existence. "And why does it matter whether your team is there or not?"

"They could hinder your rescue mission. I can't just send them away without an explanation. They're far too perceptive. I can't even send them out on patrol without permission from the government. They're new agents, and this is their first time out in the field. You're going to have to do something to distract them, like last time, while someone else enters from the back, where I will be waiting to help."

Peter crosses his arm, leaning back against the wall. "That last plan failed."

I give him a hardened glare. "This time, you know exactly where she is. Besides that, I'll be helping you while everyone is fighting at the front of the warehouse. It will work this time."

Peter glances at Spencer, who gives him a small nod. Peter returns his eyes to me. "All right. You'd better be telling the truth, Jackson. Otherwise, I'm not afraid to do what I need to do."

"Which means what, exactly?"

Peter smiles cynically. "Why don't you take a long look at your left hand, and then figure that out for yourself?"

Noah narrows his eyes at me. "How can we know this isn't a trap, Jackson? Since when can we trust *anything* that comes out of your mouth?"

I shake my head. "I know this all sounds... crazy. And I know I'm the *last* person you'd ever believe, but I promise you I'm not luring anyone. I'm not sticking around after you get Raegan out of there. The night Raegan was shot is the night Carissa left, and everything else you know about me may have been a mask I hid behind, but she wasn't. I love her with everything I have. And now I don't even know if she's alive anymore, or if Evan really knows where she is. I don't know if he's already captured her again..." I trail off, my heart aching at every possibility.

"Besides that," I continue. "Raegan is sick. Her body is rejecting food. It can't handle when she eats more than a few bites of oatmeal or potatoes. She also has a bullet wound in her right shoulder."

The redheaded girl at the table looks up sharply. "Bullet wound?"

I nod, looking at her. "Yeah. Everything about that day, minus her death, was real. I don't know what he did to help her. She doesn't seem to suffer too much, but there is a wound. It's healing, but I don't think it looks right. She needs medical attention."

I look back at Peter. His eyes bore into mine. I don't know what he's looking for, but I hold his gaze, not backing down. Finally, he breaks eye contact first and addresses the others. "He's telling the truth."

I hear Spencer sigh in relief. Peter looks at him. "We have to come up with a plan to save her. She can't—I refuse—to let her stay there much longer."

Spencer nods in agreement. "Okay. The day after tomorrow, then. We'll do things according to your plan, Jackson, but if this *does* turn out to be a trap—"

"He'll have me to deal with," Peter finishes for him.

I nod curtly. I can see his threats are not empty. He will hurt me, much worse than the stab wound in my hand this time. Because this time, he's out for revenge on anyone who gets in his way. Lucky for me, I don't plan to be caught in the crossfire of his mission against Evan.

As the others return to the table to plan Raegan's rescue, I ask Peter to speak to me privately. He steps out of earshot of the others, a miracle in this tiny apartment. For a moment, I feel bad about Noah's living conditions. But I push that aside, along with most of my feelings. "You have to hurry," I say quietly. "When I said she's sick, I meant it. Evan starved her, so she's very ill. She can barely sit up on her own. She's not going to last much longer, and she needs you. I've been giving her plenty of food and water, but it's hard for her to eat and drink. It's a shock to her system, and she's only growing weaker. I don't know if there's an infection from the gunshot wound, or if it's just the lack of nourishment. But I'm concerned either way."

For a moment, there's a softness to Peter's eyes. "Okay," he says. "We'll be there the day after tomorrow like Spencer said. Keep her safe until then. And tell her I'm coming for her."

I nod. "Of course. Do you need me to tell her anything else?"

He hesitates, thinking it over. Finally, he shakes his head slightly. "No. I'll tell her myself when I see her again. Just let her know we're coming."

I give him a curt nod. He returns to the table. I let myself out and hurry back to my car. I can only hope this will work. If not, we're all as good as dead.

CHAPTER FOURTEEN
Carissa
TUESDAY, OCTOBER 24TH, 2023

THE DOOR CREAKS AND LIGHT FILLS THE circular room outside the cells. I turn over in my cot, facing the door to my cell. I've been sleeping my life away. What else is left for me, anyway? I look over to see Spencer sliding a tray of food through the slot. He glances at me, and I sit up.

"Are you late, or has my perception of time become even more warped?" I ask.

"I was meeting with some people. A lot is going on."

I nod slightly, stumbling over to the food. Spencer stands there watching me, hands tucked in his pockets. He's waiting for me to speak, to talk about the things that are bothering me. This is our routine. He feeds me and listens to me talk about everything. But today, I get the sense he's got something *he* wants to talk about.

I take a bite of my food. Chicken soup. My mother's recipe. I want to cry. "Mom made soup?"

He nods.

"You've treated me better than we ever treated Raegan. I was so horrible to her. I can't believe I let Evan poison my mind into believing that was the right path."

Spencer leans against the door to an empty cell. "Well, I'm sure he was pretty convincing. He always is."

I nod, then swallow another spoonful. "She was so innocent."

Spencer says, "You mean she *is* innocent."

I wave my hand dismissively. "You know I don't put much stock in an afterlife. I suppose if that was in her beliefs, then maybe she is."

He doesn't say anything. I look up at him. "I can tell you have something on your mind."

Hesitating, he says, "The day Evan killed Raegan... what do you remember?"

I tilt my head. "I've told you this story many times."

He bites his lip, thinking. "I need every detail you remember."

"I was fighting off someone from the resistance. There was a gunshot and a scream. There was chaos, all around, as resistance agents scrambled to get through. I wasn't told the entire plan, another secret kept from me by both Evan and Jackson. I knew though. Deep down, I knew what it all was."

Spencer studies me for a moment, then looks away into another empty cell. "Well, Raegan is alive. Evan didn't kill her."

I stare at him, the spoon halfway to my mouth, expecting this to be some twisted joke. He always had a dark sense of humor. But this seems too dark even for him. Instead, he continues. "Jackson approached me when I went to get Peter from school yesterday. Evan's off to DC, and Raegan is still alive. He told Jackson to take care of her, but he's helping us rescue her. Uncle Andre won't help, but we've gathered a team to go in and get her. If she's alive, maybe you'll finally be able to leave your cell and return to helping us."

I drop my spoon onto the tray, unable to form any words. Slowly, I set the tray aside and rise from the floor. "Why are you telling me this?"

He shrugs, pushing away from the cell door and approaching mine. "I guess I believe you're not the bad guy in all of this. You were misled. I don't want you blaming yourself, especially if she is alive."

"Do you think you can trust Jackson?" I say, venom in my tone.

Spencer nods. "I do. He's said some other things, but I don't know if you'd be interested in hearing them."

"What could he possibly say that matters?"

"He's worried about you. And he's looking for you."

That stops me in my tracks. "You didn't tell him anything, did you?" Panic now leaks into my voice.

Spencer turns away from me. "No. No, I've said nothing. But I do think he loves you. I don't think he tricked you into believing he did. He looks lost and scared not knowing if you're okay."

I grip the metal bars of my cell door so tightly that my knuckles turn white. "Don't you dare even consider telling him anything."

Spencer sighs, meeting my eyes again. "I wouldn't do that to you. But he'll find you, Carissa. He's on a mission to find you, and he's not going to stop until he does. If that isn't love—"

"What do you know about love?" I say, regretting the words instantly when I think of his recent heartbreak, a detail he didn't spare from me. But my pride prevents me from stopping. "You've never been in love."

There's silence as I face him. He still faces me, his shoulders tense and his eyes blinking. I've hit a target I never meant to hit.

Finally, in a quiet voice, he says, "I loved Hannah. I know I would've done anything for her, even if it meant dying for her. I know I wasn't the man she needed, and getting involved with an advisor's daughter was stupid, because of the trouble it's caused for Uncle Andre. I know I'd go back and do it again because I *love* her. Even if she wants nothing to do with me anymore. And I know that Jackson would do the same for you, by how tenderly he talks about you. You can believe me or not, but you don't get to throw things at me like that."

I close my eyes to prevent the tears that want to fall. I cling to the metal bars that keep me in this cell. "I'm sorry," I say, barely above a whisper.

Spencer sighs. When I open my eyes again, I see the pain in his own. But he says, "I know you're hurting, Carissa. I know it's easier to hate Jackson than to accept that he does love you. I know that I may not know everything that's happened between you. But I saw him. He loves you."

I don't speak another word, too afraid I'll lash out again. Instead, I walk back to the shadows, to my cot, to my safety. Spencer runs a hand through his hair, sighing again. "Carissa, come on. You know you can't hide here forever. Your dad will eventually talk to you. You'll eventually be out of there, although I don't know what happens beyond that. I only know Jackson will track you here. Wouldn't you rather he knows you're safe and alive?"

"No."

Spencer says nothing else. He stays for a while longer, probably waiting for me to eat more soup, to push the tray back out. But I don't leave my cot. I don't look back at him, too afraid it will weaken what resolve I have left within me. Finally, he turns and leaves me to my thoughts. I don't touch my food, even with him gone. My mind is running through everything I can remember about that day. *How is she alive?*

When the door creaks open again later, I say, "Spencer, I need more information."

But when I get to the iron bars separating me

from my freedom, the person who greets me isn't Spencer. It's my father.

"I'm ready to talk," he says.

At this moment, every emotion that has brought me here, bubbles up inside me like a tidal wave. And just like the child that I am, I fall to my knees and cry before my father. Only this time, I don't know if he'll be willing to pick me back up.

CHAPTER FIFTEEN

Evan

TUESDAY, OCTOBER 24TH, 2023

"WE MUST ASSUME THE NEWS WILL BE taken as a slight shock. The citizens are in a state of unrest, but generally, they love me. The polls show it."

Because citizens lie. Those who don't reap horrendous consequences. But do I say this out loud? Hell, no. I listen as the president shows me the plan his advisor has created for our announcement.

I worry about what my father will think, then correct myself. I shouldn't even be thinking of my family now. They'll never accept me back, even after Sam and I complete our self-given mission of destroying the president. Forgiveness isn't going to happen. My acts have been unforgivable. And I've yet to accept that fact because though it burns me, I think of them all the time.

I nod my head, agreeing with everything he

says like the good little boy I am. I hate myself immensely. When he finishes telling me we'll be on live TV, announcing to the world who I am and what I mean to everyone, I find the courage to ask President Morgan the question that's been dancing on my tongue.

"Could I have an assistant of my own?"

President Morgan leans back in his chair. "I am willing to give you one. We have some interns looking for a promotion. I'll even let you pick one that suits your needs best."

"Actually," I say, trying to find the right words, ones that won't make me look suspicious. "Samantha was a wonderful assistant to me back in Texas. I was wondering if she could be my assistant again. You know, since I'm already pleased with her skills."

President Morgan strokes his chin. "Well, she's already been given her new mission. She'll still be close to the White House, though. You'll see her often enough. So, we'll have to assign someone else to be your assistant." He looks at me steadily. "Tell me, what are your thoughts on Samantha?"

The question is normal enough, considering my rank. However, his tone makes it much more...

personal than I would prefer. I need to keep this neutral.

"She's nice, I suppose."

"You drove to the airport together, yes?"

"Um, yes, but what does that have to do with anything?"

President Morgan has a sly smile tugging at his lips. I'm growing suspicious of his intent. "Oh, nothing. I just thought perhaps you two had a less than professional relationship outside of your mission seeing as you asked for her by name." He is still staring at me steadily, still smiling.

My eyes widen, and I can feel the rush of heat burn my face. "Oh, absolutely not. No, sir, we were strictly professional."

President Morgan nods, and I see something like disappointment flash on his face before it's replaced with his usual smirk. "Well, good to know. Now, if you'll excuse me, I have a lot of paperwork to deal with. An agent is waiting to take you to your new room."

I thank him as if I am forever in his debt and leave with whatever dignity I have left intact. Considering the conversation that just took place, I don't think I have much left at all. I follow the agent to my office on the opposite side of the White House. Once alone, I feel the urge to scream. I grab a pillow and throw it over my face before screaming into it. I can see why girls do it. It's therapeutic.

After I finish that, I find my phone. A text from Samantha sits unread. I open it.

Meet me at the café down the road when you're through with your meeting. I need to speak with you about something important.

I wonder what she wants to see me about. I change into a long-sleeved shirt and jeans. When I leave, I'm surprised there isn't any press waiting outside. It's quiet. The gates are opened for me, and I step out onto the sidewalk. I decide to walk to the café instead of having one of the drivers do it.

I blend in with the crowd of people shopping and sightseeing. As I approach the café, I see Samantha sitting at one of the outdoor tables. I make my way over to join her. She looks up at me, but her soft eyes don't meet mine. I take the seat across from her and say, "Is everything okay? I wasn't expecting to hear from you."

She sighs. "Turn your phone off."

I do as I'm told and wait for her to speak. A waitress comes by and I order a regular coffee, black.

As the waitress walks away, Samantha finally says, "I was given my mission today."

I nod. "Yes, President Morgan told me that's why you can't be my assistant. He said you'll still be close, though."

"Oh, remarkably close. They have a plan I absolutely despise. I am so disgusted with what I have to do."

I tilt my head. The waitress returns with my coffee, setting it in front of me before moving to her next table. I return my attention to Sam. "This, coming from the girl who's killed mercilessly before. What could be so horrible that it has you so shaken up?"

She exhales slowly. "I am... supposed to..." She pauses as if the next words cause her pain. Finally, she says, "...seduce you."

I choke on the scalding coffee I've just sipped. I cough for a solid minute before finally regaining my composure. My eyes widen. Suddenly what President Morgan said makes more sense. "I'm sorry, I must have misheard you because that sounded like you're supposed to *seduce* me."

She stirs her cream-filled coffee without taking a sip. "I did say that."

"I… why?"

Samantha's face reddens. "The president has some master plan. You are his heir, and since you are his heir, he wants… security. He wants to know there will be …offspring… in line for the metaphorical throne."

My face burns at this new information. I clear my throat and say, "Well... maybe this will help our plan."

She looks up quickly, skeptical. "What do you mean? I can't seduce you, Evan. You already know—"

I touch her hand. "Yes, I know. I didn't mean you have to try and win me over. I meant that it won't seem so suspicious if we spend a bunch of time together if that's what he wants. And we can plan things out for *our* master plan. We act like we're falling in love—heavy on the acting—and we do their bidding. We get enough momentum to take President Morgan down without anyone suspecting a thing from us."

Samantha sighs. "I don't know. That might be too obvious. I don't know if I can act like I'm in love with you."

I choke my coffee again. "Why is it so hard to

187

imagine that I could be a catch?"

She rolls her eyes; some of her usual behavior is returning. "I already told you it has nothing to do with you, Evan, so shut up about it already. I know we have to do this, but should we just go right for it, or should we slowly build up to something, play a little game in front of them?"

"We'll go slow," I say. Something tells me I won't mind this too much, despite my hesitations. I should mind this very much, yet I can't bring myself to be disgusted by it.

Samantha stands. "Okay. This could work. We'll start tomorrow. That's when they want me to start. I'll do what I've been asked, and you just play along. I'm sure President Morgan will be pleased."

I stand too and place a couple of bills on the table. My coffee is no longer appealing. As we walk down the street, I say, "Why do they want you to do this anyway? What is the end goal—besides providing more heirs? Because that is not happening."

Samantha shrugs. "I think they just want us to marry, to be seen together in the public eye. The president could never find a wife of his own, so at least when he announces you as his heir, it will look good to the press that you have a lover in your life. You'll look more appealing, especially if you're seen around town with me, doing what couples do." She gives me a sideways look. "He's arranging your life for you, Even, down to when we'll have these supposed heirs."

If I was still drinking coffee, I might have choked again. I cough. "As I said, that's not happening. Ever."

"No, it's not, but we have to play the part of being young and in love, and we have to play it well. We want to get this right, or else we're screwed."

My mind is sent in a flutter of confusion. I can't believe President Morgan would think this is okay, that I could just fall in love with Samantha because he arranged it. What's worse is wondering what would have happened if Samantha hadn't told me about it. Would I have believed she loved me? Would I have fallen for her?

I don't know if I want the answer to that question.

We part ways and I head back to my room in the White House. I wonder if Jackson's holding up with his newly arrived team.

CHAPTER SIXTEEN

Peter
WEDNESDAY, OCTOBER 25TH, 2023

I FIND SPENCER IN THE WORKROOM, earbuds in, and glasses on. He doesn't notice me at first until I'm standing right in front of his desk. He yanks out an earbud. "What are you doing here? I thought you wouldn't be coming back around."

"I asked my mom to bring me here. I started thinking about our plan for Friday."

Spencer sighs, removing his glasses and rubbing his eyes. "Okay, what were you thinking about?"

"How we need to be armed. I know this might be crossing some line of trust, but can't you get us into your uncle's arsenal?"

He looks at me like I'm insane.

Maybe I am.

He shakes his head. "Of course not. Look, I said I would help you gather a team. I helped you get a plan together. Hell, I'm even going inside the freaking warehouse with you and praying this isn't a trap. Because I swear, if I die, I will haunt you forever and make your life miserable."

"I don't doubt you would, but my life is already terrible. I'd be amazed if you could top any of it."

He falls silent. "I'm not going to have you feeling sorry for yourself now. I don't know how I can get access to the arsenal without Uncle Andre discovering our plans. I'm not comfortable crossing a line of trust like that. If we're discovered, my uncle will never trust me with anything again."

I sit down across from him and rest my head in my arms on the table. "You're right. I shouldn't ask something like that of you."

Spencer sighs defeatedly. "But I can't ask them to go in there unarmed. I'll figure something out."

I look up at him. His expression is unsure, but I smile. "Thank you."

The door to the workroom opens and Mr. Williams looks inside. "Ah, Peter. Your mother told me you came along today. I need to speak with both of you in the hall."

I glance at Spencer. "He didn't hear us, right?" I whisper.

Spencer shrugs. "Honestly, with him, there's no telling. Come on."

Out in the hall, I see Mr. Williams is not alone. Brett Carrol stands with him, tall and commanding. I feel my fists clench at my sides as I stare him down. This is the man who said Raegan was dead. *This is the man who gave up.*

Mr. Williams says, "I told Brett the things you discovered, and he thinks it would be unwise not to investigate, at least a little. So, I felt like you should know his team is heading out there Friday. We'll let you know what they find as soon as we can."

"Friday?" I repeat.

Spencer elbows me in the ribs, shutting me up fast.

Mr. Williams says, "It's the soonest he can gather a team."

I want to say something to make it clear I do not approve of this. But anything I say will give away the plan, and that will ruin our chances.

Brett says, "And before you demand to help, the answer is no. You screwed up last time, and you're a liability. They know you care for her. I was there for her declaration. If this is a trap, they're trying to lure you out. And we're not about to let that happen."

I want to scream that it's not a trap, but I can't. If they know what we're planning, there will be no mission and Raegan will be in more danger than before. I storm off towards the training room. It's Wednesday, which means classes start soon, but I need to punch something.

Hard.

I hear the door swish open as I'm in the middle of sending the punching bag swinging.

Spencer comes over, not getting too close. "This plays to our benefit."

"How?" I say, throwing a hard jab.

Spencer sighs. "Because they know what they're doing more than we do."

"But Jackson will only work with us. And I want to be there to save her. I screwed up big last time. I'm the reason she could have died. I should have been there for her that night. If I hadn't left with my mom, none of this would have happened. I should have fought for her more. Instead, this is the mess she's in."

Spencer tilts his head, tucking his hands in his pockets. "But we're going to bring her home. And she'll be safe."

I throw a harder punch, knocking the punching

bag off the hook. It rolls away and stops far from me. Spencer's eyes are wide as he looks at the punching bag, then at me. I exhale. "Jackson pulled me aside at Noah's apartment," I tell him. "She's not doing well. Evan has been keeping her weak by withholding food. Even though she's eating a bit now, she's only getting sicker."

"But does running in there and getting yourself killed save her? You're looking for a redemption that she's not demanding of you. She never would. She would never hold any of what happened against you. You don't understand that the only person who is mad at you right now is you."

He's right, and I hate it. I'm the only one holding myself accountable. Raegan would never hold me to this. Still, I shake my head. "I need to know what Brett is planning."

Spencer sighs, rubbing his face with his hand. "They're going over the plans now, in the meeting room."

I pace back and forth. "Isn't there a camera in there?"

Spencer nods. I smile. "So, if we happened to get into the system like you know how to do, we could watch the meeting?"

Spencer frowns. "That's pretty invasive and totally against everything I stand for."

"We don't have much more of an option. We need to get a hold of those plans. We're screwed otherwise."

Spencer groans. He looks at me and says, "I need you to know I hate you."

I smirk. "I know."

He shakes his head but leads the way back to the workroom. It's still empty. Spencer opens his laptop and types away. Soon, we're watching and listening to this meeting.

Brett sits across from Andre, pointing at a piece of paper. "It will be like the first plan," he says, "using the distraction method. I do have word that Evan is in DC, so I don't know what team has been assigned to this place now, only that Jackson Maverick is leading it. Since Jackson is the one who came forward, I can't imagine anything good coming from this."

Andre nods. "Yes. Well, I did explain that to Peter and Spencer. But I am concerned that there might be truth to this."

"And there might be. So, I'll have some agents assigned to distract the team by barging in from the front. Once they're in place, I'll take Cody, my partner, with me, and we will search the place thoroughly."

Andre and Brett keep talking, but I smile. Maybe Brett will prove himself useful after all.

"REMIND ME AGAIN WHY I'm even bringing you here?" Noah asks as we pull into the parking lot of Jackson's apartment. His dark sports car is parked nearby.

"Because he needs to know about the change of plans, and you're the only one who knows where he lives. Besides, we'll only be here for a few minutes."

Noah says nothing else, but I know he's not happy about being at the apartment of his stepbrother. We approach the door, and I knock four times. Noah sighs, glancing around. "It's unfair that a guy like him gets to live in the nicer apartments."

Before I can say anything to that, the door swings open. A shirtless Jackson, with a toothbrush in his mouth and hair that has yet to deal with all the gel he uses to style it, greets us. "Whamyouwamft?"

I smile sarcastically. "I'm sorry, I didn't quite catch that, but I have really important information that I need to give you. Can we come in?"

He nods and steps aside. Once the door is closed, he wanders back down the hall to the bathroom. He returns without the toothbrush, but still no shirt. "I said what do you want?"

"Brett has decided to interfere with everything," I say.

"You mean that FBI agent who was yelling at you the whole time you were trying to get to Raegan? Ha—I like him. He seems hardcore."

I glare but continue. "He's taken matters into his own hands. He's decided to raid the warehouse on Friday, using part of his team as a distraction while he slips by the defenses to search for Raegan. I don't trust him. So, we're going to let *him* be the distraction, and let you lead Spencer and me to Raegan while they go on that dead-end mission."

Jackson considers what I've just said and then nods. "All right. Sounds fair enough. I'm glad you came by. I have a request for you."

Noah crosses his arms. "You aren't in any position to make demands."

Jackson nods again. "I know, but there's a

young girl who's on my team. Just fifteen. She's run away from home and I don't want her involved in any of this. Is there any way you can take her with you?"

Noah begins yelling. "Are you serious? You think after everything that's happened, we're just going to—"

"Yes, we'll take her," I say, stopping Noah from finishing his rant.

Jackson gives me an appreciative look. "Thank you. It means a lot to me that you'd do this for me."

I laugh humorlessly. "I'm not doing it for you. I'm doing it for a girl who shouldn't be in this mess."

Jackson shrugs. "Fair enough."

As Noah drives me home, he rants on and on about how despicable Jackson truly is, but I don't listen. Because I saw the way Jackson's eyes softened when he was speaking about this young girl. He seems anxious to show us that he's changed, and I can see that he has. I almost trust him now. Maybe that's foolish, but I see the effort he's putting into helping us.

Noah takes me home and I feed Gunnar his dinner. My mom hasn't arrived, so I eat some leftovers and do my homework as well as I can.

Friday, the day everything goes down, is just two days away. I'm going to skip school. Nicole and Sawyer wanted to do the same and come along to help, but it would look too suspicious if we all skipped. But Nicole told me to keep her updated.

As I shut my eyes for the night, I know I won't be getting much sleep. Friday, I'm going to see Raegan again. Friday, she will be safe, and I'm not going to let anyone hurt her ever again.

CHAPTER SEVENTEEN

Jackson

MY TEAM STANDS GATHERED IN THE front lobby of the warehouse, awaiting my instruction. I called them here, and now I'm finding I don't have the words. I'm worried about tomorrow, the battle. I'm worried their lack of training out in the field is going to show up in a battle against highly trained agents of war. I want to prepare them, yet I need them caught off guard for the plan to even work. I don't know how to speak to them. Evan made it look so easy, even when he was only acting stronger than he truly was.

I finally gather enough words to make something out of my thoughts. "I called all of you here today to prepare you for the things ahead. There's so much you don't know yet, about what it takes to be an agent. You have trained with the best of the best, but you've never been put out here, on the field, on the front line."

I pause. They look bored. Already, I'm losing them. "This team is meant to patrol, to scout, to observe. I don't want any of you jumping the gun and tracking down dangerous people. I know you've trained for violent situations, but in this instance, I want us to observe."

Linley raises her hand. "What if we are under attack?"

The question catches me off guard, but it's only my paranoia getting to me. She wouldn't know anything about the plans. "Then we do our best to defend ourselves. As you learned in your basic training, you know we fight to capture. Killing is the last option. If you can avoid it, then avoid it, because once you kill someone, everything changes. You have to be careful."

Trevor says, "What if some of us have already killed someone?" His eyes hold fear, regret, and maybe even a little trauma.

"Then we move forward. I'd rather you didn't kill anyone on my watch. We're trying to keep undercover. We're a scouting team, which means we watch, we wait, and we gather the information that no one has yet heard. We patrol the city we're stationed in."

My team looks unenthused, but I'm hoping I'm saving their skins. I wonder how I'll get Linley to go with Peter and Spencer tomorrow. She seems too observant, and she doesn't like to take orders from anyone. But I can't let her get mixed up in all of this.

With the briefing complete, I dismiss them and take some food down to Raegan. She sits up on her own, more color filling her cheeks. I say, "Tomorrow, sweetheart, all your problems will be over. Well, not all of them. You'll still have to find a hiding place. But your boyfriend will be with you again."

She glares at me. "He's not my boyfriend. But are you sure they're coming tomorrow?"

I smile. "Yes, I'm sure. I spoke with them earlier today. Well, I spoke with Peter. Noah yelled at me, but I'm used to that."

Her eyes light up. "How is he?"

"Noah? Fine, I guess. He still has that ridiculous ponytail."

She scowls. "Not Noah. Peter."

I smirk. "Oh, he's fine. He looks tired, and he definitely hasn't slept lately. He's a bit irritated by everything, but he treated me well enough. I think

I've earned a little trust from him."

Her eyes get a lost look and I gag for dramatic effect. "Anyway, I think we need to see how your walking is today. You'll likely be doing plenty of that."

"I don't think I can," she says, her face taking on more of a pallor.

I approach her cot, helping her sit up. "You have to try. Once you're out of here, you can rest for however long you want. But it's that in-between, the fight to get out that you have to work on."

She nods reluctantly. Lately, I've been helping her work on her sitting and standing, though with whatever infection she has now, it's hard for her to do anything and not be dizzy. She gets slowly to her feet and I hold her up until she balances. Then she takes a few, meager steps towards the door. She lurches forward and I rush to catch her. She groans. "I knew this wasn't a good idea."

"Kid, Peter can't carry you up the ladder. I know he'll carry you as much as he can... but you'll have to help yourself, too."

She grunts unhappily, and I help her back to the cot where she lies down again. I decide to tell her about Linley. "You'll have someone going with you from my team."

Raegan doesn't move; her gaze is fixed on the chalky ceiling. "What do you mean?"

"I already ran it by your lover boy. He's okay with it. She's a young girl who ran away from home because her mom is getting married to someone else and she doesn't approve. I don't want her involved with this. She still has time to escape, and I know she'll be safe in Andre's care."

Raegan glances at me, her eyes softening. "That's sweet of you, Jackson. I knew you had a heart somewhere."

I scoff. "No, you thought I was a pigheaded ass."

Raegan shrugs, looking back up at the ceiling. "That too." She yawns. "I think I'm done for the day. I need to rest up for tomorrow."

"All right. Good night."

I gather the tray and the empty water bottles to take upstairs with me. I glance back at Raegan, but she's already faded into the dark abyss of sleep. I leave the door open, not daring to wake her by shutting it. I load all the dirty dishes and empty bottles in a duffel bag to make it easier to get up the ladder. I climb up, then carefully push the tile back in place. I round the corner of the boxes that have been carefully stacked to protect the location of the bunker's entrance.

As I turn, I find Linley sitting atop a stack of boxes near the door to the hallway. Her brown eyes find me and instantly I remember forgetting to lock the door behind me.

"Linley, I told you all never to enter this room."

Her eyes dance mischievously. There's a spark behind them—no, more than that: a flame. She's proud of her feat, sneaking in here and startling me. I can only hope she knows nothing of the bunker. She's far enough away that there's a chance she didn't see me moving the tile or leaving the entrance to it. But it's still close enough to have seen something. I wait for her to say something.

Her smile is confident. She reminds me of myself when I was young. "Well, I thought there'd be something interesting in here, but it seems all that exists is boxes that you're using to make a fort. And it looks like you eat in your fort."

I glance down at the plate sticking out of the duffle bag. Good. She didn't see anything to make her suspicious.

Relief floods through me. "Haha. Very funny.

All right, I've asked you not to come in here. You've
had your fun. Now leave."

She slides off the stack of boxes, landing
gracefully on her feet. Oh, Andre will find a place
for her at the ranch, for sure. And she'll be safer
there. Because as soon as Raegan is rescued, I'm
abandoning this place to find Carissa. And there's
no way in hell I'd leave a young girl like Linley to
suffer the same fate as me. I will not allow any more
victims. I just can't watch it happen again.

I'M SETTLING INTO MY bed, my sheets pulled
over my head when my phone rings. I curse myself
for not silencing it before coming to my room. I roll
over towards my nightstand, where it vibrates and
flashes. Not bothering to see who's disturbing my
sleep, I answer groggily, "Hello?"

"Hey, Jackson. I'm just checking in to see how
things are going."

I sigh. "Well, I was about to sleep for once, but
you've so kindly put a stop to that, so thanks."

He ignores my comment. "Have you been

caring for... my pet cat?"

I roll my eyes. "Yes, she's been fed, as you've instructed me. You know you can trust me to care for her, right?"

"I trust you entirely with her care. I wanted to make sure you aren't spoiling her."

I hear the idle threat in his tone. "No, I feed her, then I leave. Simple. Easy."

The lies fall easily off my tongue, easier than I would like. But I've lost my ability to care at this point, especially when it comes to Evan Williams. He's the worst among traitors and liars.

"Awesome. How are you?"

"Well, as I said before, I was about to sleep. How are you? Isn't it even later where you are?"

"Only an hour later. I've been taking care of things and I lost track of time. Samantha and I have been getting along and we talk a lot. It's so easy to lose track of time when you're enjoying talks with a friend."

This is starting to sound strange, even for him. "I guess that's great. But what exactly do you mean by getting along?"

Evan chuckles, and it sounds so forced that I know something is up. This conversation is no longer genuine. He says, "Well, honestly, I think I'm developing feelings for her. She's so kind, funny, and smart."

I sit up, rubbing my eyes. Obviously, I'm not getting any sleep yet. "This is Samantha Winters we're talking about, right?"

He laughs. "Yes. Who else would I be talking about?"

"I don't know, man. Look, I'd love to talk and catch up with you—really, it's the highlight of my year—but I need to get some sleep. It's been a long day. Can we talk later?"

Evan sighs slightly. "Yeah, I should probably try to get some sleep, too. I'll talk to you soon. Night, buddy."

The phone clicks and I shut it off, tossing it away from me. Nothing about that conversation seemed right. I don't know what Evan is up to, or what story he's trying to portray over the phone, but at this point, I don't care enough to find out.

CHAPTER EIGHTEEN

Evan

THURSDAY, OCTOBER 26TH, 2023

"WELL, HONESTLY, I THINK I'M DEVELOPING feelings for her. She's so kind, funny, and smart."

The words flow from my mouth, and I hate the fact that there is some truth to them. After everything Samantha has told me about her past, even knowing there's no chance she could ever feel the same thing for me, I still find that I like her more than I should. And it kills me.

I hear the sleep in Jackson's voice, the exhaustion plaguing him. Like me, he probably doesn't sleep well at night. And I know his team arrived recently. He's probably tired. "This is Samantha Winters we're talking about, right?" he says.

I laugh, but it's so forced that I don't even believe it. I know he'll see right through it, too. "Yes.

Who else would I be talking about?"

"I don't know, man. Look, I'd love to talk and catch up with you—really, it's the highlight of my year—but I need to get some sleep. It's been a long day. Can we talk later?" I can tell he's over with this conversation and probably thinks I lost my mind somewhere along the way here.

I think I have, too.

"Yeah, I should probably try to get some sleep, too. I'll talk to you soon. Night, buddy." I hang up before he can say anything else, though I don't think he was going to. I sigh, rubbing my face with my hands. Sometimes, I miss Jackson's humor. He lightened the mood, even when he rubbed me the wrong way.

I miss my parents. My mom's hugs. My dad talks with me about life, the future, his goals for the resistance... All of that crumbled when I made my decision. It wasn't like I had much of a choice. I'm protecting them and keeping them alive is what I keep telling myself, but as time goes on, the line has blurred between that idea and what I'm really doing here. Besides that, I failed to protect my sister in my thirst for power. Now she's out there, somewhere, and I don't know if she's safe.

I leave my new office and head down the hall toward my room. When I go to unlock the door, I find it's been unlocked already. I push it open to find Samantha sitting on my bed. She looks up at me and says, "This is the next step. General Khan told me I had to come in here and... I'll leave the rest to your imagination." She's referring to President Morgan's head General and closest advisor. He trained me when I first started being blackmailed. He's vicious, and the very definition of evil.

And now he wants to meddle in the ways of love. Whatever he thinks building a relationship looks like, it's been a while since he's experienced it.

I close the door behind me. "Well, none of that will be happening. So, you can leave now."

Sam stands, her relief is palpable. "Thank you."

As she brushes by me, I feel the tension surrounding her. "Unless you need to talk," I say.

She glances at me, one perfectly manicured hand on the doorknob. "Um... no. It's nothing."

I tilt my head, removing the tie from around my neck and hanging it up in the closet nearby. "Whatever you say. I mean, I'm willing to listen. Sleep won't come for me for a while considering..." I trail off, not entirely sure where I was going with that statement.

Her hand falls from the doorknob. Her hazel eyes meet mine and she says, "How can I convince Khan I'm succeeding in my mission? You're not in love with me and we've done enough pretending to last us a lifetime. Eventually, they'll catch on."

I shrug, beginning to unbutton the white dress shirt that's been causing me to itch all day. I throw it in the hamper and pull on a gray t-shirt from my closet, but not before I catch Samantha's gaze. It holds nothing within it. She has no feelings for me whatsoever. Can't say I blame her. Even I hate myself now.

"I'm not entirely sure."

She groans, sitting back down on the bed. "You're so much help."

I grab some jogger pants and step into the bathroom before changing my bottom half. I step back out into the room to find Samantha lying on her back, her feet dangling off the bed. She looks up at the ceiling. Tears fall from the sides of her face.

"What's the problem here? I know I'm horrible and the idea of having to act as if you love me is rather disgusting, but I'd like to believe you have more faith in me."

Samantha sniffles, rubbing her nose with her hand. "It's not that. I promise it's not about you. I feel like I'm cheating on Xander, even if this is all an act. I vowed on his grave never to love anyone again, not the way I loved him."

"You're not breaking that promise by putting up an act to get a job done. This is like any other job you've done before. Besides that, if you ever do fall in love again, it won't be the same way. Every person you love, you love a little differently. You can never love two people the same way."

She props herself up on her elbows. "How so?"

"You loved what he did for you then. You loved the way he loved you back. There are things unique to that relationship that will never be duplicated with anyone else. You can't break your promise to him, because there's no way to love someone else the same way."

Her eyes widen, and I can feel the tension in the room wither away, back to the shadows where they belong. "I... I guess you're right."

I sit down next to her. "And it's perfectly acceptable to not love anyone again. Because you've been too scarred by love before. I understand."

She shakes her head, looking down at her lap.

"That's the problem. I think I'm falling for someone I really shouldn't."

My heart clenches, but I don't say anything for a while. Finally, I find the strength to utter a single word. "Who?"

Her hazel eyes meet mine, and I can see the bursts of orange, the flecks of green, and the different shades of brown, all perfectly blended in her irises. The words that escape her lips catch me by surprise. "Evan Williams, I think I'm falling for you."

CHAPTER NINETEEN

Raegan
DATE: UNKNOWN

TOMORROW, I SEE PETER AGAIN. MY MIND swirls with the hope I begged it not to have. *He's going to be here for you.* The words repeat in my mind over and over, my heart soaring far from my captive body.

I close my eyes again, knowing it's not time for me to be awake yet. Maybe tomorrow is already here. I know I fell asleep when Jackson was talking to me. I feel bad, but I couldn't keep my eyes open any longer. I only meant to rest them for a moment, but when I opened them, he was gone and the door to the room was left open.

I think of Peter, the way his hair fell perfectly across his forehead. The way his hoodie smelled when he gave it to me. I feel bad now. I've thrown it in the corner of this room; his smell is no longer on it. No, a rather disgusting smell is attached to it now, thanks to the time I've spent here, unwashed.

It's his favorite hoodie, the one he always wore. Maybe it'll wash out. I shake my head slightly. He's not going to care about that. He's going to be concerned about getting me out of here again. And now, with the added weight of helping the young girl Jackson spoke of escape, I'm sure there are a lot of other things on his mind.

I open my eyes; my mind is too busy to let me get a few more moments of peaceful sleep. I want to try to sit up, but I fear what could happen. I haven't tried to sit up without Jackson in here to guide me. If I fall, I'll be stuck until he comes to bring me breakfast. But… I'm stiff. And my legs feel numb.

I want to prove to myself I can do this on my own. I don't need Jackson here to help me sit up. I've gotten stronger with every day that's passed. But I've also become sick from infection, most likely from the wound on my shoulder. I can barely move my arm anymore.

I sigh and try to push myself upright with my left arm. After a few attempts, I give up. It's hopeless. They'll be lucky to be able to get me out of here. I go back to my daydreams of Peter. It's stupid, but since admitting my feelings for him out loud, I see him completely differently in my head. His eyes are a shining gray. His smile warms my heart. I want to hug him again, for him to hold me tight like he did when we were reunited after six years apart. I want to hear his heartbeat as I lay my head against his chest.

But then... I said my feelings for him out loud. I thought I was about to die then, and I desperately wanted him to know how I feel. But I'm alive, and he's coming to rescue me. If he feels the same way, things will be different. If he *doesn't* feel the same way, things will be different. Things will be different no matter what. If it's the latter, I could tell him I meant what I said as a friend, but I'm not going to lie to him. I could never lie to him.

My body is a bundle of nerves. I feel the butterflies in my stomach trying to cause a storm within. No, even if he doesn't feel the same way, I can't let the friendship die. I *need* him.

I hear footsteps approaching and Jackson's deep voice saying, "Good morning, sweetheart. Did you sleep well?"

I groan. "No. What time is it?"

"Almost time for your freedom. I want you to

try and eat something before they come for you. I'm not sure if they'll take you to a doctor or what will happen once you're out of here, so you'll need your strength."

I sigh and let Jackson help me sit up. He sets the tray in my lap, laden with oatmeal and fruit. Although I eat slowly, I eat more than I managed before. When I've had enough, he helps me swing around and dangle my legs off the bed. I go to stand, all feeling rushing to my legs in a painful crescendo.

He takes my hands and guides me forward a few steps. I'm wobbly and I nearly fall so many times, but again, it's an improvement from before. When I'm safely seated on the cot again, he says, "They'll be here any second. I need to go back up. Just stay right here. Do you think you can stay sitting up like this?"

I nod. "I'll be fine."

Jackson rushes off, and I realize now how hideous I must look. My hair is greasy, my body stinks from a lack of showers for weeks on end… and suddenly I feel self-conscious Peter has to see me this way. But there's no going back now. And I'm ready to finally be free.

CHAPTER TWENTY

Peter

FRIDAY, OCTOBER 27TH, 2023

MY MOM COMES DOWN THE HALL TO THE living room. "Are you ready to go?"

"Oh, I forgot to tell you that Sawyer and Nicole are giving me a ride today."

My mom adjusts her earrings as she looks in the hallway mirror. "How nice. I'm glad you're reconnecting with your friends again."

Gunnar comes and nudges my hands with his nose. I pet his head idly as my mom continues. "You need more interaction with others. I'm so happy you're talking to them. I know it's hard, but you need to keep the friends you have close to you."

I nod stiffly "Yeah, you're right."

She doesn't know what we're really doing today. And she has no clue that Nicole and Sawyer broke up nearly a week ago.

My mom sighs, coming up to me and hugging me. "I'll see you tonight. Love you."

"Love you, too."

Mom grabs her keys and heads out the door as Sawyer pulls up to my house. Nicole is in the front passenger seat beside him. I step outside, lock the door behind me and climb into the back of the truck. We wait for my mom to back out of the driveway and then head out of the neighborhood. My mom is long gone down the road by the time we exit the neighborhood.

Without a preamble, Sawyer says, "Please don't die today, okay? We can't handle losing someone else."

Nicole turns in her seat. "Yeah, I'd rather you both come back alive."

"Thanks, guys. I appreciate the vote of confidence."

Nicole smirks. "Anytime."

Sawyer turns into Main Street Market and parks next to Spencer, who's waiting for me in his truck. I get out and lean into Sawyer's open window.

"I really do appreciate you two. I know it's probably a bit... hard. Being in the same truck and everything."

Sawyer looks down, his jaw clenching. Nicole's lips form a grim line. "Raegan means more to both of us than whatever's happening right now. Right... Sawyer?"

Sawyer looks up. "Yeah. Rae became one of my best friends in the short three years I've lived here. I can set aside my personal feelings if it means saving her life."

I thank them again before walking around the front of his truck to reach Spencer's. I slide in and say, "I appreciate you doing this."

"Save the mush for your girl."

I smirk. "All right, all right. Let's do this."

We leave and head down the road toward Cyrus. My heart begins to race more and more with every passing moment. I don't know what to expect, what will happen. I'm nervous and excited all at once.

Noah and Stella will be parked across the street from the warehouse, watching Brett's team and communicating with us through walkie-talkies. Spencer and I will park around the back to retrieve Raegan. Jackson will meet us back there to lead us to her.

Spencer says, "I know my truck doesn't have

much of a backseat, but I put a bunch of blankets and pillows in there so she can rest on the way to headquarters. My uncle has a doctor waiting to examine her, something he set up so once Brett brings her back, she can get the treatment she needs."

I grunt. "Yeah, because Brett did such a fantastic job last time."

"Doesn't matter. She's alive and we'll be the ones taking her back."

I want to argue, but he's right. So, I don't say a word. We pull into position, and I grab my walkie-talkie and check-in with Stella and Noah.

"What's up, bro? You parked out back yet?" Stella says, sounding bored.

"Yeah, we're in the back. Do you have a clear view of the front?"

A pause. "Yeah, we're here. It looks like we got here just in time. Brett and his crew just arrived."

I inhale sharply. Suddenly, the commotion from the front is audible from where we are. The back door opens, and Jackson peeks out, beckoning to us. Spencer and I climb out of the truck and follow him inside. We're already in the room where Raegan was held before.

Jackson says, "The door is locked, so even if some of my team decide to come around, they can't get in." He leads us over to some boxes, then kneels and lifts a huge tile behind them, revealing a ladder and a deep, dark abyss beneath it.

Spencer takes a step back and says, "This looks a bit suspicious."

Jackson raises an eyebrow. "After all we've been through, you think this is where I kill you?"

I sigh. "We don't have time for this. Jackson, you go first to show us there's nothing down there."

Spencer crosses his arms. "He'd expect you to say that. Maybe I should go first."

I glare. "No, Jackson, you go down first. And we'll follow."

Jackson nods, lowering his body into the hole and gripping the ladder. Spencer goes next, followed by me.

Being in the dark is disorienting, but I immediately compensate by using my other senses. I can hear our feet on the rungs of the ladder, echoing off the stone walls. I can hear Spencer breathing beneath me, and the subtle squeak of Jackson's leather jacket.

Finally, light begins to invade the space, first

dim, then brighter as we near the bottom. I hear Jackson's feet hit the ground first, then Spencer's. When they're out of the way, I step down onto the floor and look around. We're in a long hallway with bright lights and metal walls, so different from the welcoming atmosphere of Mr. Williams' underground space. This is almost prison-like— fitting for the purpose.

Spencer steps quickly behind Jackson now and holds a gun to his back, just as we planned. "Precautions."

Jackson holds his hands up. "I'm not lying, so I'm not worried. Open the door already and save your girlfriend."

I inhale sharply. My hand touches the cold doorknob. I twist it, but I don't push it. If Jackson's lying and this is an ambush, I could die here, and then Spencer will probably die as well. My heart begins to race as I slowly push the door open. But no ambush awaits me on the other side. Instead, I see a girl sitting on a cot. Her brown hair is limp and dirty. But when she looks up, I'm met with those blue eyes. Despite everything, they haven't lost their fire.

The air rushes from my lungs. "Raegan."

I run to her, feeling tears streaming down my

cheeks. I see tears begin to trail down her face too, leaving streaks in the grime. She flinches.

"I stink. Don't get too close."

I grab her, holding her tightly to me. "Do you think I care at this point? After thinking you were dead?"

She shudders from the sobs that overcome her. I'm not bothering to hide my own. I touch her back, her hair, her arms... not quite believing she's here. I hold her slightly away, examining her face. Her tears leave trails down her face. I wipe them away. "I never thought I'd get to hold you again."

She smiles through the tears, and I caress her face. I want to kiss her. I want to hold her close and never let her go again. I'm too afraid to let go, too afraid she might disappear if I so much as blink.

I hear footsteps, but I don't bother glancing back. Spencer's voice fills the silence, saying, "I hate to interrupt this, but. Jackson went back up to get Linley. It sounds like Brett's getting closer. I'd rather not let him know we were here, or else he'll tell my uncle. And explaining how we have the weapons is something I'd rather not have to do."

I scoop Raegan up. She's much thinner than before, much lighter. Not that she was all that heavy before. She nuzzles her nose into my neck. "I missed you so much," she whispers, and I wonder if she meant for me to hear her or not. It doesn't matter, my heart is racing.

I set her down in front of the ladder, letting Spencer go first. I then help Raegan up, climbing behind her to support her when she needs it. She's shaky, and several times I have to push her up, letting her entire weight fall back against me. She has hardly any stamina on her own. Finally, we reach the top and Spencer helps pull her out. I'm next. Jackson stands by the back door.

"Come on," he says, urging us forward. "My team is losing the battle. Brett will be here in no time."

I nod and scoop Raegan into my arms again. Spencer holds the door for us and I carefully carry her outside. Jackson follows us out. I get Raegan situated in the back of the truck. I expect to see the young girl Jackson insisted on rescuing, Linley, following behind him, but to my surprise I see Jackson locking the door.

"Wait, where's the girl? Linley?"

He frowns. "I don't know. I returned to the surface as we planned, and I couldn't find her. It seems she ran off in the chaos. She was supposed to wait here for us, but I can't find her, and there's no time now. You have to get going."

Spencer pauses by his door. "And what about you?" he asks Jackson. "Where are you going?"

"I'm going to search for Carissa. She hates my guts, but I need to know she's safe. I can't live my life obeying Evan's orders and wondering if she's even alive."

Spencer stares down at Jackson, studying him. "Why do you care about Carissa?"

Jackson looks down at his feet, and I am surprised to see the depth of the heartbreak in his eyes. "Everything in my life has been fake. She was the only thing that was real. I love her and I hate that I hurt her. I want to find her and at least tell her that. I have no clue where she is, but I can at least try to track her down." He moves to take a step away.

Spencer sighs. "You'd better come with us."

Jackson shakes his head. "Andre will only lock me up."

"Yeah, he probably will." Spencer hesitates for a moment and then takes a breath. "Carissa came home, Jackson. If you want to see her, you'll have to come with us. I can't guarantee what my uncle will decide to do, but I know you'll get to see her."

Jackson's eyes are blazing with fury. "I've been going on and on about Carissa this whole time, and you said nothing? You could have told me she was all right, at least!"

Spencer shakes his head. "She was hurting, and she's my cousin. I couldn't betray her like that. I wasn't trying to play you or lie about it. But family comes first. I'm telling you now, so decide what you want. We have to go."

Jackson is still angry, but he says, "Oh, I'm coming, all right. I need to see her again."

He climbs into the front seat beside Spencer and goes to slam the door, but then seems to remember Raegan is in the back and shuts it gently. I climb in the back with her, and she shifts slightly and rests her head in my lap. I use the walkie-talkie to communicate with Stella. "Mission accomplished. Come on."

Spencer revs the engine, and I text Sawyer our simple code word.

Success.

As we put more and more distance between us and that warehouse, Raegan grows more and more still. As her eyes fall closed again, I run my fingers absently through her hair. I don't know when we'll have another calm moment after this.

Her breathing becomes more even, and I look down at her. The steady beat of her pulse against my leg keeps me grounded and reminds me that she is alive. She's here.

She's alive.

I'm tense the whole way, cautiously looking out behind us to make sure no one is following. No one ever is, but I can't stop checking every few minutes. Only Noah and Stella are behind us, and no one in the few cars that pass us even gives us a second look.

Finally, Spencer turns off from the main road and onto a back road covered in dirt and gravel. I've never been this way to the ranch, but getting off the main road puts me more at ease.

When we arrive at the ranch, Spencer drives immediately into the underground garage. When he's parked, I carefully wake Raegan from her sleep. With my help, she sits up. I can see the weariness in her eyes, hear it in her quiet voice asking where we are. I pull her to me. "We're safe."

I slide out first, then I carefully lift her—bridal style—into my arms. Spencer is already at the main door, putting in the code and waiting for us.

229

As we make our way inside, I see Stella and Noah pull into the garage and park.

When we enter the lobby, Mr. Williams is shocked, and I can tell he's not happy.

"Brett said she wasn't there."

I refrain from saying what I feel about Brett, and instead settle for, "That's because we saved her."

Mr. Williams suddenly sees Jackson and says, "YOU!"

He takes a step forward, but Spencer steps quickly between them. "He helped us. And he agreed to come here willingly. This doesn't have to be a fight. *We* don't have to fight."

"No, but I demand you both to explain yourselves. This isn't a game or a mission. This could have been your life—your death."

Spencer doesn't back down. "I knew exactly what I was doing. You've taught me everything I know."

Mr. Williams tenses. "I didn't teach you disobedience."

He sighs and walks over to the phone behind the lobby desk. He speaks a few words, then puts it back on its base. In a few moments, two of his men arrive and hurry over to Jackson, who stands stoically as they each grab one of his arms; he's been expecting this. As the men take him away, towards the holding cells, he glances back at me and Spencer. Spencer gives him a nod, and he goes willingly.

The doctor arrives now, a small woman with long black hair and dark, almond-shaped eyes. She has me take Raegan to a small room where she can do a physical assessment.

"You need to step out of the room, Mr. Daniels," the doctor says.

Raegan is not thrilled to be left alone in the room with the doctor, but I squeeze her hand. "I'll be back in a few minutes, okay?"

"Promise?" she asks weakly.

"Promise," I say, certain. With that, I slowly slip my grasp from hers, and I walk out while the doctor begins the assessment.

When I'm back in the lobby, Mr. Williams glares at me and Spencer in turn. "What you two did is worthy of severe punishment. Do you realize how many lives you put in danger?"

I step forward. "We did what we had to do. Raegan was in danger. Brett didn't genuinely care to help."

"That's not for you to decide."

I am about to argue, but Spencer says, "Peter, don't do this. It's not worth arguing. My uncle isn't going to listen to you, and you aren't going to listen to him."

I take a few steps back. Behind me, a door opens, and Raegan's parents and my mom rush in. My mom grabs me, turning me to face her. "Are you all right?"

I brush her hands off me, stepping back. "I'm fine, Mom. Why wouldn't I be? I knew exactly what I was doing."

My mom reaches in again and pulls me close to her. My fight is with Mr. Williams, not her. She doesn't deserve my anger. I wrap my arms around her, hugging her back.

Mr. Williams crosses his arms. "This is what I'm talking about. Peter, if Jackson was deceiving you—"

I step away from my mom to face Mr. Williams again. "And if he wasn't? Raegan could have suffered for it. Jackson was the only person who knew where Raegan was being held. There's no way Brett would have found her on his own. You put too much faith in that guy. He's not out to help the rest of us."

Mr. Williams sighs, pinching the bridge of his

nose.

Spencer steps between us. "Look, neither of you is ever going to agree about what is right and what is wrong. Can we please move on?"

Mr. Williams looks at his nephew, a new hurt in his eyes. "Do we need to address how you went in there with him, using weapons from my armory? I *trusted* you, Spencer."

Spencer takes a few steps backward as if he's been shoved away, visibly hurt by Mr. Williams' words. "Uncle Andre..."

I stare at the floor. This is my fault. I should never have suggested the armory or going behind Mr. Williams' back. At least not this way.

Spencer's fists clench at his side, and I think for a moment he might turn on me. But instead, he takes a step toward his uncle and says, "You're right. I did go along with it. I went along with it because deep down, I know Jackson wasn't lying to us. He came to me first. I saw how much pain he was in, and it was *real*. I knew he was telling the truth, that he truly regretted what he'd done, and I wasn't going to let my best friend keep grieving the girl he loves when she needed saving."

My mom glances at me, but I don't meet her

eyes. Mr. Williams is silent for a long time. Finally, he claps his hand on Spencer's shoulder and gives it a brief squeeze. Nothing is truly resolved, but it's in this act I can see things will be okay. Mr. Williams says, "I'm just glad you're safe now. I'm afraid most of Jackson's team got away."

I step forward. "Speaking of Jackson... He helped us out. I'm not saying his past actions should be forgiven, but I honestly think he deserves a chance to speak now."

Mr. Williams nods. "We can look into that in due time. For now, it's safer for all of us if he stays locked up."

The doctor returns from the examination room, her face devoid of any emotion. She says, "Mr. and Mrs. MacArthur, could you join me inside for a discussion with Raegan?"

The two exchange worried looks and then hurry after the doctor. I want to follow, but Spencer grabs my shoulder. He shakes his head.

"Give them space. You lost a friend, but they lost a daughter. They need this time."

I want to argue, but once again he's right. Mr. Williams and my mom have moved further down the hall, most likely discussing what kind of punishment we're going to be given. It doesn't matter, though. I know we did the right thing, even if we did it the wrong way. I turn to Spencer.

"So… I'm your best friend, huh?"

"Well, Raegan is obviously more to you than that, so I figure the position is open."

I smirk, punching him in the shoulder. "I'm not focused on talking to Raegan about what is—or isn't—different between her and me right now. All I want is for her to heal. We'll cross that bridge when we get there."

Spencer nods. "Sounds fair enough."

I smile. "But you are my best friend. I don't think I could trust anyone else the way I trust you. Thanks for defending me to your uncle. And for not giving up on me when I was losing my mind."

He punches my shoulder now, and says, "Don't get sappy on me, Daniels, or I might take back everything I said."

But he wouldn't. Instead, he sits with me, waiting in the hall for whatever may lie ahead for Raegan.

CHAPTER TWENTY-ONE

Carissa

I HEAR THE DOOR SLIDE OPEN AND HEAVY footsteps enter the room. They don't match my father's or Spencer's footsteps, and from the sudden racing in my heart, I know something isn't right. I slowly rise from my dark corner and carefully peek through the cell bars.

Two of my father's men are standing in front of the cell across from me. They shove someone in and lock it, and I wait for them to move away.

"Know that anything you say will be used against you," one of them says to whoever is inside.

"Oh, those aren't my full rights," retorts a familiar voice, full of confidence. "Come on, you can do better than that."

The men grumble, but they don't argue.

Smart choice.

They move aside, and I see him standing there.

He's without his leather jacket, and I question whether this can be the same man. His hair is mussed up, but it still looks great. *Curse him for being so hot.*

He sighs and turns away. He hasn't seen me yet. Good. I pray he doesn't. Then again, I doubt God would spare a second to hear me after what I've done to so many people. I creep back into my corner, waiting. I hear Jackson mumble to himself, as well as the sound of his cot creaking under his weight.

The main door swings open again, and once more I listen to the footfalls.

They belong to Spencer. Jackson calls out to him. "Hey, you told me Carissa is safely here. I haven't seen her. I hope that wasn't a sick joke to get me locked up, especially after everything I've done. I need to know she's safe."

I nearly scoff aloud. Why would he care about me? He *betrayed* me.

Spencer says, "She's here. But I've been sent in here to interrogate you."

Jackson laughs. "Oh? Interesting. Well, ask away."

Spencer says, "Start from the beginning."

"I was born, and my parents were already

broken up. They weren't married, so it was easy for my mom to take off with me. I did meet my father, but he's a drunk with a drug habit, so I went ahead and moved on from that. Oh, and about seven years ago my mother got married after years of being single, and I hated the man she married, but not as much as I hated his son. Shall I go on?"

I can imagine Spencer holding his head in his hands now. I dare another peek around the corner and see exactly this. Spencer groans.

"Maverick, I didn't ask for your life story. When did you start working for the government? And when did Evan?"

Jackson huffs. "That's boring. But if that's what you want to know… I was eighteen when I started. Evan was a later initiate. Wrong place, wrong time… It was a bad situation all around. He was forced to work for the president at first, and for a long time, he was trying to prevent all of you from being killed. But then something changed in him. And after that, he stopped telling me anything. I knew from the beginning he hated working for the president. His motives were to protect his family. But then... the goodness left his eyes one day. I don't know what it is, but he's not like the Evan I met."

I try to tune out the rest of the interrogation. I know the story. I know the truth. And Jackson, surprisingly, doesn't hold out on Spencer's questions. I stay in my corner, meditating, breathing, but then I hear my name spoken from the mouth I detest.

"And Carissa? I need to see her, to know she's okay."

Spencer sighs. "Carissa," he calls, "stop hiding, please."

Betrayed, I stand from my corner and walk into the light shining through the cell bars. Jackson faces me, his eyes watering.

"Carissa..." he starts, but I turn away.

Spencer approaches my cell. "Raegan was saved today."

That catches my attention fast. I turn on him and press myself against the cell bars dividing us. "What do you mean she was saved? She's dead!"

He shakes his head, smiling wider than I've ever seen him smile. "Jackson helped us get to her, and then he was going to go on a hunt for you. I figured he'd eventually track you down and find you here, so instead, I brought him along." He grins sheepishly. "I know you're probably mad at me for that."

I cross my arms. "Yeah, I am mad. Extremely mad. You're right, he would have found me eventually, but now I have to deal with being across from him every moment of my imprisonment from here on out. I never wanted to see him again and you knew that."

Spencer shrugs. "You don't have to. You usually stay in your dark and angsty corner over there, feeling sorry for yourself. You can't see him from there, and he can't see you. Problem solved."

As Spencer turns to leave, I say, "I don't feel sorry for myself."

He glances back at me as he reaches for the door. "Are you sure about that?"

He steps out and closes the door behind him, leaving me alone with Jackson. I glance over at him and find he's looking at me.

Staring.

My anger rises. "What do you want?"

"I'm so happy you're alive," he says, not answering my question.

"You didn't think I could take care of myself out there? Is that it? Or now that you've done your one good deed for your lifetime, you wanted to try and win me back? It's not going to happen."

Jackson sighs, running a hand through his already messy hair. "No. I never thought I would win you back. But believe it or not, I still love you and I needed to see for myself that you were still alive. Of course, I knew you would be. I knew you'd kick the butt of anyone who dared cross you."

He still loves me? Highly unlikely. I shake my head. "If you loved me, you would have come with me that night instead of helping my brother continue his plans. I don't even want to know what he did to Raegan since apparently she isn't dead after all."

Jackson grips the bars of his cell in his hands, his knuckles turning white. "I do love you, Carissa, and I wanted to come with you. But your brother threatened to find us and kill us both. At the time, I took him completely seriously: he was bloodthirsty after his first kill. But it turns out he was only bluffing to manipulate you and me." His voice softens. "I never wanted to hurt you, Rissa."

I cringe at the use of my nickname. Only he ever got away with using it, and despite all my best intentions, I find myself melting a little more. I can't let this happen. Trust gets you hurt. Though I feel the tears forming in my eyes, I turn away from him.

With a steady voice, I say, "Leave me alone."

I find myself back in my corner, though now I wonder if Spencer's words truly hold merit. I let myself cry, but silently, so Jackson doesn't hear me. Soon, I find myself drifting off to sleep.

CHAPTER TWENTY-TWO
Raegan
DATE: UNKNOWN

MY PARENTS FLOOD ME WITH HUGS.

Well, mostly my mom. My dad holds my hand as I lie on the examination table in this small office Mr. Williams has set up. The doctor's name is Dr. Wu. Her hands are cold, and she's not showing any form of sympathy or caring. My mind is foggy as I resist falling asleep. The words "dehydration," "mild concussion," "and malnourished" float around the room. My dad squeezes my hand and I weakly squeeze back.

At last, the doctor finishes up and says I can go home, only because going to a hospital would be dangerous. Evan could find me again since the hospitals report every patient admitted to the government. So, it's a special diet and plenty of fluids for me, as well as rest. I'm not to move around too much yet.

My dad helps me sit as the doctor leaves.

All I want is to shower.

A few resistance agents come to see me before we leave, all in disbelief that I'm alive. Peter is the last to stop by, leaning against the doorjamb, his hands tucked in the pocket of his jeans. It's a simple act, yet I can't look away.

His eyes smile before his mouth does. He looks tired, broken.

But oh, so beautiful.

My parents step out to go tell Mr. Williams what Dr. Wu said, leaving Peter and me alone. Peter says, "I missed you."

Peter, I love you! My last words echo in my mind, but I don't know if this is the best time to bring that up. So, I say, "I missed you, too. I never thought I'd be here."

My mom returns. "It's time to go home."

I exhale and try to stand up but end up falling forward. Peter lunges to catch me, and for a moment, I feel dizzy. He helps me stand, but says to my mom, "I can carry her."

He lifts me again, bridal style, and carries me to my dad's truck. He helps me get settled in the back seat, and for once, I sit like a normal human.

My mom gets in the front passenger seat; my dad is still inside, talking to Mr. Williams. Peter helps buckle me in. When he's leaning over me, I take a risk and kiss his cheek. He pulls away, his face reddening. "What was that for?" he says softly.

I smile. "Thank you for not giving up on me."

Peter smiles shyly, the first time I've ever seen him shy about anything.

My dad arrives and I tell Peter goodbye. He touches my hand and says, "I'll visit you soon. I promise."

He closes the door, and my heart feels both heavy and light. I'm alive, Peter saved me, I'm with my family... but this is far from the safety I thought we could have. If anything, things are only going to be more complicated. I want to focus on being here, on being alive, and not on my deathbed. But there's so much more still to come...

My dad leaves the underground parking and I watch the trees go by as we drive down the road. It's a drive that seems to go on forever, but I take in every second of it. When we get home, my mom insists I take a bath, but I refuse to sit in a pool of my own filth. I agree to mostly sit in the shower, only standing when I can.

She's scared I'll fall – and she's probably right – so she waits outside the door. I sit on the floor of the tub and watch all the dirt and grime wash off me. The hot water burns my skin, but I love it. It feels refreshing. I run my hands through my hair, finally finding the strength to stand. I rub shampoo through my scalp, letting it lather, and then rinse it. I end up washing my hair two more times before finally putting some conditioner in it.

After I'm done, I feel human again, at least a little more so than before. I carefully step out of the tub and grab a thick towel to dry off my reddened skin. Maybe the shower was too hot, but at least I'm finally clean. I can only imagine the killer knots in my hair. Mom may have to help me with that.

I dress in the comfy pajamas my mom brings to me and let my hair out of its towel. My mom combs my hair as we sit on my bed, just like when I was young. Only this time we both cry, as neither of us thought this moment would ever be possible again.

Mom finishes and we leave my hair to dry. I turn to face her, enveloping her in my arms. "I missed you," I say, but the words can't begin to describe everything I'm feeling right now. Maybe nothing ever will.

Eventually, I'm dozing off on my bed, a blanket pulled to my chin. I'm in and out of sleep, chugging water during short periods of wakefulness. Mom and Dad take turns checking in on me, making sure I'm okay.

When dinnertime comes around, they bring me a meal on a tray. Dr. Wu suggested I eat light at first until my system gets used to having real food in it again. Even though Jackson fed me more than Evan did, it's still hard on my body to eat much of anything.

So, my mom brings cut fruit and water. It's enough to keep me full and ready for a full night's rest.

After I eat my fruit, my mom takes the tray downstairs. I'm sitting propped against my headboard, not wanting to fall asleep quite yet. My dad enters and says, "You have a guest, but he's willing to wait if you need sleep."

I look up. "Is it Peter?"

Dad smiles and nods. "Of course."

I smile. "Let him in."

My dad leaves and Peter enters my room. He seems unsure of himself, his eyes wandering around the room, his hands fidgeting at his sides. Finally, he stands just inside the doorframe. "Hey."

"Hi," I say awkwardly. I don't know why things are awkward now. It's Peter. My best friend. *But it's more than that now, isn't it?*

Peter rubs the back of his neck as he smiles. "How are you holding up?"

I offer a weak grin in return. "Better than I thought I would. You can sit down, you know."

He seems to relax a little and approaches, sitting on the edge of the bed. I feel a flush creep to my face, knowing now that he heard me speak the words I said when I thought I was going to die. I don't know how to begin a conversation with him right now, considering that all has been laid out.

Peter starts. "I'm so happy you're alive."

I close my eyes. "Me too. I mean, I felt worse than dead down there, but you came for me."

"Of course, I came for you. I never gave up on you. Once Jackson said you were alive, I never stopped fighting for you."

My chest and stomach flutter with butterflies. "I know you did. Thank you."

"Everything came apart when I thought I lost

you," he says softly, and his voice catches a little.

What do I say to that? "You would have been okay."

He shakes his head, then gets to his feet and begins pacing in front of me. "No, you don't understand. I was ready to track Evan down and kill him. I thought he needed to pay for what he did. He still needs to pay for the way he left you. Seeing you alive, though... It makes me realize revenge isn't the answer. Everyone told me that, but I was so set on doing something that I know now I'd have regretted." He stops and glances at me. "I'm sure hearing me say all this disgusts you."

I shake my head. "No. Because I know I'd feel the same way if the situation was reversed. Maybe not ready to kill someone, but I'd be heartbroken." There, I've said it. "But Peter, you have to know that there's more to life than our friendship. You can't let your life revolve around—"

"I love you."

I shut up fast. The blush I felt before is nothing compared to the one that floods over me now. His eyes bore into mine, and the fire within is deep, passionate, and burning. I stutter. "W-what?

"I love you. That's what you said to me before

249

Evan shot you."

I can play this off. I can say it's love between friends. I... I can't handle us changing right now. "Of course, I love you, Peter. And you love me, too. We've been friends forever. Best friends."

"Don't give me that bull crap," he says. "You meant it more deeply than just friends. I know you did. And you don't have to worry about … ruining anything between us now, because I love you, too. I've hated myself every day for not saying it back at that moment. I was too afraid. Of what, I'm not quite sure. But my biggest regret was not telling you how I felt sooner. I'm not making that mistake again."

My heart is thumping wildly against my chest. I want to scream in delight, to jump into his arms, to have him hold me close. I want to hear his heartbeat. Is it pounding as fast and as hard as mine? Yet I know I can't do this right now. I know I have to focus on getting better. On being able to fight once again. And that kills me.

"Okay. You're right. I love you. As more than a friend. But… I can't be anything more right now. I have to get better first."

He nods. I can see he's hiding the pain with a

smile. I hate that I'm causing this pain. He sits on the edge of my bed, taking my hand in both of his. "And I'll be here for you every step of the way. I will be what you need me to be."

The butterflies are building up at his touch. "Thank you. And… I'm sorry that I can't be what you need me to be."

He sighs. "You as you are now *is* enough for me. And you shouldn't believe otherwise. But…" His face brightens suddenly. "I came here with a surprise. I know you can't leave your room, so I'm going to bring it in. If you want to see, that is."

I smile. "Of course, I want to see."

Peter gets to his feet and hurries out the door. He returns a moment later with… a dog?

"Who is this?" I say, leaning forward.

"His name is Gunnar. He found me when I was on a run. I had gone to the tree and he appeared there. His eyes are like yours… I thought maybe you sent him. But I knew he would cheer you up."

The dog pads over to my bed, where he rests his head on my lap. I pet his solid little head and gently scratch behind his ears. He has a calm, friendly demeanor, and I find it comforting. "He's beautiful," I say. Gunnar thumps his tail on the floor.

Peter smiles again. "Good. I thought maybe… we could share him. If you want. I can bring him whenever you'd like."

"I'd love that." I continue petting Gunnar. When I grow weary, Peter sits down with me, letting me rest my head on his shoulder. Gunnar lies down on the floor, turns around a couple of times, and is soon asleep.

"I talked to your parents about confessing my feelings," Peter says after a while, "so this is about to get super awkward when I tell them I've been shot down."

I kiss his cheek, surprising him and myself. "Just for now," I add.

His cheeks tint pink. "I respect your need to get better, but I can't lie about my feelings for you."

I meet his eyes, my hand finding his cheek. "I'd never ask you to. I… I love you, Peter. And I don't know what that means. But… when I'm stronger, I'd like to find out."

Peter leans down slightly. He wants to kiss me, I know. But he won't do it without permission from me. My eyes meet his as I slowly lean up, our hands still tangled together between us. My eyes flutter before they close, and I feel his breath brush my lips.

My door slams open, causing Peter and me to jump apart.

"RAEGAN, YOU'RE ALIVE!" Nicole screams. Peter and I jump apart as Nicole and Sawyer barge in, unannounced.

I'm filled with excitement, despite the interrupted moment. Nicole and Sawyer are a sight for sore eyes, although my last interactions with Nicole were not pleasant. None of that seems to matter to either of us now; I'm just so happy that she's happy to see me. Yet... I'm sad Peter didn't kiss me. I know it would have been a bad idea; it would have changed everything. But I can see my own mixed emotions reflected in his eyes. His fingers still brush mine, slowly... deliberately.

"Nicole, you're not mad at me anymore?"

Nicole answers by rushing over and hugging me. Gunnar gets to his feet and moves out of the room, obviously disturbed by the screaming and commotion.

"Mad?" Nicole says. "No. No, I thought you were dead, Raegan. I don't think I'll ever be mad at you again."

Peter stands from my bed, giving us some

room. My eyes meet his, then Sawyer's.

"Sawyer, I missed you."

Sawyer smiles, but there's a pain in his eyes. Something's bothering him.

Nicole sits next to me. Her eyes are filled with tears. "I'm so sorry I didn't believe you. You were right about everything. I should've trusted you."

I hug her again. "I forgive you. I understand. I don't know that I would've believed me, either. I was distant and cold to you so suddenly. You didn't have much else to believe in. I'm sorry."

Nicole cries into my shoulder, and my own tears begin to fall. I pull away from her embrace. "I'm just... so happy to be alive. To be home."

I know I can't stay home for long, though. It will only be a matter of time before Evan begins searching for me. I'm his best-kept secret, and it's all about to be ruined for him.

Nicole wipes her eyes. "I will never doubt you again. I'm so sorry."

We hug again, then she stands. "I suppose we should let you rest."

I'm happy to see everyone, but I can't hide the weariness that is starting to overtake me. I will fall asleep in a matter of moments.

Sawyer hugs me once, quickly before they leave.

Once they're gone, Peter sighs and pushes himself away from the wall. "You need rest," he says.

I don't quite want him to leave, but he's right. He walks over and leans down to hug me. I wonder for a second if he'll try to kiss me again, but he doesn't seem to make any move. I know it might be for the better, even though a big part of me wishes he would.

I wrap my arms around him. I'm not helping either of us with this "just friends" thing, but I can't find it in me to care. He doesn't seem to care either as he holds me tightly, and his lips brush the top of my head in a soft, slow kiss.

I feel the rush of heat on my cheeks.

We stay like this for a while, but eventually, I know it's time for me to sleep. I'm fading fast. I feel my body getting weak again. I've overdone it for today. Peter pulls away and leaves my room, Gunnar following closely behind him. Peter's eyes catch mine one more time before closing the door behind him.

Being just friends is out of the question. We're

too far gone for that. But now my main concern is what will happen to my family. Evan is bound to figure out what's happened when Jackson no longer reports to him. And soon, we won't be safe here. It's only a matter of time before Evan comes crashing through our door, ready to take me again.

And I don't know if I'll have the strength to fight him off this time or to keep Peter from following through on his threat. And that scares me more than I care to admit.

My mind is still wired, but my body is utterly exhausted from everything I've endured in the last three weeks. I feel myself relax into my bed and my eyes slowly close. My mind drifts into the abyss of darkness, and I fall into yet another nightmare-filled sleep.

CHAPTER TWENTY-THREE

Peter

SATURDAY, OCTOBER 28TH, 2023

"AND FROM NOW ON," MY MOM SAYS, "YOU have to let me confirm with your friends that you are actually going somewhere with them." She sighs. "I hate that I can't trust you to tell me the truth about where you're going."

I nod, not meeting her eyes. I don't bother to tell her that Sawyer and Nicole would have covered for me if she'd asked them where we were going. Spencer would've, too. We all had a mission that day, and nothing was going to stop us from completing it.

But I understand why my mom is worried. I hugely betrayed her trust. And I feel terrible. We hadn't been talking much at the time, not since I found out about my father's upcoming nuptials. But now I know that my mom was only respecting his wishes by letting him tell me himself. It's not her fault he was too much of a coward to do so sooner.

"Mom, you don't have to worry about me sneaking off again. This was a one-and-done deal."

My mom scoffs. "Yeah, and if Raegan finds herself in another precarious situation, I know you'll rush to rescue her. So, we're not playing these games. You should have told me what you were doing."

I shake my head. "You trust Mr. Williams too much. He had Brett on the case, and for you, that would have been enough."

My mom sighs. "Honey, I know you don't like Brett. If I'm honest, I'm not a fan of his, either. But he's been doing this for years. You should have trusted him to bring her home."

I shake my head. She just doesn't get it. "Jackson's deal didn't extend to an FBI agent who would've double-crossed him." I sigh. "Anyway, it doesn't matter now. Everything is done and over with. Raegan's home safe, and that's what matters."

My mom takes a seat in the chair near the couch I'm on. She runs both hands over her face and then meets my eyes again. "Did Raegan like Gunnar?"

I smile, despite everything. "She loves him.

We're co-parenting him."

My mom smirks. "Does that mean you finally told her how you feel?"

I feel a slight heat rise to my face but ignore it. "Yes. I did. We had a good talk."

My mom groans. "Come on, tell me what happened! Is she your girlfriend now?"

My smile falters slightly. "It's a bit complicated, and I'm not going to push her into anything right now. She needs rest and probably therapy after everything she's been through. I'm not going to bring my emotions into the mix right now."

My mom rolls her eyes as she stands. "Such a guy thing to say. Come on, let's go work on making dinner. I told the MacArthurs I would bring them some food. They need a good, home-cooked meal. Besides, you should talk to Raegan's father more seriously before you move forward with anything."

My jaw goes slack. My mom laughs. "Scott MacArthur likes you, Peter. There's no problem with him. But you must be respectful. I've taught you that."

I slowly rise from the couch. "I already talked to both of her parents before I spoke with Raegan.

Can we have a subject change? Please?"

My mom's eyes darken. "Have you called your father?"

"Mom, why must you ruin a perfectly nice afternoon with topics like this? Can't you comment on normal things like the weather?"

She sighs. "It's rather dusty in the sky today, isn't it?" she says brightly. "Makes the sun look more orange than yellow."

I laugh and follow my mom into the kitchen. "Never mind. That was the most depressing attempt at talking about the weather I have ever heard. Let's just make dinner."

"You do need to talk to your father eventually."

"No, I don't. He has his own little family now. He doesn't need me and he doesn't care about my feelings. If he did, he would have told me he was about to get married. Or maybe, you know, told me he was seeing someone. We talked so much before. How could he not tell me? And he makes more time for them than he ever did for us." I'm surprised by the emotion in my voice.

My mom touches my shoulder, looking up at me. "Peter, your father made mistakes in the past.

He loves what he does with his career. What happened all those years ago are moments that made you who you are. When you and Raegan grow up and get married, you can choose not to follow in his footsteps, not to repeat his behavior. But you can choose to love your dad because you know he loves you. You know," she looks at me, "he was scared you wouldn't approve of the marriage."

"Well, I... I don't know if I do or not. But I'm not going to stop him. And who said Raegan and I would be getting married?"

My mom smirks as she pulls some chicken and vegetables out of the fridge. She hands me some bell peppers and onion. "Start chopping these and think about what I said. I'm not going to force you to talk to him, but maybe you'll change your mind soon enough. On both accounts."

I don't say anything but begin chopping the vegetables as she slices the raw chicken into pieces, putting them into a pan for the oven. Her famous chicken fajitas are the best comfort food ever; Raegan's family will love them.

She slides the chicken into the oven and begins to sauté the vegetables in a frying pan. Her cell phone rings, and she hands me the spatula. "Can you watch this while I take this call?"

I nod, and she takes her phone into the living room as if it's private.

"Hi, James," I hear her say. "How are—"

My father. I roll my eyes. Probably trying to get me to talk.

"Oh, my goodness, when did this happen? No, I didn't hear about it on the news. Anywhere in Texas, you say?"

I turn to look at my mom. Her face is white as a sheet. I turn the heat down on the vegetables. They're nearly done. My mom runs a hand through her hair. "Of course. If we see or hear anything, we will let you know immediately."

My mom hangs up and looks at me. I already know this is not going to be good. "Mom?"

"Your soon-to-be stepsister is missing."

"*What?*" I didn't know a stepsister existed, but my stomach fills with dread.

My mom comes back into the kitchen, removing the vegetables from the heat. "The woman your father is marrying, Christina, has a fifteen-year-old daughter. She's been missing for a couple of weeks and they have it on good authority that she may very well be in Texas. She wasn't a fan of the marriage and decided to leave so her mom could be happy."

I sigh, leaning against the counter. Though I don't know this woman or her daughter, I feel terrible for them. I know what it feels like to lose someone, and it hurts like hell.

"What's her name? Maybe I can get some more information on her."

"I believe he said her name is Linley."

My heart drops. My mom can tell there's something wrong. "Peter, what do you know about Linley?"

I push away from the counter and head towards the front hallway. I slip on my sneakers and my hoodie. My mom follows me. "I know she's become one of the government agents. She was on Jackson's team. He wanted us to bring her out with us. He knew she was too young and needed help before it was too late. But when we were leaving, she had run off again and we didn't have time to look for her. I need to go talk to Jackson and Carissa. Can I please borrow the car?"

Mom nods. "Yes, but please be careful. And now I have to figure out how to tell your father about this over the phone without being obvious."

I shake my head, grabbing the keys. "Don't tell him anything yet. I need to confirm. But if he can send you a picture of her, send it to me so I can ask Jackson if it's the same person."

My mom nods and grabs her phone out of her pocket. I feel my phone buzz as she sends the photo over. I hurry out to the car, get in and drive off. My heart is racing. I hope it's not the same person. Because if it is, this is going to get difficult.

SPENCER OPENS THE DOOR to the cell room and I step inside. Jackson is leaning against the bars. Carissa is nowhere to be seen, so she must be in her broody corner. I turn to Jackson.

"You said there was a girl you wanted us to help, but she got away before we could do anything. What was her name?"

"Linley Matthews."

I cringe inwardly. My soon-to-be stepmom's current last name is Matthews. I continue with my questioning. "And how old is she?"

"She told me fifteen."

I hear shuffling. Carissa has joined us. I ignore her for now. "And what did she tell you?"

"Her mom was getting remarried, and she didn't like that. She wanted her mom to be happy, so she ran away from home. I guess somewhere along the way she mixed in with the wrong crowd. Got involved with the government. She's far too young to become a robot, which is why I wanted to save her, but... you know what happened next."

I begin to pace back and forth. Jackson pushes away from the bars. "Are you all right, man? You look like you're going to faint."

I stop. "Linley is my soon-to-be stepsister, and she's been missing for a week. My father and her mother are worried sick. They live in California, and they have it on good authority that Linley is here, in Texas. I need one more confirmation from you."

I hold up my phone with the picture of Linley. She wears an all-black outfit. Her brown hair falls in waves down her shoulders. Her eyes are dark brown. He studies the picture, then nods.

"Yeah... that's her. I'm sorry, man. I should've made more effort to have her ready to leave. Then again, I didn't know she'd run off like that. I asked her to stay put where I had her hiding. And then afterward, I tore apart the warehouse looking for her. Even looked out into the fighting. Brett nearly shot me in the face, by the way."

I shake my head. "It's not your fault. But we do have to find her before she gets any more involved than she is now. You have no clue where she would have gone?"

"No. We weren't close like that. I did connect with her instantly; she was like a little sister or something. I saw a lot of myself in her – angry, hurt, depressed. And when she told me how her mom was getting married and she didn't support it, I related to that a lot."

I nod. "It's okay. I have a plan, but first, I need to make sure I do this the right way for once. I have to talk to Mr. Williams."

"I'M SORRY YOU WANT me to do what, exactly?"

I sigh. "Sir, I know I have not earned your trust

lately, but please hear me out. Jackson and Carissa were always the best at tracking people down. I know what they did, but I need them to help me out."

Mr. Williams pinches the bridge of his nose. "You want me to release two people who stabbed us all in the backs to go track down a fifteen-year-old girl who's working for the government?"

"Yes, sir. You see, that girl is about to be my stepsister, and my dad is freaking out. We have the resources to make this a successful case. All I want is for Jackson and Carissa to bring Linley back here, so we can protect her. She's not too far gone yet."

Mr. Williams stares me in the eye. "And how do we know they won't betray us again?"

"I'm willing to take that risk. I believe in them. I know they want to do the right thing. We have to give them the chance to show us they've changed."

Mr. Williams is silent for a long time. At last, I hear him mumble under his breath. "All right, Peter Daniels, I will let you use them to find your stepsister. But if they betray us or do anything to put us intentionally in harm's way, you will face severe consequences. Am I clear?"

I nod. "Yes, sir. I understand."

Mr. Williams stands up from his desk. "Well, let's give them a new mission. I'm sure they'll be extremely *thrilled* to work together again, especially after Jackson broke my daughter's heart."

"It's for the greater good."

"I sure hope you're right about that, son."

Spencer looks up when we enter the cell room. He looks at his uncle and then at me. "How the hell did you convince him to agree to this?"

I shrug. "I'm pretty charming, honestly."

Spencer rolls his eyes. Mr. Williams says, "Carissa and Jackson, I am releasing you because I have a mission for you. You will both, as a team, track down Linley Matthews and bring her back to headquarters. If you choose to betray me again, you will be shown no mercy. However, if you prove yourselves honest and trustworthy and show that you are willing to fight for our side, I will be convinced that you no longer need to be locked up."

"No thanks," Carissa says. Everyone turns to her.

"Please, Carissa," I beg. "This girl—my stepsister—she's too young to be involved in any of this. I know how hurt she is by what our parents have done. My father didn't even tell me he was seeing anyone, and suddenly I received a wedding invite in the mail. I can help her."

Carissa crosses her arms. "Of course, I'll help you, but I don't need Jackson, and I think we all know, between the two of us, who'd be more likely to betray you, Dad." She stares pointedly at her father.

Mr. Williams steps forward. "Both of you betrayed me before," he snaps. "Therefore, it stands to reason that you could both do it again. However, I'm not sending you alone. Jackson has seen this girl before, and she may be more willing to comply with him. As for him, I want him to go along with you to look out for you. Jackson is many things—"

"An ass?" Spencer says.

"A traitor?" I offer.

A heartbreaker," Carissa states firmly.

Mr. Williams sighs. "This is nonnegotiable, Carissa. You both will be going, and you will find this girl."

Carissa's shoulders slump, but Mr. Williams unlocks the cell door. He then crosses over and unlocks Jackson's. He motions for all of us to follow him out. "I'll provide weapons and secure communication devices for each of you. Peter will

269

give you all the information he has about Linley Matthews. You are to bring her back here safely. Then we will discuss what's next."

We meet in the workroom. Stella and Noah are there. They jump up when Carissa and Jackson walk in. Noah glares at Jackson. "How the hell did you get out?"

Jackson smirks. "Seems I've already received my first mission from the boss. Don't suppose you've been on a mission yet, have you?"

Noah glowers, but I punch Jackson in the arm. "This isn't about that. Stop being annoying."

Jackson sighs. "You're right. I'm a new man. And I'll prove it. Even if it's so painful."

Carissa scoffs. Her brown hair has grown slightly from the short shoulder-length cut she used to have.

We take a seat at Spencer's usual table. Spencer and I sit across from Carissa and Jackson. Carissa rests her head in her hand, her elbow propped on the table.

"All right, Peter, what do you know about Linley?" she asks.

"She's been missing for about a week, which matches the time she arrived here. She has brown hair and brown eyes. I've printed a picture for you."

I push the enlarged photo over to them. I've never met my stepsister, yet I immediately feel connected to her. I don't want to help her... I *need* to. Before it's too late.

"She likes to wear dark clothes. She's in a bit of an emo phase."

Jackson nods. "Yeah, she was in dark clothes when I met her. She was confident. Definitely capable in terms of her ability to fight for whatever it is she thinks she's fighting for. She's stronger than she looks."

"Really?" I ask.

Jackson nods. "Yeah. I feel awful I couldn't do anything more."

Spencer hands them some of the papers Mr. Williams uses for official business. "You're making up for it now. Sign these release forms stating that you accept your mission, and then you can head over to my uncle to get your weapons and communication devices. Make sure to test out the earpieces. They're new."

Jackson and Carissa sign with ease, though Carissa is visibly unenthused to be working alongside Jackson. I can't blame her, after everything they've been through together. But we need to bring Linley home.

After the papers are handed back to Spencer, I lead them to the armory, where Mr. Williams hands each of them the earpieces, a pistol, and a knife.

Jackson puts his earpiece in and stalks out of the room. I glance at Mr. Williams, who looks a bit confused.

Carissa scowls, pressing her finger to her earpiece. "Yes, you moron, I can hear you."

Jackson walks back in with a smirk. "They work."

Mr. Williams pinches the bridge of his nose and says to me, "I am questioning my decision to go along with this plan."

I laugh awkwardly. "They'll do fine, sir."

Carissa snatches the pistol and puts it on the holster on her belt, then straps the knife on her other side. She glances back up at me and says, "I will personally hold you accountable for the mental damage I am about to endure from doing this."

I shrug. "You'll survive."

Jackson holsters his pistol and knife, then says, "Let's go kick some butt."

CHAPTER TWENTY-FOUR
Raegan
SATURDAY, OCTOBER 28TH, 2023

I WAKE TO THE SOUND OF VOICES downstairs. I hear the front door opening and then shutting again. My eyes don't open yet, though I'm aware of my surroundings. Sometimes I wake up thinking I'm still in the bunker Evan held me in. And other times, I know immediately that I'm back in my bedroom, that I'm safe.

Footsteps climb the stairs, then my door sweeps open. My mother pokes her head into my room. "Raegan?"

I groan. "I'm awake."

"Michelle brought some of the fajitas she made last night. I don't know if you're hungry."

I'm not hungry. The idea of food is a nauseating thing. The doctor said to stick to mostly bland food: toast, rice, some fruits, and water… but then I catch a whiff of dinner. And suddenly, I feel like I could be a bit hungry.

"Maybe a small amount?" I say, beginning to sit up.

Mom nods. "Okay. I'll bring some up."

I wish I could go sit at the table. Bed rest is boring. It's only been two days, but I'm already going crazy. Yet I'm too exhausted to even try to move out of bed.

Mom returns with a tray. On it is a glass of water and a plate of food. She's given me a small serving of beans and a small serving of chicken fajitas.

I take a small bite; this tastes so much better than toast and butter. Mom smiles. "I can sit here with you if you'd like."

I nod, my mouth too full of food to respond. She takes a seat on the edge of my bed. We haven't said much to each other, both of us unsure how to fill the space. I have questions about what's gone on, but it seems my parents want to hide things again, just like they did before I knew of the resistance.

I take a sip of water, gathering my nerve, then I ask, "What have you and Dad been hiding?"

My mom smiles sadly. "You've only just gotten back. I don't want to add to your worry."

"But something is going on," I say.

She runs a hand through her hair. "You're right. You can't… stay here."

I sigh in relief, almost laughing. "Is that all? I knew that already. It would be too dangerous. Evan could find me here if I stay too long."

My mom's eyes don't meet mine. I pause. "There's more?"

She nods. "Andre has a hidden bunker far from here, far from headquarters, in the middle of nowhere. It's not like a normal bunker, but he wants to send you there."

Another underground prison. Except it's the key to my safety. I don't like the idea. I'm terrified. But I don't say that. I need to be strong. "Okay," I say.

"But we can't go with you."

Now all my resolve to seem okay disappears, sapped out of me. "What?"

My mom stands. "The more people who believe that you're dead, that we're still grieving, the less likely it is that any of us will be in danger. We have to keep the act up."

Any part of me that was hungry is gone. I push the tray aside. "I can't go back down," I say, my heart beginning to race at the idea. "Not alone. I can't…"

My mom opens her mouth to reply when Peter appears in the doorway. My mom looks over, and says, "Oh, hello, Peter. I'll give you two privacy."

She gets to her feet and rushes out of my room. Peter looks at me.

"What was that about?"

I shake my head, hugging myself as I begin to feel the anxiety shake me. "My new living arrangements."

My heart still races, beating wildly against my chest. Peter tilts his head. "What do you mean?"

"I can't stay here too long, Peter. Eventually, Evan will try to find me, track me down, and drag me back before his secret is out."

Peter frowns, stepping further into the room. He doesn't meet my eyes. "I knew eventually you'd have to be put in hiding, but… but where will you be going?

"Andre has a bunker… somewhere far away in the woods. He wants me there."

"What? No… no, he can't do that to you.

Doesn't he even realize—"

"I know," I say, cutting him off a bit more harshly than I intended. Softening my voice, I say, "I don't like it, either. My parents can't come. I'll be alone again."

Peter takes a seat on the edge of my bed. "No, you won't. I refuse to let you be alone like that. I will be there as often as possible. You will not do this alone."

I look up at him. "Really?"

"Really," he says firmly.

There's something else dancing in his eyes. Worry. Fear. Apprehension about something. "Is something else bothering you?" I ask.

Peter sighs tiredly. "I need to tell you something."

The seriousness in his tone makes me lean forward slightly, reaching for his hand. "What's wrong?"

Peter looks out the window of my room, but whatever he's looking for isn't outside that window. His eyes finally meet mine again and he says, "It's about that girl we were supposed to bring back. She's my soon-to-be stepsister."

"What?"

Peter runs his free hand through his hair, a gesture that shouldn't have as much power over my heart rate as it does.

"My father is getting married. He didn't tell me he was even *seeing* anyone. The lady he's marrying has a daughter. And that daughter is the girl that Jackson wanted to save from becoming a government agent."

I squeeze his hand slightly. "Where is she?"

He doesn't answer for a while, looking away. Finally, he says, "I don't know. But we're going to find out."

IT'S LATE AND MY mind is still racing. I stare up at the ceiling, my body exhausted. But sleep won't come to me now.

There's no screaming to fill the silence. But everything buzzing in my head does a good job of replacing it.

After Peter told me everything about his father and his soon-to-be stepsister, I didn't know what to do.

We talked a bit more, and he listened to me talk about the bunker I'll be going to. He understood my fear.

I must have finally slept because sunlight now filters into my room.

I feel so useless, lying here, not able to move.

I attempt sitting up, something I've been practicing in the hours I've been lying here alone. Today it's a bit easier. My back presses against my headboard. I don't feel all that dizzy today. *Maybe I could...*

Before I can change my mind, I slowly position myself to stand from the bed. I've walked a little, with help. But I need to do it myself. The process is painful. My legs are numb, not used to moving around much. My head feels like it's spinning when I do finally get to my feet.

But that all subsides as I steady myself, a hand on my dresser for support. I don't move for a solid minute, just focusing on standing. Finally, I inhale, preparing myself for what I'm about to do.

I take a few steps.

Then a few more.

My hand slides off my dresser as I stand on my own.

I make it to my bathroom, use the toilet, and finally look at myself in the mirror. The sight is hideous. My eyes have dark purple circles under them. I look like a skeleton with skin. My hair is thin and disgusting. I look away.

I'd cry, but that takes too much energy from me. Instead, I close my eyes and brush my teeth, enjoying the fact I'm doing it all on my own.

I hear my mom come into my room. "Raegan?"

I'd closed the bathroom door before relieving myself. I slowly make my way back over to the door, open it, and lean against the doorjamb for support.

My mom is shocked. "Raegan... you're..."

I smile. "I know I'm not supposed to. But I had to use the restroom and I... I needed to do something myself."

My mom envelops me in a hug. "How does it feel?"

"Good... I don't want to lie back down yet."

She kisses the top of my head. "Okay. Then you don't have to. But if you start getting fatigued..."

I nod. "I'll go back to bed if I do. I just... want to feel normal. Before everything all changes again."

"We won't send you to the bunker until you feel better. Andre already said we'll wait until you gain strength. We just have to be careful in making sure we keep up appearances."

Keeping up appearances shouldn't be too hard. I wouldn't want to go outside anyway. I'd be dragged back to Evan immediately if I were spotted. And I most certainly have no intention of going back there, to his cruel imprisonment.

The doorbell rings and my mom says, "Michelle said she was sending Peter with some more food... Would you like me to send him up here to see your progress?"

"Yes, please."

Mom leaves and I return to the bathroom, trying to make myself look presentable. Now that I know how horrible I look, I'm self-conscious.

My bedroom door brushes open, and Peter says, "Raegan?"

I step out of the bathroom, walking on my own.

Peter's smile is enough to make me melt. He walks over to me and puts his arms around my waist, pulls me close. I press my cheek to his chest. I hear his heart beating faster and faster, in sync with my own.

"Hey," he says."

"Hi," I say shyly.

"You're standing," he says.

"I am."

He rests his forehead against mine, then says, "I guess I shouldn't be holding you like this. It's not helping the 'just friends' approach we're going for."

I wrap my arms around his neck, pulling him closer.

"That's not helping, either," he says softly, his breath brushing my face.

My dad clears his throat, and we jump apart. "Am I interrupting anything here?"

"No," we both say quickly.

Peter rubs the back of his neck. "We were just…"

My dad smiles. "The door stays open, okay?"

"DAD!" I feel my face turning red.

My dad was never the overprotective type, but he loves to tease me. I rub my hands over my face. "Why did you come up here?"

My dad sets a tray of food on my bed. "Your breakfast. And to make sure the door is open." He pats Peter's shoulder and then saunters back out the door.

I'm mortified. Peter starts laughing. When he finally stops, he looks at me. "I'm just glad your parents trust me. This could have been awkward."

I sit down on the bed and take a bite out of the buttered toast on my plate. "Was it not already awkward?"

He smiles. "No. No, that's just your dad being himself. It's funny how people were making that joke our whole lives but it's only bothering you now."

I feel my face going red again. Peter comes and takes a seat by me on my bed. Suddenly, he's serious again. "How are you feeling?"

"Overwhelmed. Scared. The sooner I get better, the sooner I'm shipped off to some bunker. I don't like the idea of going underground again."

He puts his hand over mine. I look up at him. "And what about you? What's to come of the search for Linley?"

He shakes his head. "Nothing yet. Jackson and Carissa checked in with Mr. Williams last night, but only because they stopped at a hotel. Carissa made it extremely clear they were staying in separate rooms."

"Can they be trusted? I know Jackson helped

you get to me, and I do believe he's changed. But what about Carissa?"

Peter shakes his head. "She's acknowledged her errors. Evan guilted her into things and she thought she was protecting her family by doing what he asked. She now knows how wrong she was. Trust me, if either of the two of them has changed, it's her. But I agree with you. Jackson is a changed man, too, and they both will work hard to find her."

"I hope so. I'd hate for someone so young to be brought into the government ranks."

Peter sighs, nodding his head. "Yeah. I'm just so pissed at my dad for not telling me he was even dating someone."

I frown. "I'm sorry."

He shakes his head. "It doesn't matter. This is nothing compared to the hell you just went through."

I touch his knee, causing him to look me in the eyes. Behind the steel gray is a pain so deep. His father's actions have hurt him too much. "Just because my hurt is different doesn't mean what you're going through is any less painful. What you feel is justifiable to the situation. Your dad, whom you lived with for most of your life, didn't even bother to tell you he was getting married, let alone dating someone. I think I'd be pretty mad, too."

Peter's eyes soften. He covers my hand with his own. I feel the calluses that have formed on his palm, but his hand is still comforting and warm. "I thought he and I were close, but since I moved out here, he only ever wants to talk business with me, always asking me when I will go to college and what college I will go to. He's offered me a summer job and an internship at his company, and a full ride to college if I accept. And I know I'd be crazy to turn down something like that, but I... I don't want to run a business. I don't want to go to college right after high school. Maybe not at all. That's not what I want for my life. And maybe I don't know what I want yet, but I want it to be my decision, not his."

"It's okay," I say. "To not have a clue about what you want, I mean. You're eighteen. You have so much more life ahead of you."

He smiles. "Okay. Enough about my pain." His smile falters as he looks away.

I tilt my head. "What's wrong? I can see something's bothering you."

"I don't want to bring up bad memories for

you, but… what happened that day? We all heard the gunshot and the scream."

My shoulder still gets phantom pains, even more so when I think about that day. I look down at my lap. "Evan did shoot me, as you know. And I did scream from the impact. And then shortly after, I blacked out. When I woke up, he was bandaging my arm, and I was in this weird room. It was in the bunker, the one he left me in. He said I lost a lot of blood. And ever since, I was kept in that room, only given one meal a day. Sometimes I thought he might poison me, so I only ate when I couldn't take the hunger anymore."

Peter is quiet for a few moments, and then he squeezes my hand. "I want him to pay for everything he's done."

"I know you care about me, Peter, but I'd never want you compromising your morals over me. Evan isn't worth the time."

Peter nods, but says, "Jackson said Evan is about to become the president's heir. The president never married and has no children. So, he's going to announce Evan as his heir to the country. We're screwed. Badly."

Before I can reply, my dad is in my doorway

again. We both glance over, letting go of each other's hands that we didn't notice we were holding.

My dad says, "Just making sure the door was still open. We're all friends here, right?"

I tilt my head at Peter. "Well?"

He smirks. "Yes, sir. Friends."

My dad gives Peter a stern look and then a tight smile before turning and heading back down the stairs. I say, "What was that all about? Am I missing something?"

Peter is still smirking. "Oh, nothing important."

"Tell me."

"Fine," he says. "My mom said before we continue with—well, whatever we're doing here, I needed to talk to your dad and get his permission."

"And what are we doing?" It's my turn to smirk. I can see a rosy tint coming to Peter's cheeks.

He winks at me. "You tell me."

I want to address the elephant in the room: we can't be only friends anymore. Too much has been said between us. But there's the sound of more footsteps.

To my surprise, Spencer appears in the

doorway. "Finally," he says to Peter. "Bro, do you even answer your phone anymore?"

Peter reaches into his pocket for his phone. "Oh. Sorry. What's wrong?"

Spencer sighs. "There's been a breakthrough. We need you to come to HQ." He looks over at me and smiles kindly. "Hey, Raegan. Sorry to steal him so soon."

I smile. "It's okay. I understand."

Spencer nods then turns to leave. "I'll be waiting in the truck."

Peter rises from beside me to follow him. I grab his wrist, and he turns towards me. "You never answered the question."

He smiles. "You were supposed to answer."

I lower my voice slightly as he steps closer. "I want to know what you say first."

He leans down so we're eye to eye. Our noses touch. My eyes flutter but I don't let them close.

"Then I guess you'll have to wait until tomorrow when Spencer isn't rushing me out."

He kisses my forehead and stands up straight again, the smirk never leaving his face. I can feel the intense blush on my cheeks, even after he leaves. That boy will be the proverbial death of me. And is it so wrong to say I don't mind?

CHAPTER TWENTY-FIVE
Jackson
SUNDAY, OCTOBER 29TH, 2023

THE MOTEL WE'VE TRACKED LINLEY DOWN to is shabby at best. Carissa sighs as if she doesn't want to get out of the car her father let us use. My car, which was left back at the warehouse when I took off, is too obvious for this job. This beat-up old car is simple and unassuming. No one would suspect anything from us.

Carissa looks out her window. I reach out to touch her arm but think better of it. She's not willing to forgive me yet. And I honestly can't blame her. I hate myself for putting us in this position.

"Are you ready?" I ask.

"No. This is the motel I came to when I was nearly out of money. The manager and I had a bit of a… disagreement."

"So, you tried to leave without paying the full bill?"

Her blue-green eyes meet mine, though she is not amused by my comment. I know her too well and she hates it. I clear my throat to prevent the laughter from passing my lips. "Well, you did dye your hair back to your natural brown. It was silver before. He may not recognize you."

I leave out the fact that her hair makes her look hot and that I love her natural color. It wouldn't be appreciated.

"When do you think I dyed it, genius?" she says, opening the car door. "However, this is bigger than any of that. Our job is to find Linley, so let's get going before I change my mind."

I follow Carissa into the small building where the manager's office is. A young boy, maybe seventeen, sits behind the desk, scrolling on his phone. I roll my eyes. He doesn't realize how closely he's being monitored by the government through that thing.

Carissa clears her throat. The boy looks up. "Oh, it's you again."

She glances at me before looking back at the boy. Before she can open her mouth, a middle-aged man comes around the corner. "Ah, back again?"

I decide I should speak. "Hello. We're looking

for a friend of ours."

The manager comes to stand behind the desk. "Okay. Do you know what room they're in?"

"If we knew that, we wouldn't be in here," Carissa mumbles under her breath.

I nudge her arm slightly, hoping she gets the message. "No, but we have a name. Linley Matthews."

The manager types something on the computer but shakes his head. "No one by that name is staying here. There is another motel about six miles north of here. Maybe you have the wrong place."

I keep my cool. If I were hiding out at a motel, I'd change my name. "Well, we have a picture of her. Maybe you've seen her?"

I hold out the printed photo of Linley. The manager nods. "Ah, yes. That girl did come in, but her name was not... what did you say again?"

I shake my head. "It doesn't matter. She uses different names. Do you know what room she's in?"

"She's not here anymore. Ms. Knight checked out two days ago."

Carissa perks up her ears at that. "What name did she use?" she asks, finally saying something without any hint of snark in her voice.

The manager hesitates. "That is considered classified information. You did say you were friends of hers, right?"

"Yes," I say, although I know that can't be enough for him to give us anything. I reach into my back pocket for my wallet. I may need to bribe the man.

"Her name, as documented in our files, is Gwendolyn Knight. Her ID said she was nineteen. She left two days ago, though where she was heading, we haven't a clue. Not that it is any of our business. Maybe give her a call, see where she's at."

I nod. "Thank you, sir. We appreciate it."

Carissa follows me outside again, her arms crossed. When we're a safe distance from the building, she says, "I told you."

"Yeah, but that was shady of him to give us the information we need. He can't prove we're friends with Linley."

Carissa marches past me to the car. "Probably doesn't care. This place is so disgusting. But now we have a name. We need to try some area hotels and check to see if anyone with that name has stayed in any of them. She's faking everything – and how the hell did she get the money for a motel anyway?"

I shrug. "Come on. We just need to find her."

We drive around to other motels nearby, checking the name, but Linley – aka Gwendolyn Knight – hasn't been to any of them. I begin to wonder if she's left the area altogether. We may have a tougher situation on our hands.

We expand our search and pull up to a hotel closer to Cyrus. We find "Gwendolyn Knight" stayed there for one night. Another guest tells us she ate dinner with "Gwen" after seeing her sitting by herself in the dining room, looking lonely. They thought she was younger than nineteen. I don't dare tell the woman she's right. We learn Linley was heading to a job in Cyrus, and that's when we realize she likely went back to the warehouse.

As Carissa and I get back in the car, I say, "This is like old times. You and me tracking someone down. Of course, we're fighting for a different team now, but it brings nostalgic feelings back, right?"

Carissa scoffs. "This is not like old times. Old times were when I loved you."

We're at a stoplight. I touch her hand, causing her to meet my eyes angrily. "Tell me right now you don't love me anymore. After everything we've gone through together, every mission, every battle... If you can tell me you don't love me, then I won't fight for us anymore."

Her eyes shine with tears she refuses to let fall. "I... I can't tell you that. Of course, I still love you. It's not a switch I can just turn off after all this time. It takes time to let love go."

Someone honks at me and I realize the light is green. I take off, speeding away towards the warehouse, the place I'm dreading returning to. My hands grip the wheel tightly; my jaw clenches.

After a long, painful silence, I take the risk of breaking it. "Why let time take away everything we built up? Okay, I made a bad decision. I stayed with Evan because I didn't want you hurt. I couldn't live with myself if I was the cause of any pain. Yet it seems I hurt you anyway. But I helped Raegan get home. Doesn't that prove to you I'm trying to change who I am?"

She's silent. I glance at the radio clock. We've traveled all over the place and it's getting late. I pull over to a small motel. Even though we're close to the warehouse, we can't do anything if it's dark. And driving back to the ranch wouldn't look good. The motel looks relatively clean from the outside.

Carissa gets out first. I follow her. The manager rents us two rooms and we part ways for the night.

After a shower, I change into the pajamas I packed in my mission bag and lie on my bed in the dark, staring up at the ceiling. The sounds of military trucks fill the night air, as well as gunshots. I jump every time.

My mind is on Carissa and everything I did wrong. She'll never forgive me. But maybe it's time I forgive myself, instead of seeking hers. I did what I had to do to protect her. Even if she never sees that… she's alive. And that's all I care about.

I don't know when it happens, but somehow, I find the solace of sleep. It seems like just moments later that I'm waking up to the sunlight filtering through the sheer curtains. The city is awake and alive out there, but I hardly hear a thing.

I get dressed and meet Carissa in the lobby, where we check out and head back to the car, parked in the motel's lot.

When we get in, she's the first to speak. "I've done some thinking."

"I have, too."

"Would Linley have gone back to the warehouse? I mean, it seems a bit odd for her to go back where she was running away from."

Oh. I hide the hurt from her. I guess I had my hopes up that she thought of me last night as much as I thought of her. I shake my head slightly. I made a promise to myself that I wouldn't think like that. I need to be stronger. "I think she would because it's safer there than out here in the open. And I don't think she was running from the warehouse specifically."

"Then what was she running from?"

"The chaos. The fighting. She's scared about the life changes her mother is making. She came here to get away from that."

Carissa grunts. "Why would she sign up to be an agent of the government?"

I'm about to answer, but the truth hits me. "She wasn't. She was hiding."

"What are you saying?"

I push the gas down a little more, weaving through traffic. "I'm saying she didn't come here to fight in a war. She hardly knew anything about what was going on when she first arrived. She's only hiding in what she probably thinks is some gang. We need to find her. There's still hope she can be rescued before the government signs her into

297

their service."

We both fall silent for a while, until Carissa asks, "What if we're already too late?"

I shake my head, "That's not an option. The mission is to save her."

"But… we can't discount the fact that it's been days since anyone has seen her."

"I can handle those odds," I say, ending the conversation.

We will find her.

I will make sure of it.

CHAPTER TWENTY-SIX

Evan

"WHY WON'T HE ANSWER?"

Samantha groans. "Face it. Jackson abandoned you. He's long gone by now. Who knows where he went?"

I sigh. For the past few days, I've called, texted, and even emailed. Nothing. I should have known he'd try to leave, probably to look for my traitorous sister. But that leaves me to wonder what's gone on back home.

I schedule a meeting with the president. We're announcing the big news this weekend. I still have time to fly back to Texas and check on things. I explain the situation, leaving out the details that would get me killed where I stand.

"I need to fly back and check things out with headquarters."

"Why don't I try contacting Jackson myself?" he suggests. "I'm sure he's busy, and maybe he doesn't have time for your calls. But he has to answer to me."

It's not a bad idea, but I know the more involved President Morgan is, the more likely it is I'm screwed. "Let me fly back. If he's there, I'll talk to him and then come straight back here. It'll just be a couple of days. Besides, it might be good for me to check in on his team and make sure they're in tip-top shape and meeting all the requirements."

President Morgan nods. "True. All right, we'll get you out there. But Agent Winters has to go with you."

"Of course, sir."

I say nothing to object because this will help with the plan to look like we're slowly falling in love. I hate that this is what it's come to. I cringe at the thought of trying to go along with the president's plan. Especially after her confession about falling for me. We haven't been able to talk much like we used to after that. I don't know if it's my head playing games, but something feels very off.

Either way, the flight is scheduled using one of

the president's fancy jets. Sam and I leave that evening. We don't talk much on the plane, as I know everything is being recorded. Instead, we make neutral small talk about nothing. We give the hidden cameras something to look at. That's it.

When we land at the airport, I rent a car and we drive thirty minutes to the warehouse. It's exactly how I left it: trashy. Jackson's car is, remarkably, parked out front. Maybe he is busy and didn't have time for my calls. Maybe this flight is all for nothing.

At the door, we're greeted by some new faces. Most are much younger than us, but some are older, closer to our age. Everyone looks ready to pounce until they see it's me. They already know who I am meant to be.

The oldest of the group, who looks to be in his early twenties, approaches. "It's a pleasure to meet you in person, Agent Specter. What brings you here to our warehouse?"

I force a smile. "Well, we're doing checks on every base, and I also came to see Jackson. Where is he?"

The boy frowns. "Oh. He left a few days ago. At first, we thought he might have been captured when we were attacked, but we have since discovered that he left willingly and that the attack was a distraction for us so he could get away."

So he could get away… or so someone else could get away? My heart drops at this, but I keep my cool. "Attack? Tell me more about this attack. And what's your name?"

"Trevor. I've kind of taken the lead here since I'm the oldest, but if you are going to put someone else in charge, I will gladly obey orders. As for the attack, it happened suddenly. No one expected it. Resistance agents descended upon the warehouse. We fought back. They didn't take any of us, thankfully. We were able to push them back. It was odd. They didn't seem to be looking for anything, either. That's why we assume it was a distraction organized by Jackson to abandon us."

I glance at Samantha, whose face reflects my confusion. "I'm going to leave you with Agent Winters for now. I will talk to President Morgan and see what he says. Excuse me."

I'm nearly running to get to the storeroom. The steel door is still locked. I unlock it with the key I kept. Inside, things look mostly as I left them. But the back door is no longer covered in boards. As I get closer, I see the tile has been moved. She could still be down there. I climb down the ladder, but soon my fears are confirmed. This new development could ruin everything.

When I'm back above ground, I quickly call President Morgan.

"Sir," I begin, "there's been an unexpected wrench thrown in our plans. Jackson abandoned this place with help from the resistance."

I RETURN TO THE main hall, eager to assign a new leader and get out of here so I can hunt down Jackson. Of course, I should explain things to Samantha first. And I don't imagine this going very well. I pull her aside to my old office so we can talk. Her arms are crossed, and she looks coldly at me.

"First you leave me with a team of newbies, then you think you can just pull me in here for… what, exactly?"

I sigh. "I've lied to you about some things. A lot of things."

Unexpectedly, her expression softens from enraged to curious. "What do you mean?"

303

"I didn't kill Raegan MacArthur. I faked the entire thing and put her in the bunker under the storeroom, where I kept her weak, tired, and barely alive. I didn't have the guts to follow through with my mission. Jackson knew that, and he was here taking care of her. But now they're both out there somewhere, and if the president learns of this, I'm screwed."

Samantha is silent for a while. I don't dare meet her eyes for fear of finding a wave of new anger and betrayal there. Instead, I feel her hands on my shoulders. I look up. I don't acknowledge the electricity racing up my spine. After Sam told me she might be falling for me, I backed away. I didn't know if it was true. I still don't. Part of me believes it can't be. She told me she didn't feel like she could ever fall in love again. But… this feels right.

"*We're* screwed if he finds out," she says, squeezing my shoulders. "Like it or not, Evan, we're a team. We need to find them. I don't understand why Jackson didn't abandon the place and leave her to rot down there, but we will have our answers soon enough. For now, you need to confirm with President Morgan that Jackson deserted so he can assign a new leader here."

"I told him," I say, studying her face for a moment. I find freckles I never noticed, and little golden flecks in her eyes. But what I don't find is feelings. "Is it hard to feel so alone?"

The words are out before I can stop them. She steps back, hugging herself. I feel cold again. But instead of turning away and leaving, the way she usually does, she answers. "I've been alone for so long now that I don't know what it feels like to have company. I see the look in your eyes. I know the feelings you have for me."

I look away from her, studying some nonexistent fiber on the floor. I feel exposed. She continues. "And it pained me that I couldn't be what you wanted me to be sooner. It killed me that I was given a mission to play with your emotions, that I'm supposed to act like I'm falling in love with you. But if you want the truth," here she pauses and her gaze searches mine for a moment, "I know I'm falling for you. But I'm too broken to be what you need. It has nothing to do with you and everything to do with me. I feel as though I'm playing with your emotions."

I shake my head, standing from my perch on the edge of the desk. "No. You are not controlling this game. What they've done to us is sick and twisted. They're practically arranging my love life for me. If I hadn't been paired with you, it would have been someone else. To be honest, I'm glad it's you they chose for this because I can trust you."

Before anything else can be said, a knock at the door interrupts us. I'm thankful, needing a break from the heaviness of it all. I open the door to find Trevor and a young girl standing outside.

Trevor says, "This is the girl who ran away during the attack, but she returned a while ago. We've been hiding her here."

The girl looks young, mid-teens at most. Her hair is dark brown, and her clothing is black. Her face is devoid of any makeup. Her eyes look bloodshot as if she hasn't slept well in a few days.

"What's your name?"

"Gwendolyn Knight."

I reach to shake her hand. "Evan Williams, but you may know me as Agent Specter."

She doesn't react much. She must not have been with the agency long. Samantha and I follow the two to the main hallway. As we walk, I come to a decision: I'll make the choices here. This way, President Morgan can see my leadership prowess.

"Well, Trevor," I say when we get to the lobby, "I've decided that since you're the most experienced one here, you will take over the leadership of the team. From here on out, you will patrol and report back to your commanding officer. He or she will tell you what to do if you stumble across anything odd or resistance-related."

Trevor agrees, of course, but for some reason, Gwendolyn frowns. Was she hoping for the position? There's no way I'd put such a young girl in charge of the team, as much as I see her leadership skills. I can already see how strong she is.

Samantha hands me a clipboard. Each recruit's name is on this list, except for Gwendolyn's. I glance up at her and a light bulb goes on in my head. She's a stowaway. But I don't think she's from any resistance. I can see her full obedience to this team.

"Gwendolyn, can you explain why you aren't on this list?"

"Because I snuck in."

Her honesty is brutal, and her tone is rude.

I like her already. "Well, you know we could have you imprisoned for that. The penalty for infiltration is death."

Her face shows no fear, only clear defiance. I can't hide the smile that comes to my face. There are risks in accepting someone who isn't on any list made by the government, lists confirmed by the president himself. To let her in could be a mistake.

Yet I see there's a stubbornness about her, something that prevents her from showing her fear in the face of knowing she's breaking laws by being here in front of me now.

Finally, I say, "But because you've been a good sport, we'll test you and get you admitted to the agency."

She gives me a curt nod as if she's expected this her entire life. Samantha shakes her head at me from behind the group, but I ignore her for now. She doesn't see the potential Gwendolyn has. And we will need someone young to become my heir when I'm running the country.

CHAPTER TWENTY-SEVEN
Carissa

"IF SHE'S BACK AT THE WAREHOUSE, WE need to get there as soon as possible. We can't just wait nearby for her to come out."

Jackson shakes his head. We're parked across the street from the hell we left behind. I know he's scared to go back in because of his team, but it's too dangerous waiting around out there. We're only losing valuable time.

"We have to get in there, Jackson," I say, trying again. "We know she returned to the warehouse the other day. If we want to secure our freedom and prove our loyalty, not to mention save a young girl from making the same terrible mistake we did, we have to try."

His brown eyes look deep into mine. I want to break the connection. I want to turn off what I feel when I see him. He's different now. But it's a good difference, and I don't want to admit it.

"If I go in there," he says, "they'll want to know why I left. They'll detain me and question me. And I don't want to get roped back in."

I sigh. "I won't let that happen."

"You can't control what I do, Carissa. And you can't control what *they* do. You know that."

We're silent for a moment; the air between us is tense. Finally, I say, "You said you want to show me that you're in this with me, that you'll stay by my side. Prove it by going in there with me. Because whether you come along or not, I'm going."

He doesn't look at me, nor does he make a move to shut off the car. I guess I should have expected this. I slip my earpiece in as I open my door and get out. I slam it, to show him I'm mad. It's a petty move on my part, but oh, so satisfying. The traffic is light this time of day, so I cross the street with ease.

I see Jackson's car still parked in the lot. Another car is parked next to it, but I assume it belongs to one of the team members there. I sneak up to the door, my hand hesitating just above the knob.

"Are you going to open it or not?" Jackson whispers in my ear. His breath brushes against my skin.

I smirk. "I was giving you a chance to prove me wrong. Now let's do this."

He followed me over. He really does want to prove he's on my side. How can I deny it now? I shake my head slightly before opening the door.

I need to focus. We get the girl, then we talk about our future if there is one.

I pick the lock as quietly as I can. It takes a few moments before I hear it unlock. I open the door, but no one is around. We step in silently, quietly shutting the door behind us. No one is in the front lobby, meaning they'll be somewhere else in this prison. I carefully lead the way, keeping my steps quiet. I check a few offices near the front; all are empty. I rifle through some papers on one of the desks, but there's nothing of importance. Evan most likely took anything with meaning. We go cautiously down the opposite hall, and I suddenly hug the wall. I can see the team over near the steel door that guards the storage room. But with them, I see the two people who make my blood run cold: Evan and Samantha.

My eyes widen, and I'm in a daze. Jackson grabs my arm and pulls me in a mad dash back to the door. We almost make it to freedom. His hand is on the knob. But suddenly I'm yanked backward, away from him. My hands are restrained behind my back. Jackson turns around, reaching for me, and is quickly captured himself. We're taken back down the hall, though I put up a fight.

Evan smirks as we're marched over to him. "Ah, here are the two deserters now."

Jackson pushes away the guy restraining him. "Bro, what are you talking about? I didn't leave you."

Evan laughs, but it's not a humorous laugh. It's the kind that sends a chill racing up your spine. He turns to our captors. "Okay, put them in the room over there so I can deal with them."

I'm roughly shoved from behind; I stumble slightly as I'm pushed toward the door. From the sound of the scuffle behind me, Jackson is fighting against his captor. I don't fight. I want to know what exactly is going on here. And if we're going to succeed in getting Linley out, we can't take the risk of getting ourselves killed.

The recruit shoves me into the room, and

moments later Jackson is pushed in as well. I feel numb. This is where the lies began, and maybe this is where they will end.

Outside the doorway, Evan turns to the young recruits. "Everyone go about your business while I handle these traitors. Don't worry; everything will be fine."

The team walks away, though a boy glances in at us once more before he finally leaves. Samantha follows Evan into the room, sticking close to him. I watch them both with careful eyes.

"Jackson Maverick," Evan says, all calm, cool, and collected. He's been gone for too long. "You say you didn't desert us, but then why would you be peeking around the corner with my traitorous sister?"

Jackson clears his throat. "Well, I—"

"Save it," Evan says. "Nothing you say will work with me this time. I know you far more than you think. I only care about one thing, and I want you to tell me the truth. And just maybe you'll be able to salvage any hope you might have of living past today."

Jackson shares a look with me, condemning himself. Evan continues. "Where is Raegan?"

"I don't know."

"Don't give me those lies. I know you helped her escape. So... where is she?"

Jackson looks to his feet. I look at my brother. "We'll never tell you where she is. You'll never find her, either."

Evan sighs, shaking his head. "So be it. You know, I wanted to help you out. But just remember when you're on execution row, you brought it on yourselves."

He starts towards us. I'm ready to fight, but Jackson shakes his head and says, "No, darling. It's over."

I face him. "What do you mean? We can get out of here."

He shakes his head. "Even if we take them down, there's a whole team out there ready to finish us off."

Evan grabs me hard, pushing me against one of the pillars that hold up the ceiling. This alights Jackson's anger, ripping the calm from him in an instant.

"Don't you dare touch her like that." Quick as lightning, he steps over and head-butts Evan in the jaw. Evan staggers away from me but doesn't fall.

Samantha just watches coldly from the side, although she flinches slightly when she sees Evan is hurt.

Evan swings back at Jackson, but Jackson ducks. He then yells at me. "Get out of here!"

I hesitate and then make a run for the back door. That's when Sam starts to move, but she doesn't seem to be trying awfully hard. I kick the door hard enough, it swings on its hinges. I run outside and almost collide with a girl standing in the alley. Could it be...

"Linley?"

She turns fast, the shock evident on her face. "How do you know my real name?"

I sigh. "There's no time to explain. Can you grab the lock pick tool from my pocket?"

She does as I say and asks, "Why are you handcuffed?"

"I'll explain in a moment. Can you pick the lock?"

She smirks. "I'm great at picking locks."

In a few short moments, my wrists are free. I rub them carefully, then say, "Come with me. Please."

"Why? I don't know you."

I glance back at the door. No one's come for me yet. "Trust me. I know Jackson."

Linley is hesitant, but I don't give her an option. I grab her arm, forcing her to run with me to the front of the building. The traffic is still light, so we run across the street to the car. Then I remember: Jackson has the keys.

I groan. Running my hand through my hair, I look inside the window – and see the keys sitting on the seat.

I sigh in relief as I open the door and tell Linley to get in the back.

She hesitates. "You could be kidnapping me. How can I trust you?"

"Because… I know Jackson, but I also know your soon-to-be stepbrother and he wants you safe."

Linley steps back. "This is about getting me home, isn't it? I don't want to go home."

"And you don't have to. But it's not safe to discuss this here. We have to go."

Suddenly, there's the sound of gunshots coming from the warehouse. My breath catches in my throat and I pray to whoever will listen that Jackson was not on the receiving end of those bullets. This seems to scare Linley enough to hop in the car. I get behind the wheel, crank the engine, and drive us away down the road, somewhere distant enough to be safe.

When we're out of sight, I pull off into the parking lot of a store. Linley says, "Are you okay? You look pale."

I nod. "Jackson... he's still at the warehouse. We've been searching for you for a couple of days. Those gunshots..."

Linley's eyes widen. "Can't you call him?"

Of course. "You're right. My father gave us secure communicators." I can only hope Jackson remembered to grab his.

I press my finger to the button and say, "Jackson, can you hear me?"

It rings like a normal phone. I hear a ragged breath. "H-hello, darling."

"You're okay!"

"Um... define 'okay'?"

I pause. "I heard the gunshots. Were you...?"

"Yes, but nothing vital. I hope you drove away."

"I did, but I can come to get you if you're able to get out. Please tell me you got out."

Jackson exhales. His breathing sounds labored. "I… I was shot in the abdomen and I pretended to pass out immediately. They left the room, so I crawled over to the back door, but I'm in the alley. It won't be long before they find me. Just go. I need you safe."

"No," I say firmly. "We're coming back for you."

"We?"

"I have Linley," I say. "She's safe. I'm coming to get you. Just hang tight."

Jackson is silent for a moment. "Not much else I can do."

I hang up and tell Linley to buckle up. I pull out of the parking lot and speed back to the warehouse. I notice when I pull in that Evan's car is gone. Cautiously, I drive up the alley. Jackson is lying on his stomach, a pool of blood forming under him.

I get out, telling Linley to stay inside the car. She ignores me and clambers out behind me. I kneel next to Jackson, helping him roll onto his back. I lift his shirt.

He winces and says, "If you wanted me to get my clothes off, you just had to ask." He gives me a weak grin.

"Don't flatter yourself," I say. I rip the sleeve off my shirt and wad it against the wound, trying to staunch the bleeding.

"We have to get you to a hospital."

Linley and I carefully help Jackson up. He groans from the pain. With difficulty, we get him into the car.

When we're safely on the road, I call Spencer from my earpiece.

"Hello?"

"Spencer? We need you to meet us at the hospital."

"What happened?"

"We have Linley, but Jackson's been shot. I need you to come and get Linley so you can take her to HQ."

"I'm on my way," he says.

Jackson says, "No, no hospital. I'll be fine."

"You will not," I tell him. "Now shut up so I can figure out where we're going."

I can hear Spencer scrambling for his keys. "Which hospital?"

"The closest one to us is Cyrus Methodist Hospital. So that one."

Spencer promises to be there as soon as

319

possible and we hang up.

Jackson's head rolls to the side as he starts to lose consciousness. Linley says, "Is Jackson going to die?"

I shake my head. He can't die. Not now. "Not on my watch he's not."

Linley seems a bit frazzled. I can't blame her. The only person she ever had any connection to is sitting behind her in the back seat, bleeding out of his gut. I feel broken for her and broken for myself. The reality that Jackson could die suddenly hits me hard, and it takes everything in me not to cry.

"Rissa...if this is it... you need to know—" he begins. His voice is very weak.

"This isn't it," I snap. "You're not dying on me now, Jackson."

He grunts, moaning in pain as he tries to move around.

"Stay still," I say.

"Darling, this could be the end. I... I'm already struggling...to breathe. Let me talk."

Linley has curled up in her seat, her face against her knees. I want to be doing that now. I want to panic, to cry, to scream, anything to show how I feel right now. But I can't. I need to be strong for her. I need to be strong for Jackson. And maybe… maybe I need to be strong for myself.

"I…I will always love you."

The words bring tears to my eyes, and I can't stop them from falling. I blink rapidly. *Focus*, I tell myself fiercely. I can see the hospital up ahead. The car's tires screech as I make the turn and pull up in front of the emergency entrance. I tell Linley to stay put and watch Jackson while I go get help. I run into the lobby and see heads turning toward me.

"I need help," I shout. "My boyfriend's been shot."

A nurse rushes up to me. "Where is he?"

"I drove him here. He's in my car. Please, you have to help me."

The nurse touches my shoulder. "It's okay. Calm down. Lead us to him."

Some EMTs roll a gurney behind me as I lead them to the car. Linley steps out once she sees me and opens the back door. Jackson is lying still now, all color drained from his face. I curse under my breath as they move him to the gurney. His shirt is soaked with blood; my makeshift bandage had no effect. They rush him into the hospital, with Linley and I running after them.

A doctor stops us before we can follow them down the hall. "We have to get him to the operating room right away. From the looks of it, he's in critical condition with a lot of blood loss. Hang tight here in the lobby. We'll come to get you when we have more information."

I'm sobbing now, unable to be strong any longer. "Please. Please save him."

The doctor nods. "We will do everything in our power to help him."

A nurse leads us to a private waiting room. Linley takes my hand in hers as we follow her down the hall. Her face is without any emotion. We sit down, side by side, and the nurse closes the door as she leaves. I take in her company now; soon Spencer will be here, and she'll leave with him.

Linley studies me. I feel her eyes on me even with my own closed. I practice my breathing, but nothing is working to calm me down.

I... I will always love you.

Why didn't I say it back?

Finally, Linley says, "So you're Jackson's girlfriend?"

"It's a bit complicated," I say.

Linley nods as if she understands. Maybe she

does. Though she's only fifteen, I can see the wisdom of an old soul in her brown eyes. There's so much more to her, and I can see she feels alone in this world. Something I know Jackson relates to very well.

A little while later there's a knock on the door and Spencer comes into the room, but he's not alone. My dad and Peter are with him. I rise to meet them and suddenly I'm in tears again. My dad envelops me in his arms and I collapse against him, sobbing into his chest. The hard realization that I love Jackson hits me, and the thought of losing him is too much to bear alone.

After a few moments, I'm able to control my emotions, taking a little step back, and wiping my eyes. Peter approaches Linley, who is still sitting on the cushioned chair. He sticks his hand out to her.

"Hello, Linley. I'm Peter. We're supposed to be siblings soon."

She gives him a once-over before finally shaking his hand. Timidly, she says, "Hi."

Spencer runs a hand through his hair and leans over to me. "How did a young girl like that get mixed up in this?"

Linley hears him and gets to her feet. "I lied my

way into staying. I didn't get recruited into anything. But I knew about the things that were happening because my mother used to be a part of a small rebellion in California. She stopped once she and my father divorced four years ago."

Dad looks uneasily around the waiting room. We're the only ones here, but it's not safe to talk about any of this right now. "We need to wait until we go home before we have this discussion." He turns to me, a soft expression on his face, and hugs me again.

I say, "I never thought you'd forgive me."

"My dear, I forgave you the moment you came back home. But I couldn't reward your behavior with comfort. You've proven to me that you can be trusted with so much. Jackson has, too."

"I… I'm scared.," I say, unable to stop myself.

He holds me tighter. "I know you are."

I squeeze him tightly and then step back. Spencer settles comfortably into one of the cushioned seats now. I tilt my head. "I thought you were taking Linley back to HQ?"

Dad steps past me. "Yes, Peter and I will be taking her back. But I don't want you to be alone while you wait for Jackson to get out of surgery.

Spencer's going to stay here with you."

Spencer nods once as if to stop me from arguing. He knows me too well.

Linley turns to my dad and Peter. "I'll tell you everything I know. I'm ready to be safe. But please don't send me back to my mom. She's going to be so mad at me."

Peter smiles. "Don't worry. Everything is going to be okay."

They leave, and I sink into a chair next to Spencer. My heart is still racing. So much blood was flowing out of Jackson, and the image will never leave my mind.

Oddly, Spencer chuckles. I turn my head to look at him. "What?"

"Nothing. It's just... you're denying to yourself how much you care about Jackson. I know he betrayed you and broke your heart, but he only wanted to protect you. Evan didn't give him many options."

A new wave of tears rushes quickly down my face. I look away, not wanting Spencer to see me cry. He's right. What happened that night... only a month ago... wasn't Jackson's fault. And Jackson may never know I love him, too.

I think about my brother. How dedicated he used to be to my father's resistance. He never gave any indication that he'd disagree with our dad.

"Do you think Evan is evil?" Spencer asks, trying to distract me.

"Well, all that crap about protecting us is probably not far from the truth. But his logic behind it all has become so twisted. He's doing things that he'd never normally do, even if it was to protect us. There's something more he's after now. Power. Raw, unfiltered power."

He nods. "Well, the worst part is we don't know where he went."

Then my stomach lurches as I remember. "He... he's going to try to find Raegan. He asked us where she was, and we wouldn't tell him anything. That's when Jackson started to fight him, and I got away first."

"Uncle Andre has it covered. Once he heard about Jackson being shot, he ordered Raegan to be taken to headquarters. It's not the safest, but she's not strong enough to be moved entirely from her home. And Evan's not stupid. He won't come around headquarters because he'll know he'd be captured easily."

I give him a look of surprise, but I know I can't question him more about this. We aren't in a secure place to talk about this stuff. I nearly suggest we go outside, but I can't leave. I'm tethered here as long as Jackson is here.

I must fall asleep at some point because I feel Spencer shake me awake as a doctor enters the room. His eyes look tired; his long white coat makes him look like a mad scientist. I realize it's the same doctor who stopped me in the hall earlier. He holds out his hand to me.

"I'm Dr. Jameson."

I shake his hand. Spencer does as well. Dr. Jameson says, "Are you the only family here for Mr. Maverick?"

I nod. "Yes. He has no one else. I'm his girlfriend and this is my cousin."

I figure the more truth I speak, the easier this will go, and the easier it will be for us to make a clean getaway.

The doctor nods. "All right. Well, I need to be frank with you. Jackson is not doing well. We were able to stabilize him, but he lost a lot of blood. We won't know how he's doing until he wakes up, but we've moved him to the ICU. If you'd like to see him briefly now, you may. But if you're not immediate family, you'll need to leave by nine p.m."

I'm the closest thing to immediate family Jackson has, so if this guy thinks I'll be leaving, he has another thing coming. But I don't dare say that out loud.

Dr. Jameson leads us down the hall. I hug myself, scared of what I might see. Spencer wraps his arm over my shoulders, letting me lean into him. We step into the room and I see Jackson lying on one of the beds. He's surrounded by machines, and there are oxygen tubes in his nostrils. His face has more color than before, which is good, but his eyes are still closed.

The doctor leaves us to visit. I brush the dark hair off Jackson's face. I can see some bruises from when he was fighting. I kiss his forehead, then hover near his ear, tempted to whisper the words he so bravely said to me. But I will not be a coward. I will speak those words to him when he wakes up, so he can hear me. And we can plan our future, our goals, our everything. I will wait for him as long as it takes.

CHAPTER TWENTY-EIGHT
Peter
SUNDAY, OCTOBER 29TH, 2023

LINLEY SITS IN THE BACKSEAT BEHIND Mr. Williams, watching as the world goes by. Her head rests against the window, and her fingers trace absent circles on the door. I can see the defeat in her posture, the way she doesn't seem to care anymore. And though I know next to nothing about her, I want to help.

"Linley, have you met Emilee yet?"

"Yeah."

I smirk. "She's super annoying, right?"

Linley looks up at me, a shy smile tugging on her lips. "A little, I guess. When we met, she talked a lot about her boyfriend. I guess she thought we could have 'girl talk' or something, but I'm not interested in boys."

I laugh. "Emilee always talks about her

boyfriend. Don't worry, you'll eventually get used to it."

"I guess I'll have to. I suppose my running away didn't stop them from getting married, did it?"

I turn in my seat. "No. It seems like you've brought them closer together. But you weren't the only one who wasn't told this was happening. My dad sent me an invitation to the wedding in the mail. That's how I found out. And I lived with him most of my life. I felt betrayed, just like you feel right now."

Linley sighs. "Do I have to go back?"

"Probably. They're flying in to come see you, at least. Don't be afraid to tell them how you feel. I've told my dad how I feel. We... we aren't talking right now. But that shouldn't be how your relationship with your mom is."

Linley shakes her head, anger in her eyes. "My mom has never understood me. She wants me to be more girly, and less, well, the way I am. I like my oversized shirts and my black clothes, but she wants me in frilly dresses and makeup. She wants me to find a boyfriend. I don't want any of that. Not right now."

I nod. "And why is that?"

"I know what's going on around us. My mom used to be in a small resistance before she and my dad got divorced. Sometimes, she still helps them out. And she's always been so open and honest with me about it. It probably sounds dumb to you, but I thought if I could get in with the government, I could be a double agent of sorts, getting information the resistance might need."

Mr. Williams glances into the rearview mirror to look at her, then back to the road. "You're fifteen, right? Why would you worry about this kind of thing?"

Linley's stubbornness begins to show through again. Her eyes regain that initial spark I saw in them when we first met in the hospital. "Because if I don't do anything, how am I any better than the enemy? I know I'm young, but I'm smart. I'm not going to sit around and wait to see what happens when I get a little older. It could be too late by then."

Mr. Williams and I share a look as he pulls into the garage at the ranch. As we begin to descend, Linley sits up in alarm.

"It's tight in here. What if it collapses?"

I look back and smile. "It's okay. It's how we

get down into HQ. At least, for now. It's not entirely safe here, but it's safer than where you could've been."

Once we're out of the lift and parked, Linley calms down a bit. We walk to the lobby door together and go inside. Mrs. Williams greets us and introduces herself to Linley. She then takes Linley upstairs to get her settled.

Mr. Williams looks at me. "I was wrong about you, Peter."

I look back at him. "What?"

"You are very impulsive and hot-headed, but I'm realizing that your quick thinking has saved two lives now. Lives I never believed could be saved. I want you to know how sorry I am."

I don't know what to say. I'm stunned because I knew I was defying orders. "Thank you, sir. I know what I did wasn't right. But I don't regret anything. I couldn't just leave Raegan. Not even if the chance of her being alive was slight. But I don't understand why Brett and his agents didn't look deeper into whether she was truly dead. They're the FBI. I would think they'd know to look further."

"That's the issue I've struggled with," a new, feminine voice says. A woman with a long red braid approaches us. At first, I don't recognize her. Then I realize it's one of Brett's agents. Ailey.

Mr. Williams gives her a small smile, sensing the tension. "Hello, Ailey. What are you doing here?"

She fidgets with the hem of her hoodie. "I came because I couldn't remain quiet much longer."

Her Irish accent adds an edge to her voice. "There is something that has bothered me about that day. When we entered the room where Raegan MacArthur was supposedly killed, there was indeed blood at the site. But any good agent knows blood doesn't always mean death. I began searching the room for any possible escape hatches, but Brett told us to stand down. We left after only five minutes. When we returned, he told you she was dead. But there was no hard evidence of that."

Mr. Williams is silent. So, I speak. "You mean he didn't try to find her, even if it was a recovery mission?"

Ailey shook her head. "No. He didn't let us search. He's our superior, so no one questioned him. I think we all assumed we'd be reporting back here for our next steps to find her. No one knew he was claiming her to be dead until he did it."

Something isn't sitting right with me. To be fair, I've never liked Brett. But now that some of my worries are confirmed…

Mr. Williams nods. "I will make sure this is looked into. Thank you, Ailey." She doesn't move to leave, so Mr. Williams says, "Is there something else?"

Ailey flinches slightly. Finally, she says, "I did my own investigation and found out that Brett might be working for the president. Not as an undercover resistance member, but as a spy. Sir, I think he's spying on the resistance to give the government information. I don't know for sure, but I'm concerned I could be right."

Suddenly, everything starts making sense. Brett's insistence on Raegan being dead could have been because he knew Evan's mission *was* to kill her and because he probably believed she was dead. And he knew that by searching further, it would only convict everyone involved.

Mr. Williams is quiet for a moment. And then he says, "Tell me, Ailey. Do you know where Brett is?"

Ailey shakes her head. "No, though I suspect he's back in D.C. by now."

Mr. Williams frowns. "Thank you for coming forward. I will make sure Brett can't come back here until we know what is going on."

Ailey seems satisfied with this and leaves.

I look at Mr. Williams. "Though every ounce of my being wants to say I told you so, I'm shocked that he was working for the government. I just thought he was arrogant."

Mr. Williams sighs, rubbing his face with his hand. "It seems every thread I thought held this resistance together are the very threads that will make it come apart."

"Peter?"

I turn, finding Raegan coming from the workroom. I smile, wrapping my arms around her. "What are you doing here?"

She holds me tight, her arms around my waist. "Evan is looking for me."

I freeze. "What?"

"Evan is looking for me again. He was on his way to my house."

She starts to shake as she cries softly into my chest. I hold her firmly, glancing back at Mr. Williams. "She's not stable enough to go to the bunker."

He nods. "I know. That's why she's here. Security is on high alert, but Evan would have to be a fool to show up here now. Her family will stay here for the night, where it will be safe. I've urged your mom to come here as well. We should probably get to your house for you to get your things. It won't be for long, just long enough that he can look around and see you both are gone."

Raegan finally lets me go. I wipe the tears from her face and say, "I'll be back in a few hours. It's going to be okay. I'm not letting him get you again."

She nods, and I reluctantly walk away, following Mr. Williams to his truck.

IT'S LATE WHEN MR. WILLIAMS drops me off at home. Curfew is nearly upon us. I rush into the house, ready to gather our things. My mom is sitting on the couch, and I can tell by the look on her face that something bad has happened.

"Mom? We need to hurry."

She jumps, startled by my presence. "Oh, Peter. I'm sorry. I know but… there's a letter for you."

336

I approach the coffee table. A white envelope with my name across it sits there. But the problem is not the envelope itself. No, the problem is that it's from the government. My heart nearly stops. "W-what is that?"

My mom looks nervous. "I didn't open it, so I don't know for sure, but I know there is only one thing that..." She trails off.

My heartbeat quickens as I rip open the envelope, hoping it's nothing. Yet as I read the letter in its entirety, I realize Mr. Williams didn't intervene on my behalf in time. My eyes prick with hot tears, but I blink them back. I have to be strong for my mom. I read and reread the words over and over, wishing them out of existence. But here they are, signed by the president himself. "I... I've been drafted."

The tears begin to fall from my mom's eyes. She rests her face in her hands. "Everything I ever feared. My son... I failed you."

I kneel to hold her, but she's sobbing now. I stay strong for her sake, but I feel like punching the wall. I can't leave. Not after everything that's happened.

I read the letter again.

337

Peter Daniels,

Congratulations. You have been selected to take part in the draft of the United States Military. In three days, an army truck will pick you up at your home and take you to the training facility you have been assigned to. Please be advised that you may bring no personal items, save for one item of your choice. We will provide clothes, shoes, weapons, and the like. You do not need to bring these. We look forward to seeing you soon.

Sincerely,
President Fredrick Morgan

I have three days before my life is sold. How am I supposed to go on missions? How am I supposed to go with Raegan to the bunker, as I promised?

My mom's sobs have quieted, but the tears still fall. Gunnar pads quietly into the room and leans against her leg in a futile attempt to comfort her.

My questions have no answers, and my head spins with everything I must do now. I can't run from this, or I will end up dead. But if I accept my fate… I'll be dead just as fast. There is no escape.

There is no refuge.

Three days. That's all I have to say goodbye. Those are the last few days where my life will be mine.

CHAPTER TWENTY-NINE

Evan

IT'S MIDNIGHT WHEN I PULL UP IN FRONT of Raegan MacArthur's household. Conveniently, Peter Daniels' home is just across the street. Both houses look quiet, the occupants likely asleep. It is after curfew and, unlike me, they don't have a pass to be out here in the night.

I slide out of my rental car, shutting the door as gently as possible. This will not be easy, but I refuse to be defeated like this, caught in my lies.

I walk up the front lawn to Raegan's house. All is quiet. It won't play to my advantage to have absolutely no noise, but I don't have much of a choice.

I kick the door in, and it breaks from the hinges easily. I glance around outside, to make sure no one saw anything, before walking in. The house is dark, and no one seems to stir. I search downstairs, finding no one. The master bedroom is clean, and Raegan's parents aren't here.

I climb the stairs, though my hope that I will find her is dwindling fast as I realize my father must've already prepared for this.

There's a bathroom, a linen closet, and then a bedroom on the second floor. All are void of people.

I scream in rage, knocking some pictures from the walls as I make my way back downstairs.

I repeat this process with Peter's house, but I already know that they won't be here. I already know that my father planned to hide them until I'm out of town again. I won't be able to get her back.

But that doesn't mean the president will ever know she's alive. Not if I can help it.

With Jackson dying, or even dead, that only leaves Samantha who knows my secret. The resistance won't want the president to know Raegan's alive. It would only backfire on them as well.

For now, I accept that I have lost this battle.

But only because I know that I've already won this war.

CHAPTER THIRTY
Raegan
MONDAY, OCTOBER 30TH, 2023

I HEAR THE BIRDS CHIRPING OUTSIDE MY window. It's a sound I never thought I'd hear again. I slowly sit up. It's still a harder process, but the fact I can sit on my own is something else I never thought would be possible again.

I take a deep breath. Then another. All is peaceful right now. And I know it can't stay that way for long. So, I take this moment, this feeling. I let it fill me up with a new hope I didn't have before.

Coming home early this morning after learning Evan skipped town wasn't the best experience. Our front door was kicked in and broken. Pictures had been torn from the walls and shattered on the floor. But I was so weak from the car ride and the stress that I couldn't stand any longer and went to bed.

Even though it was only a couple of hours ago, it feels like it was days. My sense of time has yet to come back in full.

I hear the soft knock, then the gentle brush of my door opening. I look over at my mom. She smiles, carrying a tray of food. "Good morning, honey."

I smile. "Good morning. Why are you bringing my food up here?"

My mom sets the tray on my lap. "I know you've been doing a great job getting up and down the stairs. I just don't want you overdoing it."

I begin to eat the fruit she's prepared for me. My appetite has increased, which means I can begin eating larger portions of food and even start eating some meat. I know my strength is coming back. Even my arm feels slightly better. It's stiff, and the bandage that is plastered to my shoulder doesn't help with mobility, but it's healing.

After I eat, my mom helps me get ready for an appointment with the doctor, the same one that saw me the moment I got back to headquarters. She comes to my house once a week to check on me and see how I'm progressing. I still can't leave the house. Mr. Williams wants us to keep up the ruse that I'm dead because if word gets out that I'm alive, Evan may try to come for me again.

When she arrives, Dr. Wu gets straight to work. She checks my vitals, my weight, and my shoulder.

She's cold and quiet, as usual. Finally, she says, "You've gained ten pounds since you last saw me. You're growing stronger and your shoulder is healing nicely. You won't have to wear bandages for too much longer. We'll get it changed out to a clean one today, and then you can rest some more. If your shoulder begins to act up or hurt, I can get you a sling, but it's not pertinent to your healing."

I'm excited to hopefully get the bandages off soon. Doctor Wu has my mom help me take off my shirt. Then Doctor Wu returns with the clean gauze and some of the spray she used on the bullet wound before. She wraps the wound from my shoulder to just above my elbow.

Then she says, "You should be good to go, although we'll have to meet one more time to look at the healing process of your shoulder."

"Thank you, doctor," my mom says. She walks Dr. Wu down the stairs to the front door, and I hear them exchange a few final words before the doctor goes on her way. I step into the bathroom to look at myself in the mirror. My shirt is still off; my shoulder looks weird with the new bandages. I hear footsteps approaching. I figure it's my mom, so I say, "This new wrap feels weird."

I turn to look out into my room, only to see Peter. I scream, quickly shutting the bathroom door.

Peter says, "Sorry! I didn't know."

I'm breathing heavily. He just saw me... in my bra.

I pull my shirt back over my head and step out, my cheeks red with embarrassment. Peter takes me in his arms and says, "I'm sorry. I didn't mean to do that to you."

I bury my face in his chest. "It's okay. I was just... startled."

We stay like that until I'm no longer embarrassed. Peter helps me down the stairs, a slow and steady process. My mom greets us in the living room before she heads into the kitchen to begin working on lunch. Neither of us dares mention the incident from upstairs.

I start to feel a little woozy. I must have overdone it with the stairs. Peter must sense this; he helps me lie down on the couch, and I rest my head on his lap. He brushes his fingers through my hair, which is more relaxing than I care to admit.

Quietly, he says, "This is all platonic."

I smirk. "I doubt that."

He chuckles, and I close my eyes, savoring this moment. I see a white envelope on the coffee table. I don't recall it being there before I lay down.

"Peter," I say softly.

He looks at me. "Yes?"

"What's that envelope on the table?"

He doesn't say anything for a moment, but I feel the sudden tension in the air. I glance back at him. His eyes are full of fear.

"Raegan, I don't know how to tell you this."

I sit up, ignoring the dizzy feeling in my head. "Tell me what?"

He sighs. "I've been drafted."

My heart nearly stops. I feel my eyes widen and my mouth falls open. "What do you mean? I thought Mr. Williams had gotten your name out of the system."

He shakes his head. "It's a long process to do that. He wasn't quite done. My name was pulled before he could finish."

Hot tears prick in my eyes. "But...you can't leave. What about school? What about the resistance?"

What about us?

He looks on the verge of tears himself. "I skipped school and met with Mr. Williams this morning. There's nothing he can do. But he wants me to use this as my first mission. He wants me to gather information on the training style and the people who might be an immediate threat."

I've lost my ability to speak. I feel the tears trickling down my cheeks now. Peter wraps me in a hug, kissing the top of my head. He won't be here to help me in the bunker as we thought. I'll be alone again. But even worse, I may never *see* him again. And I can't bear that thought.

"Raegan, I need to tell you exactly how I feel about… about you."

Pulling back, I wipe my face with my sleeve. "You did tell me."

He shakes his head. "No, I mean… I love you. Leaving you is going to be the hardest thing I'll ever do. We've only just been reunited, and I'm being ripped away from you again. I need to know you won't wait for me. There's no guarantee I'll come back."

I feel a fresh wave of tears. "Peter, I can't… I can't promise that."

He smiles softly. "I know you can't. But you

347

need to know these may be... may be our last moments together. I don't know what's going to happen. I know I will fight every day to see you again. To be in your arms again and to hold you in mine. But for now... I have three days. Three days to be completely honest about everything. I'm not confused about how I feel for you, Raegan. I know I love you. And I always will."

He holds me again, kissing my forehead, my nose, my cheek. He stops, our faces hovering just inches apart. Our eyes meet, and there's a pause. Finally, I say breathlessly, "What's stopping you?"

That's all it takes. His lips are on mine in a perfect kiss, conveying every emotion we have. My tears mingle with his own; his hands caress my face. My left hand is on his shoulder; my right hand rests on his thigh.

We break apart, breathless. He rests his forehead against mine, eyes still closed. I study his face, wanting to see every detail, every mark, scratch, and scar. He smiles, eyes still closed.

"I can feel you watching me," he says.

I blush. "I want to memorize everything I can about you."

His eyes open, meeting mine. "I love you."

"I love you, too."

CHAPTER THIRTY-ONE
Carissa
MONDAY, OCTOBER 30TH, 2023

JACKSON HASN'T MOVED. HASN'T WOKEN up. The only thing proving he's alive is the heart monitor that beeps in a steady rhythm. The doctors come infrequently. On the first night, they tried to make me leave at the appointed time. But they soon learned it was better not to argue with me.

I eventually sent Spencer home. I couldn't keep him here. And, frankly, it didn't look good for Jackson. The doctors tried to warn me, but I didn't listen to them. Because deep down, I know he's in there.

Some nights, I curl up next to him on the bed instead of sleeping in the chair.

I'm dozing in the chair now when I hear the door open. A nurse comes in, followed by Spencer and Peter. I sit up straighter. "What are you two doing here?"

Peter glances at Spencer, then at me. "I came to see him before I have to go."

I'm confused. "Go? Go where?"

Peter looks pained. "I've been drafted."

My eyes widen. "I thought my father removed your name."

He sighs. "I thought so, too. But apparently, there was an error. We don't know what happened, only that I got the letter saying I'd been selected. I leave in a couple of days. Your father has decided to use this as my first mission. I have to gather intel for him."

I don't know what to say, so I don't say anything. I don't know how to convey how sad I am for him.

Peter rubs his neck with his right hand. "I hate to bring this up, but is there anyone I should look out for?"

I exhale slowly. "Well, you're going to want to avoid General Khan at all costs. He's a ruthless man with no morals, no conscience. He will do whatever it takes to get to the top. He's the biggest ass-kisser of any of the generals. You don't want to cross him. Ever."

"Got it," he says. "Anyone else to avoid?"

"Besides Evan? Well, Samantha Winters is another one to avoid. She was on our team back at the warehouse, working as his assistant. But she's an assassin. Avoid getting on her bad side. She had become pretty protective of my brother in the last moments I was with them. I don't know if anything is going on between them, but they were always having closed-door meetings in his office."

Peter says nothing for a moment, processing everything I've given him. Spencer comes up beside me, touching my shoulder gently. "You really should come home and shower. Maybe take a nap. He'll be okay if you're not here for a couple of hours."

I shake my head, looking back to Jackson's motionless form on the bed. He's hooked up to all kinds of machines. His face is so pale, it almost doesn't look like him. "I can't. If he wakes up, I need to be here for him."

If? I said *if.* I can't be giving up hope now. I'm the only one with hope for him. He needs me. Even in his comatose state, he needs me. I can't leave while he's helpless. He wouldn't leave me if the roles were reversed.

Peter goes to Jackson's bedside. "I don't know if you can hear me like this," he says. "But thank you for helping me get Raegan back. And for hunting Linley down. I know she appreciates it, too. She asks about you a lot. When you get back to your feet, I want you to help her. She's going to need someone there for her."

We're all silent for a moment. Then Peter approaches the door. "I've got to go. More packing and preparing."

I get to my feet, cross the room, and hug Peter tightly. He hugs me back. I'm unsure when I'll ever see him again. We finally step apart, and he soundlessly leaves. I turn to Spencer, who is leaning against the wall.

"Didn't you give him a ride here?"

He shakes his head. "No. Raegan let him use her truck. I came to relieve you. I'll sit here. Why don't you take my truck home, get a shower, and maybe some food? Then, after you're refreshed, you can come back up here, and we'll switch places."

I begin to object, to tell him thank you, but no. However, he holds up his hand and says, "Your dad said he needs to talk to you. Today. And it needs to be in person. He told me to come up here. I know this argument would be pointless otherwise and I wouldn't waste my time engaging in it. But he seemed serious."

I glance at Jackson again. My heart aches to hear his voice once more, to look into his dark eyes, to feel his hand in mine.

"Why isn't he awake yet?" Spencer asks, so quietly I don't know if he means for me to hear it.

I open my mouth to answer, to repeat the things the doctors tell me when I ask the same questions. But I don't believe the small stories they give me about comas and blood loss. While they have a point... well, Jackson should be awake by now if everything is truly okay.

"I honestly don't know why he's not awake right now," I finally say. "But I want to be here to see his eyes open, to see him breathe by himself and not because a machine is pushing air into his lungs."

Spencer pushes away from the wall. "I know you do, but he'd want you to take care of yourself, too."

"I hate that you speak about him like he's dead."

Spencer shakes his head. "He's not dead, and he's not going to die. But something deeper is the issue here. And until he wakes up, you have to do everything you normally do, including looking after your personal hygiene. Now, I can hand you the keys and let you drive yourself home, and you can come back when you've finished. Or I can drag you back home and we'll leave him on his own. Your call."

I scowl. "Fine. Give me the keys. But I'll be back as soon as possible."

"I know," he says. "I wouldn't expect less of you."

I take the keys from him and make my way through the many hallways. Once I'm outside, the bright sun beats down on me, something I'm not fully prepared for after days in artificial light.

I find Spencer's truck and climb into the driver's seat, but I find I don't have the strength to start it. Everything hits me at once, and at last, I give in to the tears I've been holding back for so many days now. When I finally gain control of myself, I put the key into the ignition and shift the truck into drive. I'm ready to see my parents. Ready to feel their arms around me. Ready to feel the comfort of a burning hot shower.

I'm ready for all of this to be over.

But the war has only just begun.

CHAPTER THIRTY-TWO

Jackson

DATE: UNKNOWN

"YOU DISAPPOINT ME."

"You're disgusting."

"I hate you!"

I don't know where I am. I only know everything from my past swirls around me. I know that I'm hurting from words that echo in my head. I find I'm standing in a desert, the bright sun beating down on me, burning my skin. My arms are protected by my leather jacket, but my face is fully exposed. I try to look down at the sand beneath my feet in a pointless effort to protect my face from burning, but it doesn't matter.

I hear my father yelling at me, his words echoing in my mind over and over. "You disappoint me. If you can't support my happiness, then you can leave."

I don't understand where this is coming from. An apparition of my father appears in front of me, repeating the same sentence over and over.

I run away, but the sand shifts under my feet, slowing me down. I stop in front of another apparition. This one is of a girl I liked in high school. I remember going up to her, after having prepared some sort of speech. I wanted to ask her to prom. But she shoots me down. "You think I'd want to show up to the most magical night of our lives with you? You're disgusting."

The words sting as if they are fresh, but the wounds have long since scarred over. I turn away from this ghost from my past and find myself facing yet another one. This one is Noah. To be honest, I regret many things that we've said to each other. I wish I could fix things between us, and change the way they are now. We may not like that our parents married in the way that they did, but we can overcome this.

The ghost of Noah wears an expression of revulsion as he stares me down. "I hate you! You've ruined my life, Jackson."

Those are fresh words, from when I tried to kiss Stella and she landed a jab to my jaw. It happened when we were in the garage, leaving at the same time that day. He yelled at me for trying to even touch her. I can't blame him.

I fall to my knees as more ghosts of the past surround me, their shouts and words echoing, overlapping in a deafening chorus of horrible things I have suppressed in the deepest parts of my mind.

I yell out. "Make it stop! Please."

I don't know who I'm yelling to, or what power this entity has, but the apparitions all disappear in an instant. Suddenly, I'm facing a mirror. I see myself.

But I'm not myself. I'm in a hospital bed. Spencer is standing against the wall across from me. Carissa stands at the foot of my bed, arguing with him about something. I can't hear their words, only see their lips moving. Eventually, Carissa takes a set of keys from Spencer and leaves. *She doesn't want to leave me. She still cares.*

Carissa is stubborn, one of the many things I love about her. I watch as Spencer paces at the foot of my bed. His mind isn't in this room. It's somewhere else. The image in the mirror warps to show me where I'm at now. Except that this version of me looks angry.

"You can never do anything right, Jackson," it says. "You might as well give up now. You're so close to death anyway. Letting it take you would be simple, easy. You like the simple things, remember."

I take a step back. How can I let this image in my mind talk to me like this?

"No," I say firmly back to my reflection, which seems shocked. "I won't stop fighting. If there's one thing I've learned in all of this, it's that you can't always chase the simple life. You have to fight for the things and the people you love. And I'm not going to let myself die like this. I *will* keep fighting."

Mirror Jackson sneers at me. "You know this will be a painful journey, right? You'll never be the same when you wake up. Are you sure you don't want to let death consume you? You're so close to it anyway."

I cross my arms. "I'm positive I want to live. I need to live for the ones I love, and for the ones I need to make amends to."

Mirror Jackson rolls his eyes. "Whatever you say. Just don't say I never warned you. You fight this battle and see if you think it's worth it. I'm out of here."

The mirror shatters, the pieces falling around

my feet. I lean down to pick one up, but I feel strange now as if my mind is splitting into many different fragments. I feel like I'm falling over, but I'm not. I stagger as I try to walk away across the desert. The mirror, the glass, all of it fades.

I fall over; my body meets burning-hot sand. Then, everything is dark once more.

CHAPTER THIRTY-THREE
Raegan
WEDNESDAY, NOVEMBER 1ST, 2023

MOST OF MY DAYS ARE SPENT SLEEPING. When I'm not sleeping, my parents help me downstairs to eat, to watch TV with them, to just sit with them and feel like a normal human.

But at night, I can't sleep. I lie awake, listening to the sounds of the night. The patrol trucks. The screams. I lie awake until morning and then sleep all day.

Tonight, everything is silent. All I can think about is what Peter told me two days ago.

Drafted.

We spent all of today together. Tomorrow morning, he'll be whisked away and forced to join the army he hates. And I'll be left behind, hoping and praying I'll feel his kiss against my lips again. That his arms will hold me again.

I can't fall asleep. Not with my mind replaying

every memory with Peter. Every moment. Every touch. Every kiss. He's kissed me a lot in these past couple of days.

Just as I get lost thinking about it again, I hear a tap on my window. I sit up, staring at the curtains. There's a shadow there. I rise, slowly. I don't know whether to run to get my parents or see what's out there. Carefully, I push the curtain aside. Peter is smiling back at me, holding onto the tree that's outside my window. I grin and open the window.

"You're going to get yourself killed," I whisper. "How did you sneak over here?"

"Very carefully," he says. "I couldn't sleep, and I know you said you don't sleep well at night either."

He climbs in, closing the window behind him. I wrap my arms around him, and he holds me. His voice is low. "I wanted one more moment with you."

I look up at him; the moonlight reflects in his eyes. But behind the smile, behind the strength, I see a boy scared out of his mind. I see Peter as he is, not as the mask he puts on.

"You don't have to pretend to be okay," I say, barely above a whisper.

He leans down, and my eyes instinctively shut.

"I know," he breathes before our lips meet. He kisses me softly, slowly. Our hands clasp together, then his hands break gently away and caress my face as I hold onto his waist. He pulls away for a breath, taking my right hand up and kissing each finger, then my palm.

"I don't want to be apart from you again," he says.

My eyes fill with tears, and I see that he, too, is struggling not to cry. I lean up to kiss his cheek, but he turns his face and we're kissing again, holding on to each other.

It's our last night.

It's all we'll have.

Finally, we break. Peter rests his forehead against mine, his eyes still closed. "I should probably try to get some sleep."

I take his hand in mine and say, "We both should. But…"

His eyes open and he looks deeply into mine. "But what?"

"I…" I don't know how to say this. "I don't want you to leave."

Even in the dim lighting, I can see his face flush.

"What?"

I shake my head slightly. "Not like that. Just lie with me."

He smiles and nods. I lead him over to the bed. We both lie down on top of the covers. We talk for a long time about the future we would make together if only he wasn't being taken away.

"We'd have an apartment at first," he says. "Pet-friendly, for Gunnar. We could make it look however you want."

I smile, resting my head against his shoulder. Our fingers are intertwined between us. "I'd love that."

But dreams are not always meant to be reality. And that's what hurts me the most.

"Peter... what if we ran away tonight? Far from any of this. No government, no resistance. Just you, just me."

I know we can't do this. There's so much danger in the idea of it. Yet... it's alluring.

"I have a mission," he says sleepily. His arms wrap around me now, his face buried in my neck. He places a gentle kiss there. I shiver.

"But if we could... would you?"

"In a heartbeat. Where would we go?"

I pause. "We could just roam. Pick up odd jobs here and there. Fight for a way to be free. Run from all the madness."

His breathing has become steadier. I, too, begin to feel the pull of sleep. I fight it, wanting to hear his answer. Because if he wanted to, we'd go tonight. We'd break the curfew. We'd run from the fate that holds us apart.

"I'd love that, darling," he says against my skin. "But we can't just run from what's chasing us. We can't give up fighting if we ever want to truly be free. There's no freedom in running. Only an extended time limit."

My heart aches at that. But he's right. I shift slightly to my side. He holds me close, and soon we're both falling asleep together. I never thought I'd sleep by Peter's side… not like this. But it's comforting. And if this must be our last night, then I will savor every moment.

But for now, we sleep.

THURSDAY
NOVEMBER 2ND, 2023

I DON'T KNOW WHAT time it is. I just know that

there's still no sunlight when I awaken. I hear a rumble outside, but I don't focus on that. I focus on the feel of Peter's arms around me. It's comforting, this feeling. I run my fingers down his arm, memorizing the feel of his skin with mine.

Suddenly, there's a pounding against the front door of my house. It's loud, threatening.

Peter's arms tighten around me, protective. He's awake, breathing erratically now. Then my mom screams and yells as footsteps pound up the stairs. My door is thrown open and Peter is yanked from my bed.

I scream. "Peter!"

His arms are shoved behind his back. The soldier in charge says, "You thought you could hide from us?"

Peter shakes his head. "No! I wasn't trying to hide. I just wanted to say goodbye to my girlfriend one more time."

Ignoring his protests, they drag him down the stairs. I sit up and swing my legs over the edge of the bed, regretting it instantly as a wave of vertigo takes over. I ignore it and get to my feet, stumbling down the stairs behind them. My mom tries to stop me, but I push her hands away and chase them outside. I need to see him one more time.

Peter's mom is outside, crying. I see two duffle bags being thrown in the back of the army truck. Peter is released from the soldiers' grip, and he runs to his mom. She hugs him, clinging to him. I stand with my arms around myself, wearing just the skimpy tank top and shorts I wore to bed. The cold air bites at my skin, but I don't care.

Peter crosses back over and folds me into his arms. "I will come back for you, Raegan," he says, for only me to hear.

Tears stream down my face. He leans down to press a kiss to my lips but is yanked away before he can. I scream. "NO!"

But no one hears me. I fall to my knees as they force Peter into the truck. He calls my name. "I love you, Raegan. Never forget that."

I cry harder as they drive away. A crowd has formed outside. Peter's mom collapses on the ground, sobbing. My mom comes to me, helping me up. "Raegan—"

She doesn't finish because I throw myself at her, crying as though my heart will break. "Why him, Mom? Why?"

"I...I don't know, my love. But I know he'll

fight every day to come back here. Don't worry. He's strong."

I feel a heavy numbness taking over me. One thing is for certain: if Peter is going to fight for me, then I'm going to fight for him. I'm going to get stronger so I can return to the resistance. I will fight to save Peter. He did the same for me. And I'm not going to let him down.

CHAPTER THIRTY-FOUR

Evan

NEW PEOPLE FILE INTO THE ROOM. I STUDY each person, but I'm on the lookout for one person in particular. These young soldiers all look scared. *Good.* They should be.

Finally, I see Peter come in. He's the only one looking confident, and defiant.

I hate him.

I go down the line of people. My job is to check them, see what they've brought with them, and make sure they aren't hiding anything. So, I do just that. No one has been brave enough to bring a weapon of their own, however, and I'm disappointed that I don't get to confiscate anything or scare them further.

I finally find myself in front of Peter. He stares me down, not afraid to look me in the eye. As much as I hate him, I know he will be one of the best soldiers this agency has seen. We'll just have to break him down first.

My security detail rummages through his two black duffle bags as he continues to stare at me. I notice in his hands a small, silver object. "What is that?"

"It's none of your concern."

I rip the item from his hand, hoping to receive a reaction of sorts. He raises his hand to strike back but hesitates. Then his arm lowers. This will be too easy.

I study the object in my hand, a simple silver keychain. Then I study it more closely. He tenses. It's a flat rectangle with two simple initials carved into it. *R+P*. I realize it opens like a locket, with a picture frame on either side. One holds a picture of a young Peter with someone I assume to be a young Raegan. The photo on the other side is a more recent photo of them together, lying on a patch of grass and smiling, likely at the camera used to take this picture. I can tell it's recent because Raegan looks a bit weak, a bit thin. It's a test to see if I will keep my cool.

I look at him, our eyes meeting in a glare of

369

mutual hatred. He looks more amused as if he thinks he has some sort of power over me, a way to blackmail me into thinking that he could threaten what I have.

He's a fool if he thinks I'm going to let him get to me.

I hand him the locket back, pinning him with one more glare. "Looks harmless."

He grunts in response. My security has moved on to the next set of duffel bags. I pin Peter with one final glare, a warning of sorts, before following my officers.

Peter thinks he can win this battle, but he doesn't know I've planned every detail of this war. He may have gotten his girl back, but I've ripped them apart once more, despite my father's intent to remove Peter's name from the roster. Of course, my father was successful in that. But he forgot all about my personal mission of revenge.

And as long as Peter's here, I will make his life hell.

Peter Daniels has no clue what's coming. And his little girlfriend won't be here to return the favor of saving him. No, after I'm through with these recruits, they won't have any desire to return to their old lives. They'll be so devoted that they'll fight hard for our cause, harder than they've ever fought for anything in their lives. They won't be human, but machines dedicated to winning this war.

As I continue down the line of recruits, only one person ends up being dragged away for bringing a knife. Such a small crime, but a huge consequence for defying orders.

I'm rather surprised no one else dared something like that. Some of them even seem excited to be here. I glance down the line one more time. Everyone stands at attention. Everyone except Peter, who glares at me. Defiance will get him nowhere, but I let him believe he has that small balance to cling to. It won't be long now.

The war may already be won, but it's far from being over. And the president doesn't know this war will end in his death.

And I will be the one on his metaphorical throne.

ACKNOWLEDGEMENTS

Wow. To finish one book and publish it is an accomplishment, but to have two out there in the world, for people to love, to hate, to hold, to cry over, to smile at, maybe even laugh it... That's a crazy feeling. I don't know if I'll ever get quite used to it if I'm honest. It's a very surreal feeling.

First off, I thank God for giving me this ability to write, to read, to know words, and to have them in my heart and soul. This gift of writing is something I hope to never take for granted.

Next, I want to thank my family. My parents for always believing in me, my siblings for their constant support, and for my family always being there and supporting me, no matter what. I don't deserve the family that I have, for sticking by me through everything and for always putting up with me no matter what. God really blessed me.

Next, thank you to Faith, my critique partner and best friend. Thank you for always going through my books after I finish up edits to make sure I didn't miss things. And for squealing and screaming whenever I come up with a new book idea. Thank you for giving me the honor to hear about all your book ideas, too. And for being my friend first. Thank you for obsessing over The Raven Cycle and Shadow and Bone with me, constantly, and never tiring of my constant rants about books.

Thank you to Abbie for helping me out with formatting woes and answering all my questions, of which there were many. You always went above and beyond in helping me and I can't thank you enough.

Thank you to my editor, Jen, for always pushing for my writing voice over everything else.

Thank you to Megan McCullough for once again making an outstanding cover that goes beyond my wildest dreams.

Thank you to the blogging and Instagram community. To name everyone would be to fill an entirely separate novel, so please know that if you have ever talked to me on Instagram, Twitter, or by email, you have been a part of everything. I know I'm no longer blogging, but each of you has been a fundamental part of my journey, teaching me things and supporting my writing. Thank you for the support for How We Rise, and the excitement for United We Fall. It's here, it's yours, and I hope it's everything you wanted. It's everything I needed.

And thank you, dear reader, for picking up this book and giving it a chance. I hope you love it.

ABOUT THE AUTHOR

 Brooke Riley started her writing journey at fifteen when she had an idea about a world falling to ruin. Though the books have come a long way from their original conception, she has found refuge in writing books. A lover of books and an avid bookworm, words have always been somewhere ingrained in her soul.

When she's not writing, she's dreaming up new worlds, making playlists, or hanging out with her family.

To keep up with all her writing endeavors, follow her social media!

- Instagram: @thebrookeriley
- Twitter: @thebrookeriley
- Website: www.brookeriley.substack.com

www.ingramcontent.com/pod-product-compliance
Lightning Source LLC
Chambersburg PA
CBHW051532100726
47898CB00005B/1662